Other books by the author:

Raven's Realm Series
Raven's Child
Windows to the Soul
Chaos Within
Immortality
Darkness Falls

Women of Ravenwood Series
Fallen
Unspoken Oaths

Gods & Dragons Series
Brothers
Victory
Beyond Valhalla

Immortal Series
Whispers of the Immortal
Tears of the Immortal
Soul of the Immortal
Fall of the Immortal
Echoes of the Immortal

ECHOES

OF THE

IMMORTAL

Immortal Series
Book Five

M.J. Spickett

NORTHERN GEM
PUBLISHING

First Edition Northern Gem Publishing (2024)

ISBN: 978-1-998318-06-3 Electronic Book
ISBN: 978-1-998318-09-4 Paperback
ISBN: 978-1-998318-10-0 Hardcover

www.mjspickett.ca

Library and Archives Canada Cataloging in Publication
Spickett, M.J., 1976-, author
Fall of the Immortal / M.J. Spickett
Issues in print and electronic formats

I. Title.

Dedication

To Priya and Ashley, who kept me encouraged and focused while writing. To Jayden, who put up with my craziness and continues to do so as I keep writing. And to Andrew, one of the best editors I've had the pleasure to work with.

AUTHOR NOTE

MJ Spickett is a Canadian Author. Most locations within her novels focus on Canada and England, and, as such, words and spacing may appear differently than they would in America. For example, we like to use "U" and "Z" in many of our words, for example "honor" (US) and "honour" (Canadian), or "organisation" (US) and "organization" (Canadian). We write grey with an "e" not with an "a." My editor is also Canadian and is helping me keep to Canadian standards. As well, although it is normal for Americans to use a single space at the end of a sentence, Canadians tend to double space. This also makes it easier to read and give an extra pause to help readers digest what they just read and better comprehend it. These are not spelling or formatting errors but simply the way we are taught to read and write.

Canadians tend to be a complicated group but that's also what makes us special.

To my Canadian readers...celebrate your uniqueness and continue writing.

Chapter One

Darkness and a whispered chant were the first things to greet her when she woke. She blinked as she turned her head, trying to peer through the darkness to see where she was. The darkness was not her friend. It was where the demons hid, ready to devour her soul and tear her away from this plane to the next. She did not want to leave this world. It was home. It was where she was meant to be, and yet, she could not hide in the darkness. That was their realm. She needed to find the light before the creatures found her.

Reaching out, she tried to find her way through the darkness. She was laying in a slightly tilting bed that felt as if it was moving, the jostling having been what woke her in the first place. The cool air that filled the tiny space was steadily becoming warming, far too warm for her liking. It made the darkness even worse, near suffocating. Her small hands touched something hard and metallic above her. She felt along it, noting that it was curved with small bumps and what felt like little boxes, but not handle. It was like a coffin. Had she died? Was she dead? Why could she still hear the whispers if she was dead?

She heard other things now, voices that were not part of the darkness, but warm with life. They were close, just outside the coffin. She hesitated a moment before slapping the roof of her prison. There was a pause in the others' conversation. It was only momentary, but they undoubtedly heard the thump of her hand. She hit it again, harder this time and began yelling. It was dangerous. The Shadows may hear her. For all she knew, she could be in this coffin for her own safety, but it was small, the air becoming far too warm, far too fast. And it was dark, unbearably dark. She needed out. She needed to be in the light and these people were the only ones able to free her.

She threw all her weight and strength into hitting the ceiling of the coffin, screaming, and begging for the people outside to hear her and help. Their voices became louder but so did the whispers. Fear knotted in her heart, but she couldn't stop, not until the lid finally swung open and two bewildered faces stared down at her with wide, questioning eyes.

"It's a child," the woman stated. She looked to be in her mid thirties. She glanced toward her partner who seemed just as confused. "Why would they have a child in one of these tubes? Are there more?"

"I don't know," the man confessed. He glanced toward the other tubes they were moving, the worry growing on his face. "We should leave her in it and call the boss. He'll know what to do. Ow!"

The woman hit his shoulder with enough force to startle him. "We can't do that," she snapped at him before leveling a nervous smile at the child in the cryogenic tube. "It's okay, honey. We won't hurt you. Let's get you out of there and find someone who can help you."

The girl shied away from her touch and pushed herself into a sitting position. She looked around but wherever they were, it was still too dark. There were too many shadows in which the creatures could take refuge in. She could hear their whispers. They knew she was awake and coming for her. She wasn't safe anymore. She was only safe in the light. She needed to find the light. Where had it gone?

Her breath hitched as something in the distance fell. She grasped the edges of the open tube tightly, fear dominating her.

"It's okay, one of our people must have dropped something," the woman assured. "Relax. Jared, radio the head-office and tell them we...er...found someone. Come on, hun. No one's going to hurt you. We have a small office close by. We can have some hot chocolate and wait for our boss to come down and..."

It was getting closer, moving swiftly through the shadows toward them. The hairs on the back of the girl's arm raised as the energy in the room began to change. The man and woman must have felt it. They glanced around the room in nervousness.

"It's coming," the girl warned as she stood up.

"What's coming?"

She didn't know how to explain it. The man grabbed her and lifted her out of the tube, placing her on the floor. She grabbed his hand and the woman's and tried to pull them toward the light but neither one would budge, both too busy asking questions that could wait. Frustrated, the girl pulled away from them and began running toward where she saw light, ignoring their calls to stop. The Shadow was coming. There was no stopping it…all she could do was avoid it.

Instinct alone caused her to pause long enough near doors to turn on lights. They were bright, washing away the darkness behind her long enough for her to make it to the next corridor and possibly saving those who found her. She ran long and hard, a mental map in her head that she couldn't recall ever having. Everything looked alien to her, yet she knew where she needed to go. She rushed into one of the labs, turning on the bright cold white lights, then headed toward the decontamination chamber, activating it before stepping inside and locking it behind her. Every inch of the chamber filled with impossibly bright white light. It should have hurt her eyes, but it didn't. It felt warm and safe, just as the tube had once been before it flooded with darkness. She didn't know how that came to be, but she was safe now. If the light touched her, the darkness could not.

She leaned against the far wall and slid down it until she was sitting, then stared out through the glass window into the lab. Screams could be heard in the distance as the Shadow found the people working in the base, slaughtering them as it hunted for her. She closed her eyes and covered her ears, fearful of what she may see if anyone should try to take refuge in the lab as she did. They would be safe if they came. There was enough light to vanquish the demon, even if only temporary. No-one came. Not even the people who found her. She was alone and that thing was still hunting her as it had been before she was brought to this place…before they put her and her Mommy to sleep. Her Mommy was likely dead now, too.

She was alone.

Alone.

Panic filled Alex, jostling him awake, his heart racing and terror filling every inch of his being. He automatically reached out for Lucas, sound asleep next to him, to make certain he was awake and assure himself he was awake and no longer sleeping. It had been a long time since he had his last vision, nearly a year since the Celestial had freed him and left the planet, but this one was all too vivid, as if he could reach out and touch the child he had seen. It wasn't a past memory but something that felt as if it had happened mere hours ago.

He reached for his smartphone on the nightstand, not surprised when a moment later it rang with a government number appearing on the screen. Pursing his lips, he reached for his prosthetic leg, carefully slid it over the stump of his right leg, then climbed out of bed as he finally accepted the call. It was never good when they called this early in the morning, but they knew to wait and not hang up if he didn't answer immediately. Yes, he and Lucas typically awoke early for their various teaching careers or to care for the vineyard, but three in the morning was a little early for either of them.

"Alex?" a familiar voice asked.

A smile lit Alex's face as he padded into the kitchen. "James, what's going on? You don't normally call this early in the morning."

The man on the other end let out a relieved breath and small chuckle. "No, and you know I wouldn't unless it was important." He took a deep breath. "Do you still get those visions you used to talk about?"

Alex didn't answer. He regretted ever mentioning them when he was interrogated after being freed by the Celestial. Instead, he made a grumpy sound, indicating he didn't want to talk about it.

"Yeah, sorry, dumb question," James amended, understanding. "Are you near your laptop or a tablet?"

"One sec," Alex answered.

He instinctively knew what James wanted to show him. He went to his office, set the smartphone to the speaker function, then quickly logged onto his laptop. A new email automatically popped up from James and he clicked on the video link. Security footage from some sort of abandoned lab began to play. He watched in silence as some sort of tube was opened by two maintenance people, revealing a frightened young girl inside. She was pale, fair too fair of skin to even be classified as Caucasian. Her skin was almost alabaster, so pale as to be albino. Her hair matched, appearing snowy white. He studied her appearance for a long time. If one was to look at her from a mythological standpoint, she could almost pass for what some believed elves looked like, but Alex knew better. This child was not an elf but rather a Celestial of some sort, except Celestials were made of pure energy and this child was flesh and blood. A hybrid perhaps? The Celestia by which he had been possessed, had been trying to breed, and it wasn't the only one. What if one had managed to impregnate a human female? Was this their offspring?

He watched, half expecting the child to feed off the two people who discovered her, despite what he had seen in his vision. Instead, she ran away, begging them to follow her before darkness moved in from the upper right hand of the screen. It moved like a blanket from one side of the screen to the other, blacking out everything in its path. The familiar whisper of the Shadow creatures sounding like nothing more than radio chatter before the people began screaming in agony as they were torn apart.

Alex felt a tightness in his chest as he remembered witnessing the ferocity of the Shadows attacking and killing people around him, the bloodshed far more horrific than if a pack of wild hyenas attacked a defenseless and injured antelope. His hands curled into fists, and he momentarily closed his eyes, trying to shut out the sight and sounds of the Shadows victims. He wanted to skip ahead but knew he couldn't without potentially missing something important. The scene changed to other security cameras that were following the girl as she ran down the corridor, pausing only long enough to hit every light switch she could find and flooding the area around her in bright white light until she reached a lab. Then, surprisingly, she dashed into a

5

decontamination chamber, locked herself inside under enough more blindingly white light, and cowered in a corner where no shadows could reach her. Lights burst outside the lab, the creature destroying the lights as it chased after her, but once it reached the lab it could go no further. The decontamination chamber had a back up generator and as long as someone or something remained inside it, it could not be turned off. The lights inside would remain on for up to a week even if the power went out.

The kid was smart. She knew exactly where she had to go to be safe. Now it was a matter of figuring out who she was and how to get her out of there safely – provided she wasn't their enemy. Alex had yet to meet a Celestial-human hybrid and he honestly hoped never to encounter one. His goal was to leave what the Celestial had done to him behind, but he knew that would never happen. He was tied to them as much as they were to him. The fact he agreed to work with Interpol and the United Nations to stop any potential threat from the Celestials was the only thing keeping him out of an American prison. He ran a hand over his ruined right ear. He had far too much experience with these beings.

"Where is this?" he asked James, knowing that James would have no information about the girl.

"You'll never believe me," James answered, sounding a mix of excited and cautious.

Alex took a deep breath as locations all around the world began to play in his mind. "Try me."

"NORAD. And no, not the new base in Winnipeg or even the hidden one under the old radio base in Sudbury."

Alex waited, hating the growing excitement in James's voice. Some people really didn't understand the danger these creatures posed. Not just the girl but the Shadow being obviously hunting her. Right now, they seemed confined to the lab but if they got loose...

"North Bay," he answered, not wanting to play the guessing game.

"You're no fun," James whined.

"It's three in the morning and you sent me a video of a child being hunted by a Shadow while it slaughters maintenance people. What part of that is 'fun'."

"You're right, you're right," James conceded. He sighed before finally getting back to business. "But yeah, it's the North Bay underground base. You know the story. It's been decommissioned and everything of value is being moved to the new one inside Winnipeg. The people down there are our movers. Most are members of the military and a few civilians. Everything was going fine until there was a power outage two days ago. Then strange sounds began echoing through the base. Maintenance went to check it out while the movers began taking the tubes to the trucks. That's when this happened. It was the first and only tube to open. Shortly after, they were attacked by this…darkness…and killed. All thirty-some people underground at the time. All but this girl. Whatever is chasing her doesn't like the light. We sent people down afterwards, flooded the place in LEDs, but she won't come out for us. Anyone who tries to go near her…she's locked the whole thing down. She won't come out."

Alex nodded absently along with him as he rewatched the beginning of the security footage. "What are these tubes?"

"We weren't sure at first, but they look to be cryochambers. There appears to be about a dozen of them, maybe more."

"With people in them?"

"Only two had people…living people at least. The one with the girl in it and another with a woman. She died in the power outage. There were three more, but they were practically mummified. I'm trying to get the records to find out who they are or were. The rest were empty and never activated. It's like they were prepared to put more people on ice but never made it that far."

"NORAD is the North American Aerospace Defense Command. Why would they have labs and cryochambers?"

"Beats me," James answered honestly.

7

Alex frowned and played through the security feed again. This didn't make sense. Why would NORAD house cryochambers and labs? Why did they have this girl on ice, and for how long? It wasn't what the base was meant for. If anything, it was meant to be a warning system should North America be attacked and could house several hundred people in their underground bunkers. There was an air base above it and rumour had it that there was a tunnel that led right into the heart of North Bay that could be used to evacuate people from the city should it ever be needed. Of course, North Bay was much larger now than when the underground bunker was originally built, and not everyone could take refuge there, but the idea was sound at the time of its creation. It still didn't explain what he was looking at. If anything, he should be looking at old computers and radio equipment, not a girl hiding in a decontamination chamber in the middle of a lab with a Shadow hunting her.

Unless it was built over a temple.

Alex felt as if he was about to be sick, his mind delving into past horrors and trauma caused by the discovery of the alien underground temples. They may appear Aztec in nature but were anything but.

He fought to keep his voice steady. "Has anyone investigated the bowels of the base? Was a temple found? Ruins?"

James's voice sounded far away when he answered. "No. There's none here. Once we got the lights on it was the first thing our people searched for. There aren't records of one either."

Of course, there were no records. There wouldn't be. Not if the government was keeping it secret and had been for decades. They wouldn't want anyone else knowing about it. That meant he would have to go and find it himself. The Canadian Shield was the best place to hide a temple. It was thick and provided a protective layer. It was perhaps the most powerful tectonic plate on Earth.

"Alex...I know you really don't want to get involved again...but we need you. This girl...she's going to starve to death if we don't get her out. You're a teacher. You're good with kids."

8

He was right, she did need him. Alex could feel that. He could almost hear her calling out to him. It was why he had had the vision. She was calling out to others like her for help. He was not a hybrid but a host for a Celestial. He could hear her plead to them, regardless of whether he wanted to or not.

"You'll be guarded the whole time. We're not going to let you go in alone," James continued. "We'll pay double your usual consulting fee."

Alex closed his eyes and listened carefully. Not to James but the *Other*, those voices that could not be heard by normal ears but by those connected to the world beyond. It was quiet save for one small voice and the whispers of the demon hunting her. No-one else was coming for her. None of her kind were answering her. She was alone.

"Lucas and I will be there in a few hours," he finally answered.

A sigh of relief escaped James. "Thank you. I'll get a room booked for you and a plane and…"

"We'll drive," Alex countered. "North Bay is only three hours away. We'll be there before you have a plane gassed up and ready to get us. Besides, the last thing I need is Lucas taking another panic attacking when flying out of Espanola."

A small laugh met him but they both knew that the runway at the small airport outside the Town of Espanola was less than desirable for someone with a fear of flying like Lucas Griffith had. They could make do with driving to North Bay. If they got a start within the next hour, they could beat morning traffic.

"Are you sure?" James asked. "Look, I know all this may be a little upsetting. I don't want you driving upset or rushing up here. You have some dangerous stretches to drive past, especially given the time of year. I can send a helicopter."

"We'll be fine. We have the jeep."

The other man was hesitant for a moment. "Alright. Be careful."

9

"We will."

He ended the call with James and rewatched the security footage again. He wished he had a live feed but knew that was foolish. If he did, he would not be able to leave his monitor if he had a live feed of what was happening with the hybrid. The girl was only safe if she stayed in the light, but now that she was outside the cryochamber, she also needed to eat. Being a hybrid meant she likely ate like a normal child, but if no one could get near her, let alone inside the chamber, it was only a matter of time before she starved to death. He wasn't sure if he could help her, but he could at least try. After all, he was perhaps the only person on the whole planet even remotely like her.

He got up and began making coffee. He and Lucas needed to fully wake up before they hit the road. Whether Lucas agreed to go with him to North Bay or not, he had to get to the child before the Shadow did and find out if there was another temple hidden deep under NORAD. Given everything that had happened over the last five years or so, and the discovery of alien temples hidden all around the world? Finding one hidden under the City of North Bay would not surprise him.

Chapter Two

N o," Lucas responded before Alex could finish telling him what was going on. "Absolutely not."

They sat at the kitchen table, coffee in hand and a hastily made breakfast in front of them both. Alex dug into his food, knowing full well how Lucas was going to react to the news they were going to North Bay. Or at least Alex was, but he knew Lucas well enough to know that his husband would not allow him to go alone. At least not when a Celestial was involved. Regardless of Lucas's misgivings, Alex was leaving as soon as he finished eating and made sure the dogs had fresh water and food. It was late Autumn; the vineyard and winery didn't need his attention right now. The latest harvest was waiting for a good frost before being picked for their new line of Ice Wine. It was still a trial-and-error process but would be fine left alone for a few more days.

"I wasn't asking your permission, I was asking you to come with me," he pointed out. He paused midway bringing his forkful of scrambled eggs to his mouth and gestured toward the other man. "I could have just taken off like last time, but if I recall, we both agreed never to do that again."

Lucas's food sat before him untouched, the man instead staring at Alex has if he had grown a second head. "You're talking about going to a site where a Celestial may have possessed a child. If you don't recall…one of those things possessed you, and nearly took you to space! Not to mention the killing spree it took you on. Do you even know the end body count? I can't even fathom it."

Alex pursed his lips. He did know the body count. He remembered every single face of the people the Celestial had used him to feed from and then kill. His hands shook as the memory of being sacrificed to the Celestial and then possessed, his body used for the creature's own gratification, came bursting into his mind. Sometimes he could still feel it moving around within him. It took great effort to keep his hands from shaking. His breath hitched, but he quickly played it off as a cough. Lucas knew how to trigger him, but Alex refused to have a panic attack simply because the other man did not want to be involved in anything to do with the Celestials. Alex had no choice. He couldn't run and hide from what had happened to him. He may be free now, but this child wasn't. If she was possessed, or some sort of hybrid, she was in trouble and calling out to him. He had to answer.

"Fifteen sexual-related encounters and two-hundred, twenty-one deaths at Area 51. Not including those killed when the Vaults broke free of the temples and flew into space," he answered Lucas matter-of-factly. "And I didn't include those killed before the Celestial possessed me, or Jefferson when he took my place."

Lucas gave him a long, slow blink before putting his coffee on the table, obviously thinking he had the upper hand but quickly losing it with Alex's confession.

"But that's not what's happening here, Lucas," Alex plunged ahead, not giving him a chance to formulate a new argument. "I can hear this girl. I can see what she sees. She's being hunted by one of those Shadow beings. She's alone and afraid and trapped herself in the only safe place she could find. No one can get to her, she won't allow them, and the Shadow is picking them off one by one. I need to get to her." He took a deep breath as Lucas processed his words. "I'm going, regardless of what you say. My only question is…will you come with me?"

The older man said nothing for a moment. He stared at Alex then shock his head slowly, not saying "no", but simply unable to believe the situation they were in. It had been well over a year since they last dealt with Celestials, and both had been hoping to never have to again but expecting to at some point. Celestials had lived on Earth for hundreds of thousand of years, hidden in underground temples or possessing people and living amongst them. They existed all around the world, some hidden in plain sight. Their presence only became known last year, despite many cultures believing in them, most seeing them as gods and Sky People. In many ways, the Celestials were the creators of humankind, but at some point, mankind rebelled. The Celestials went into hiding, some burying their temples underground while others had new temples built over the old, then took new names and forms.

"What if it's a trap?" Lucas pointed out. He stabbed at his bacon with suppressed anger and anxiety. "What if this girl is just bait and you're being drawn back for another Celestial to possess you."

Alex raised one brow, a small, amused grin lifting the corner of his mouth. "I suppose that's possible."

"I mean this is NORAD," Lucas continued, his objections turning to speculation. A sure sign he was folding. "Why would they have a kid there, let alone labs? When did it become Canada's version of Area 51?"

He sent Alex a glare as he chewed his bacon. Alex only grinned in return. Lucas's face pinched in obvious distaste as he continued to aggressively stab at his food then angrily chew it before finally give a small snort.

"Fine! We'll go, but if I so much as see one temple or Vault or possessed person, I'm dragging you out of there, no matter how much you kick and scream. I have ways of subduing you."

Alex's grin only grew. Lucas was good at subduing him. They had an entire room dedicated to such things.

Seeing Alex's grin broke the aggressive mask Lucas was trying to portray. "I should subdue you now. That'll end this whole thing. Drag you to the basement, tie you up and have my way with you until you forget this whole nonsense." His lips tugged into a sly smile. "Maybe I..."

Alex stood and rounded the table. He pressed his lips to Lucas's and licked the little bit of egg that lingered on his bottom lip before taking his plate away from him.

"When we get home, you can pound into me to your heart's content, in *any* position you want, but first, we need to save this child," he breathed against Lucas's lips. He pulled away and placed the dishes in the sink to wash them. "Now go get dressed. We're leaving in ten minutes."

A small growling like sound escaped Lucas, but after he finished his coffee, he got up and did as Alex requested.

When they first got together many years ago, Lucas would take forever getting ready and finding just the right outfit to wear and making himself look just right. That had changed since they moved into the cabin and began their own vineyard and winery. He still took his time when teaching classes or going off to do lectures and consultations, but he had gone from fitted dress pants and suits to jeans and t-shirts when working at home. Sometimes, like today, he slipped back into a military mind set and wore dark cargo pant with matching long sleeve shirt and jacket. Alex shook his head at the sight of him. The way Lucas acted when it came to the Celestial was as if they were going to war. They could be, but it seemed highly unlikely, and Lucas was simply overreacting. Alex didn't comment on it though, at least he was coming along. Alex could have done it alone, but he felt safer with Lucas by his side. He had been kidnapped, sacrificed, and possessed and nearly killed over the years, most of those things while he was separated from Lucas for one reason or another. Having him by his side lowered the chances of it happening again.

It was still dark outside when Alex went out to fill the food dispenser for the dogs and make sure the water dispenser connected directly to the outside tap was not frozen in the cool weather before locking up the back doors. The dogs had a large, heated doghouse next to the main house where their food and water was sheltered from the elements. They would be fine for a few days and their neighbours knew to check on them if Alex and Lucas were gone more than forty-eight hours. Nonetheless, Alex gave them a call to let them know they would be gone a few days and to call if there are any problems. He threw an overnight bag in the back of the pickup while Lucas took the driver's seat. Once Alex was seated next to him, they pulled out of the drive and headed into town. They would have to go through Espanola to get to Highway 17. From there, it was a straight route to North Bay.

He pulled out his tablet and connected it to the in-vehicle Wi-Fi, then pulled up the blueprint files for NORAD. It had every layer of the Aerospace bunker, but they were several decades old, the only blueprints available for the public. To Alex, that alone was enough for him to suspect there was something the government or army was hiding. Blueprints like this didn't normally fall into public domain unless a base was being fully decommissioned, or they were hiding something much larger so that they used the blueprints as a distraction. It was like sleight-of-hand. Have people look one way while what was really going on happened elsewhere. Or he could be overthinking it and the base really was being decommissioned. The labs could have been something that was not initially planned, but became part of the bunker and was either forgotten or overlooked. Cryostasis was something many governments had been toying with over the decade to preserve people of great importance. There were places all around the world with people on ice in hopes of somehow curing them of whatever they died from, and potentially bringing them back to life. It made a weird kind of sense that Canada would have the same thing. They may have been putting hybrids on ice to experiment on them and figure out their DNA, or something more sinister. Like taking blood samples to find ways of healing people. That was what happened to Lucas after the Celestial had healed him. The general at Area 51 had been willing to drain him dry to get enough of his blood with which to experiment. That could have been happening to this girl and her mother, and anyone else in stasis.

He bit his lower lip but kept his thoughts to himself on the matter. The last thing he wanted was Lucas to get even more upset about this mission than he already was.

"Should we call Elizabeth and tell her what's going on?" Lucas asked, startling Alex.

Alex bit back a curse as the tablet fumbled from his fingers. He caught it before it fell out of his reach and carefully connected it to the holder on his side of the dashboard. His heart was racing and palms sweaty. Not from the question but the visualization of Lucas being tied down and blood drained from him. He had not seen it happen but that didn't stop the image from playing through his mind. This girl was only a small child. Human or not, she would not survive losing as much blood as Lucas had.

He sat back and shook his head.

"No," he answered. "She's visiting her parents in Sault Ste. Marie. We'll be home before she gets back."

"I don't like taking off without her knowing," Lucas countered.

Elizabeth was Alex's best friend. They had known each other most of their lives, and she had been with them since the discovery of the first temple in British Columbia. Normally, Alex would agree to calling her and letting her know what was going on, but she needed time with her parents, something she rarely got with work. Besides, they were only going to North Bay, not Ottawa or any far-off land. They weren't off hunting temples or fighting terrorists. They were trying to help Interpol get a little girl safely out of a decommissioned underground bunker with a potential Shadow creature in it. It should be easy. Nothing to concern her with, really. And if they did need her then Interpol would send a plane to get her, getting her from Sault Ste. Marie to North Bay in under an hour compared to the five hours she would have to drive. For now, let her enjoy her time with her family.

The sun was rising as they took the by-pass around Sudbury, painting the sky bright white before fading to a soft indigo and baby blue. A good sign for their drive as it meant no snow and warmth by mid-afternoon. Alex refrained from studying the blueprints and instead checked the live feed from the lab to see if there were any changes with the girl. He could still feel her panic and hear her voice whispering in the back of his mind. He knew she was still in the decontamination chamber, there was no need for a visual, but he felt better seeing her.

16

"That's her?" Lucas asked, glancing away from the road for a moment.

Alex nodded. "Yeah."

"How old would you say she is?"

He shook his head. "It's hard to tell from this angle, and James didn't make much sense. Sounds like she may have been on ice since the 1970s."

Lucas hummed softly. He pulled off the highway, surprising Alex as they pulled into the drive-through of a local coffee shop.

"What are you doing? We don't have time…"

"We're making time," Lucas countered before Alex could object further. "Look, we're only an hour out and I need another coffee before we go through yet another one of Interpol's long-winded meet-and-greets. You know whoever is leading the charge will be lecturing us about safety and protocols for an hour before we go into the bunker. Or worse, expect us to prep their team on everything we know about the Celestials and hybrids, despite this being our first. Short of drinking a dozen energy drinks, I'm not sure how we're going to make it through this…again. I don't know about you, but I need to gather my thoughts along the way."

"Yeah," Alex agreed.

He felt the same, even if he didn't want to admit it, let alone over think it. All he wanted was to get in, get the girl, and get out. They could figure the rest after. Unfortunately, Lucas was right; whoever was leading the team would drone on about the mission long before it started or expect them to prep their team for them. Another coffee was needed. Alcohol would be better.

They didn't have to wait long to place their order or receive it. Within seven minutes they were on the highway again with caffeinated beverages and sweet treats that neither one would normally eat unless on a long drive.

North Bay was half the population of Sudbury, but the layout was completely different with the vast majority of the downtown core situated long Lake Nipissing and had been an important military location during the Cold War. Nevertheless, it was picturesque with older buildings, some painted bright colours, lining the downtown core. Lucas located the building they were to meet with Interpol and pulled into a free space in front of it. It was still early, most businesses not yet open.

"Please tell me they have us booked into a decent hotel if they plan on us spending the night," Lucas grumbled as he looked at the bright red and blue facade of what Alex assumed was a restaurant.

Alex couldn't help but laugh at that. "Since when did you like anything that they booked for us?" he countered. He opened the door and climbed out, shooting Lucas a wide grin. "You'll just book something better anyways."

Lucas frowned at him as he got out as well. "The last place was a dive."

"The last place was Las Vegas, and Elizabeth said it was fantastic."

"A room is not a suite."

"If it's clean and has a bed, be happy."

The older man rolled is eyes in annoyance. "Have I taught you nothing about luxury?"

Alex gave him a sideways look. "Luxury is only worth it if you have time to enjoy it. Something we don't have."

He pulled open the door and waited for Lucas to pass through first, only for Lucas to pause in front of him with a pointed look.

"There's always time for luxury, love," Lucas told him in a low, sultry voice that made the hairs on Alex's arm stand on end and his groin tighten with sudden longing. "After we get this girl to safety...I plan on showing you why a suite is so much better than a simple

18

'room'." His lips brushed close to Alex's ear. "I packed a special bag for you tonight so I can properly punish you for dragging me here."

Alex bit his lower to suppress a moan. He should have known there would be a catch to bringing Lucas with him. Not that he was complaining. On the contrary, he was looking forward to Lucas "punishing" him. The problem was, he now had a hard-on and wasn't quite sure how to hide it.

"I hate you," he breathed against Lucas's lips.

Lucas glanced down the length of Alex's body to the obvious erection in his pants then back up with a huge grin. "Maybe if you're good, I'll fix that little problem in the bathroom. Mind you, it would be amusing watching you lecture these people with a raging hard-on. I guess we'll have to see just how good you are."

Alex's nose wrinkled in distaste. "Son-of-a...uh..." He squeezed his eyes closed as Lucas patted his groin. "Seriously?"

"Behave...I'll fix it later."

He growled under his breath and adjusted his coat to hide his erection as best he could as he followed Lucas into the restaurant. Of all the places for Lucas to torment him, this was neither the place nor the time, although it wouldn't be the first time that they had sex in a bathroom. There was a certain thrill to potentially getting caught, however, not so much fun when they had to meet with Interpol or members of the Canadian government. Alex could list dozens of times where such a thing was not appropriate. Normally, Lucas agreed with him, but it would seem he was either intent on getting Alex booted from the mission or embarrass him in some way. Or Lucas was just horny and was upset they hadn't done anything that morning. Some days Lucas was hard to read, others, he was an open book.

They found the Interpol team waiting at the far end of the restaurant with several leading generals of the Canadian military. They stood and shook Lucas's and Alex's hands. Alex shifted his satchel to keep his groin covered, utterly embarrassed by the tightness in his jeans. He slightly cursed Lucas while keeping his face a pleasant mask. Lucas was going to pay for this.

"Ladies, gentlemen," he said in greeting before sitting down and crossing his legs.

Lucas sat next to him and immediately laid a playful hand on his thigh. Alex shot him a glare. Now was not the time to be tormenting each other. He gave his husband a hard kick to the shin with the heel of his foot. Had Lucas been sitting to his right it would have hurt a lot worse given the construction of his prosthetic. It was reinforced steel, custom built to allow him to walk and run with ease. It could break bone if Alex kicked hard enough. Lucas had learned that the hard way when their foreplay got a little too rough. It was an accident, but Lucas had started sitting on his left side soon after. Landing in the hospital due to a sex injury was like a badge of honour to him. Ending up there with a fractured shin from being kicked by a prosthetic took a little more explaining than a broken wrist or groin injury. Being stuck in a cast for six weeks afterwards…well it let Alex be top during that time. If Lucas kept teasing him, they might be reliving those six weeks real soon.

"I filled Lucas in on what was going on in the NORAD bunker and the little girl that is hiding down there," he began. He ignored Lucas's hand caressing his thigh. "Can someone give us more information? Maybe explain why these capsules are down there and why they contain people? I take it these were civilians?"

"Perhaps I can," a woman with salt and pepper hair answered.

"This is General Caldwell. She has been the head of NORAD since the base was moved above ground in 2006," James explained.

Caldwell nodded and stabled her fingers as she leaned her elbows on the table. "I'm sure you know the history of 'The Hole'. The complex was constructed in the 1960s, two hundred metres under the earth as a bunker strong enough to withstand a Soviet nuclear attack. It was originally the home of SAGE, a series of super-computers that interacted with our American counterparts. All this was done due to the strength of the Canadian Shield which proved to be the perfect armour to withstand a nuclear strike. It's cooled by Trout Lake." She took a breath and sipped from her mug of coffee, wetting her lips before continuing. "In addition to housing the super-computers, the Hole was designed to support four hundred people for up to one month if nuclear war did happen. It has a cafeteria, gym, medical bays, offices, a barber shop, and countless meeting rooms…some of which were later converted to labs to test what plant life could survive and regrow after nuclear war."

Alex nodded. So far what she said made sense and corresponded with what he knew about the underground base.

"In the mid seventies a strange series of murders took place in North Bay. Women were turning up dead, their hearts torn from their bodies, all while having sex. It wasn't long before we realized we were dealing with a serial murder and rapist. None of his victims survived…except one." She nodded to James who pulled up a file on his laptop and turned it for Alex and Lucas to see. "Arianna was only seventeen when she stumbled into the local hospital with no memory of ever having sex or how she got pregnant. Her parents had disowned her, claiming she ruined their family name by getting pregnant in high school. She even took a lie detector test to prove her innocence."

"You knew her," Lucas stated. His hand stilled on Alex's thigh.

Caldwell nodded. A shimmer of tears dotted the corner of her eyes, but she blinked them away before they could fall. "She was my sister. I tried to defend her, but kids could be cruel. Once word got out that she was pregnant and kicked out of her home, they were ruthless. I was already part of the Armed Forces by then, and training at this base. I risked my career by smuggling her into the Hole. Even forged her credentials just to make sure she was safe." She paused, sorrow and anguish written all over her face. "Everything was good until she went into labour. She was found by one of our civilian technicians and rushed to medical bay where they had to perform an emergency C-section. She didn't survive. Due to the…strangeness of her child, her body was placed in a cryochamber to preserve it."

Alex's brow furrowed. "I thought you said the mother died in the power outage?" he asked James.

21

The Interpol agent looked just as confused as Alex felt. Alex pursed his lips but kept from commenting further on the woman's death.

"How did the girl end up in one?" he asked instead. His hand curled around Lucas's. Something felt off with what they were being told.

The General shook her head. "I was told she died as well. I only saw her as a baby, but it was obvious she wasn't human. None of them were."

"Them?" Alex repeated in surprise.

"The other three bodies," James explained. He pulled up images of the men in who were also dead. "At first, they appeared human, but one is clearly alien in nature…the others may have been its hosts. The blood samples came back the same as yours did after being possessed. The Celestial altered their DNA."

Alex held up his hand. "Wait, that one there is like the child, he's a hybrid, not a Celestial." He tapped the left side of the screen. "The one you called a host, may have been his father, or even the host that helped father him. Does any of their DNA match the girl's?"

"His does," Caldwell confirmed. "I killed him."

"Wait," Lucas interrupted. "Is no one going to mention the fact that this little girl entered a cryochamber as a baby and is now…what, five or six? Shouldn't she still be an infant?"

Caldwell shook her head. "No. The cryochamber slows the blood flow but, depending on the settings, it does not completely stop growth. She was kept in a sterile lab set up, away from where I was stationed, and would have been constantly monitored. Depending on the settings, she would have been allowed to grow slowly. Essentially, she's a newborn in a child's body."

Alex's brow furrowed in confusion. "A newborn with complete knowledge of the layout of the complex, including how to operate the lights, the Shadow-being chasing her, and that the decontamination chamber was the safest place to hide?"

"I don't know. It has something to do with the Celestial," Caldwell told him. "All I know is we need to get her out of there."

"And what will you do once you have her?"

"Give her the family and home she deserves."

Something felt off. Alex searched the General's gaze, but she seemed to be telling the truth. This child was her niece, the last remaining part of her sister. It made sense that she would want to take her in after losing her sister and being led to believe her niece had died as well. Nonetheless, something felt wrong.

"So, how are we going to deal with the Shadow-being? I'm guessing you've never dealt with one before," Lucas inquired. He squeezed Alex's hand, silently supporting him.

"We had no clue such a thing was even in the base," said General Atkins, who sat next to Caldwell. "We don't even know how or when it got in."

"Shadows are exactly like their name," Alex explained. "They move in darkness, sticking to the shadows and using it to track and attack prey. They don't normally attack humans unless we invade their territory. They serve the Celestials."

"Which means it could have come in with the hybrid and host."

Alex shook his head. "No, it would have slaughtered everyone before the hybrid was put on ice. It would have been more recent, perhaps when the Celestials evacuated the planet." He paused and tapped his left foot nervously. "Or...he was there before the bunker was even built. So, I must know...was NORAD built over or around a temple? I know it's built in the shape of a figure eight. Was that due to a temple or Vault?"

"Vault?" Atkins asked in surprise.

"A rectangular shaped chamber. Aztec hieroglyphs etched into the metal."

The men and women around the table looked at each other in confusion.

"I can honestly say that nothing like that was ever found," Atkins assured.

Alex hummed softly to himself, unsure if he believed Atkins or Caldwell. There was a reason the Shadow was down there. It would not have invaded a human space without reason, let alone go into a killing spree. It made no sense for it to hunt the remaining hybrid, so why was it? He wouldn't get any answers until he reached the girl. It was only a matter of time before the Shadow reached her. They were racing against the clock and time was quickly running out.

Chapter Three

The tunnels were flooded with light, ensuring there was no places for the Shadow-being to hide. The main set of floodlights were connected to one of three armored vehicles moving slowly down the tunnel. No one was willing to take a chance of letting the creature escape into the city where it could hide in any pocket of darkness and move around the city with ease, even during the day. There was no telling what it would do, but given what they had previously faced fighting a hoard of the creatures in the past, it could be devastating. The problem with Shadow-beings was that they had no physical form. They could kill and rip people apart, but there was no way to fight them, except by removing the darkness as best they could. There was no telling where it may be hiding.

Alex sat next to Lucas, silently wishing they could light up the interior of their vehicle as they were the tunnel. It seemed unbearably dark inside the Hummer. It didn't matter that it was armoured. If the Shadow wanted in it would get in. It did not have a corporeal form. It was like a ghost, able to move through solid rock. The only thing that could stop it was intense light.

He closed his eyes and took a deep breath. It would be okay. He had faced off against these creatures before, even controlled them for a short time when the Celestial possessed him. Perhaps he could control it again. There was still a part of the Celestial within him, there always will be, it was what allowed him to feel and see what the child did. She was afraid, very afraid. If she was a hybrid, she should be able to control the Shadow. The fact it was hunting her instead was disconcerting. Why would it hunt her rather than serve her? What exactly was the military doing with her and the others in the

25

cryochambers? The General's story simply didn't ring true to him. There was something else going on.

A small smile lifted the corners of his mouth when Lucas's hand wrapped around his, his husband instinctively knowing the anxiety Alex was feeling.

"Are you sure you want to do this?" Lucas whispered. "These are trained soldiers; they can get her out."

"We don't know her powers. We don't even know if she needs to feed or how," Alex pointed out. "They could get her out and end up being killed. The hunger can become all-consuming."

"Even at her age?"

He nodded. "She may not be sexually mature or need to mate, but that could mean she needs to feed even more. She's been in the decontamination chamber for a long time…she could potentially take down an entire squadron in her need to feed."

Lucas was silent for a moment, his brows furrowed as he thought. "Wouldn't it make sense for her to allow one person near her to feed? Lure them in, then lock everyone else before they can stop her?"

Alex had thought the same thing. It didn't make sense to completely block herself off of a potential food source. "Maybe her fear of the Shadow has overshadowed logic. Then again, she is a child. She'll have to come out soon or risk starving to death."

He squeezed Lucas's hand. The girl could only fight her nature for so long before the need to feed became overwhelming. Lord help whoever was with her when that happened. If he could reach her first, he may be able to temper that hunger, find her another food source. He wasn't sure what could substitute a human heart, but he would find a way.

The vehicles stopped in front of a huge metal door. One of the soldiers in the lead Hummer and hurried toward it, pulling the nineteen-ton steel bank vault style door, the first of three that they would have to pass before finally reaching the old NORAD bunker. It swung open with ease. They were on the move again a few seconds later, pausing on the other side long enough for the soldier to close and lock the door behind them before jumping back into the lead vehicle. Alex's chest felt as if it was in a vise with its closure and a feeling of claustrophobia filled him. He had no issue with being underground; most of his research was done underground, but this time he felt trapped, sealed in with only one way out.

They went through the same procedure twice more before reaching the inner sanctum of the bunker. Soldiers and Interpol agents exited the vehicles, weapons drawn, as if bullets would have any affect on a Shadow-being.

Alex rolled his eyes as he walked past them. "Stow the weapons," he snapped, annoyance laced through each word. "If the creature attacks, guns won't save you. You'll be wasting bullets."

"Then what do you suggest we do?" General Caldwell demanded.

He gave a shrug. "Keep your flashlight handy."

"Swell," she grumbled. Nonetheless, she signalled for her people to stow their weapons then slung hers over one shoulder. She gestured toward a corridor on the left. "The lab is this way," she said, taking the lead.

His eyes narrowed as he watched her, but he didn't object. She knew her way around the bunker, he didn't, and despite his misgivings, she was the person in charge. He was starting to wish Elizabeth was with them. She would tell him he was overreacting and what he was feeling was merely due to what happened in Puerto Rico and Area 51, not due to Caldwell herself. It was hard for him to trust the army, any army, after that. He kept his face a mask, refusing to reveal his misgivings to those around him. Only Lucas was able to see through the mask. He gave Alex a reassuring look, trying to quell his fears.

The bunker was showing its age. The walls were a slate gray, the reinforced metal not painted, and some areas showing a rusty brown from moisture, proof that the bunker was no longer actively used. It was almost a shame to have the lights on. If they did decide to recommission it, or convert it into something else, there would be a lot of deep cleaning and repainting needed to make it welcoming to guests and employees. As it stood now, it was cold and foreboding. The grimness of the bunker vanished as they neared the section that hosted the labs. They passed through a huge cavern. It was almost like entering another realm, leaving one of darkness and decay for one that was shiny and gleaming white, untouched by time.

The labs were still being used.

Alex's stomach twisted, his anxiety growing. There was more going on here that Caldwell was letting on. The fingers of his right hand absently began tracing sigils in the air, a habit he had picked up while possessed. It brought with it a sense of calm, shielding him in a way from the outside world, as if forming some sort of bubble. It allowed him to focus on something other than the agents and soldiers around him. He noticed things the others did not. In his mind's eye he saw the girl run ahead of them, pausing only long enough to turn on the lights while anxiously turning around as if to see if she was being chased. Alex paused where she did and turn around to look back as she did, trying to see what she saw. He could feel the darkness chasing her even if he could not see it. It was still there, just out of sight but ready to pounce.

"There is an external generator that keeps the base powered, separate from the city grid, correct?" he asked as they continued forward.

"NORAD has its own power supply," Caldwell explained, her grey eyes sweeping along the corridor for any sign or threat. "The whole country could go down, but this facility can continue running on its own for decades to come."

"What are the labs used for now?" Lucas asked, obviously noticing the difference between this section of the bunker compared to the main section. "Kind of hard to claim it's been decommissioned given the pristine condition."

James glanced him, giving a small nod, noticing this as well. Caldwell didn't respond, neither did any member of her squad.

Alex frowned, the sigils he was tracing becoming larger, movements quicker. Something almost electric shot through him, an energy of some sort. He inhaled sharply, momentarily thinking someone had hit him with a taser, but no such thing happened. He had done it himself, created an energy all his own. His fingers curled into a fist, forcibly stopping himself from tracing more sigils before something else happened. Whatever he had just done, was not something he wanted others to know about. It could be dangerous, a residue effect from the Celestial. He did not want to end up in a lab himself, with doctors and scientists trying to figure out what it was which will only lead to more blood-work and testing, something of which both he and Lucas had had enough off. Whatever he had done, he would have plenty of time to figure it out later.

They reached the lab where a dozen more soldiers and lab technicians were waiting for them, many stationed close to the decontamination chamber, as if ready to pounce should the child finally come out on her own. She was pressed against the far back corner of the chamber, her knees pulled up to her chest and face pressed against them, clearly frightened and trying to keep her distance from everyone. Considering the number of armed men and women in the room, she had every right to be frightened, even if there was no Shadow-creature after her.

"Report," Caldwell ordered as she strolled into the room and took charge.

"She hasn't moved in hours," reported one soldier.

Alex's eyes narrowed in annoyance as Caldwell went to the chamber and began knocking on the reinforced glass, calling to the girl as if that would get her to respond.

"I'm pretty certain that's only going to frighten her more," he said, grasping the woman's hand when she went to knock again. "May I?"

She made a face, obviously not happy, even though this was the reason Alex had come. Then she made a sweeping gesture for him to try.

Alex gave the woman a sideways glance before kneeling next to the chamber at the child's height and gently rapping on the glass.

"Hey there," he said, keeping his voice soft and pleasant.

He tilted his head slightly and reached out to her with the strange psychic bond they seemed to share, and placing his hand on the glass, sent calm and peaceful energy to her. It took several moments but she eventually lifted her head and gazed at him with wide, pale eyes. They were multifaceted, like the Celestial's, but held no power, only fear. She wore only a shift, a white nightgown that almost matched her hair. Her skin was so pale it was almost translucent and shimmered under the intense lights. She stared at him, first in fear and then curiosity, her mouth opening in awe.

"Hi," Alex whispered, a small smile lifting his lips.

She shifted out of the corner and crawled toward him. Then she sat on her haunches and placed her hand on the glass as well, lining it up to Alex's.

"Hi," she whispered in return.

"Can you come out?" he asked.

She shook her head.

"Can I come in?" he tried instead.

She hesitated for a moment then slowly nodded.

Lucas placed a hand on Alex's shoulder. The gesture startled the girl who immediately scrambled back into her corner. Alex bit his lower lip. He wanted to curse Lucas for scaring the girl, but that might make matters worse.

"This is a bad idea," Lucas warned as Alex went to the entrance. "What if she attacks you?"

"She won't," Alex assured. He sent reassuring thoughts to the girl, promising she was safe, and he would not hurt her.

"You don't know that."

The funny thing was, Alex knew she wasn't a danger to him. He could sense it. She wasn't like the Celestial. Perhaps it was her human half. Whatever it was, he didn't feel danger from her, only fear. He let his breath out slowly and squared his shoulders. He would be lying if he said he wasn't scared. He was terrified, but not because of the girl harming him, it was due to all these soldiers and agents and the idea of one of them being foolish enough to try grabbing her the moment he got her out. Or worse, the Shadow-creature making an appearance and attacking them all. A part of him wanted Lucas to go in the decontamination chamber with him. In there, all three of them would be protected.

The heavy door slid open. The girl stood as he entered but stayed pressed against the far wall. She was small, perhaps three and a half feet tall and slight of build, almost elfish, except her ears which were perfectly human. Her eyes were captivating. Despite warning everyone not to look her in the eye, he could not help but do so himself. He remembered when he was possessed and looking at his reflection in the mirror, how alien his eyes had been when the Celestial was in control. This was different. The child was not trying to possess him or even control his mind. If anything, she was trying to determine if he was safe just as much as he was trying to determine the same of her. She was so scared if was heartbreaking. What had she endured while trapped in the cryochamber? There was more going on than Caldwell was telling him, he could feel it, almost see it in the girl's eyes.

He moved toward her slowly as the doors closed behind him, his hands risen in front of him as if he was approaching a wild animal. He hated thinking of her in such a manner, but until he knew for certain she would not harm anyone, he had to. It didn't matter what his heart was telling him.

"My name is Doctor Alex Jackson," he said in introduction, stopping several feet away from her. "I'm a…"

"Doctor…" she repeated, as if she knew him.

She hugged herself and tried to press herself back in the corner while making a small wailing sound as if she had been injured, despite no one touching her. Using his title may have been a bad idea. She obviously knew what a doctor was even if Alex was not that sort of doctor. He was an Anthropologist and searched for ancient and lost civilizations. That was how he had found the underground Celestial temple in the Rocky Mountains. He was not a surgeon or medical doctor. Something told him the child had experience with them as well as lab technicians. His stomach churned with the possible implications. There was much more going on here than he and Lucas were being told.

"I'm not like them," he said gently, mentally sending her an image of peace and calm. "I won't hurt you."

It must have worked. Much to Alex's surprise, pulled herself out of the corner and launched herself into his arms. She clung to him, her small arms wrapping tightly around his narrow waist. She pressed her face against his stomach as she shoulders began shaking. Something seemed to snap into place the moment they touched. It was as if he was meant to find her, as if this was somehow destiny. His whole body shook from the force of it, like energy rippling through her and into him, much stronger than the sigils earlier. Surprised, Alex pulled her away for a moment, wiped away her tears, and stared at her in awe. Then, feeling that she needed protection and comfort, he picked her up, letting her wrap her arms around his neck. Her grip was impossibly tight, but Alex didn't try loosening it. Instead, he rubbed her back as he spoke soothingly to her.

"It's alright," he promised. "I've got you now. Everything's going to be alright. I promise." He pressed his cheek to her head. "It's okay."

Holding her with one arm, he activated the door and exited the chamber. Her grip on him momentarily tightened in fear. He continued whispering to her, promising to protect her, even if that meant against the very people that came with him and Lucas. Walking back into the lab, he nodded to Lucas, assuring him everything was okay. There was a worried look on his face, but also a hint of something else…admiration and perhaps longing. Alex raised a questioning brow, but Lucas shook his head with a small, whimsical smile. Alex couldn't help but return it. It felt kind of nice caring for a child, being charge with protecting and comforting them. It had only been for a few minutes but he could almost see himself as a father, even if it meant adopting, something he and Lucas had discussed.

He adjusted his hold on the child, prepared to carry her all the way to the awaiting vehicles when Caldwell suddenly strode up to them. She didn't say a word, only grabbed the child by hair, yanking her head to one side before Alex could stop her. Then she injected a syringe full of some strange liquid into the girl's neck. The child gave a surprised cry and tried to jerk away, some of her pale hair being yanked out in the process as she yelled and cried. She became wild in Alex's arms as he tried to pull her away from Caldwell without hurting the child more. Her long finger clawed at his back as she tried to escape the General but within moments, she began blinking rapidly and shaking her head, fighting against the affects of the drug. Soon, she slumped in Alex's arms, her head resting against his shoulder, gentle breath ruffling his hair, unconscious and now dead weight.

"What the fuck?" Alex snapped. He stepped and placed a hand protectively over the injection site. "She was calm. There was no need to drug her!"

"That Shadow thing is still out there, and it's attracted to her. If it can't sense her, it won't attack," the woman argued as she threw the syringe on a table.

"On the contrary. If it's out there and protecting something, it will attack anyone that gets in its way."

Her eyes narrowed and lips pursed as if she was going say something further. She gestured to the two medics that had accompanied them. They stepped forward with a gurney. Alex bit back a curse. He glanced at Lucas who gave a small nod, encouraging him to let them take the girl. His hold on her tightened, his fingers curling in the thin fabric of her nightgown. A protectiveness he had never felt before filled him. He didn't want to let her go, didn't trust

33

these people with her, even if Caldwell was her aunt. He didn't really have much choice though. They didn't have time to bicker. The Shadow-creature was still out there, and sleeping or awake, the girl was being hunted by it. Everyone in the bunker was at risk, as was the city if it escaped. While he wanted to place his entire focus on the hybrid in his arms, she would have to wait until they were safely back in the city.

Taking a deep breath and letting it out slowly, he laid her on the gurney and stepped out of the way as the medics checked her vitals before strapping her to it. She looked incredibly tiny and defenceless. The urge to protect and take care of her only grew in Alex. His breath hitched when Lucas wrapped an arm around him. His heart raced just a little as he felt Lucas's lips press against his temple in reassurance. Alex's shoulders slumped as he leaned into his husband. He didn't like giving the child up but Lucas was right, even if he did not speak a word; the girl didn't belong to him. He had no claim on her. He certainly wasn't her father. He could never have children, but for a moment, a very brief moment, he felt like a father forced to give up his child. Where the thought or sentiment came from was beyond him. It probably had something to do with having been possessed by a Celestial and one of its kind had fathered her. They may not be related by blood but they shared a bond, one as strong, or stronger, than what Caldwell shared with her.

He felt strangely empty without the child in his arms as they their way back to the entrance. Lucas stayed next to him, still fully armed with a fully automatic rifle like the soldiers, knowing Alex's moods could shift as quickly as the weather. It was part of his Post Traumatic Stress Disorder caused by all the horrors he had faced because of the Celestials and temples and those that sought both.

They followed behind the gurney, Alex unwilling to be too far from the hybrid. Nothing impeded their path. No flickering of lights or shadows where there should be no shadows. It felt oddly quiet and still, almost dead. It was as if they were walking through a tomb where before there was a sense of energy and life, despite the decrepit look of the main section of the bunker.

The hybrid was placed in the back of the middle vehicle, armored van that doubled as a mobile medical facility. Alex moved to climb into the back with her but before he could, Lucas was pulling him toward the vehicle they came in while Caldwell climbed in with her niece.

"Something's off," Alex grumbled as Lucas sat next to him.

He buckled himself in then leaned against the door, trying to get a look at the van ahead of him. Why couldn't he shake the need to be with her and protect her? What had the Celestial done to them?

"The Shadow is likely lurking in the darkness," Lucas mused as the Hummer caravan began to move. "The flood lights will stay on until we're out of the tunnels."

"Yeah," Alex murmured.

"Alex," Lucas sighed. He placed his hand on the younger man's lap. "She's safe. No one's going to let anything happen to her. I promise."

"You can't make that promise. No one can."

His husband caught his chin between his thumb and forefinger and gently turned his head so they faced one another. "Baby, I promise you, she'll be alright. It's these soldiers and agents you should be worried about. We don't know how she feeds. If they let her stay awake and the hunger hit...she could kill everyone here without a second thought. She may not even be able to control it. Caldwell did the right thing knocking her out. Getting her back in a cryochamber where she's safe from the Shadow and everyone is safe from her, may be the best bet."

Alex's mouth fell open to argue but stopped. Lucas was right. They had no clue what the girl was capable of. Just because she hadn't attacked or fed off of anyone didn't mean she wouldn't. Caldwell had her best interests at heart. Alex had to trust her, regardless of what his heart said.

"Don't worry, it's going to be okay," Lucas assured. He took Alex's hand and gave it a squeeze. "Let's get out of here, and once we're clear and able to go to our suite…I'll make you feel better."

Alex rolled his eyes but grinned. Lucas knew how to make him feel better, even if it was a little "unconventional". He squeezed Lucas's hand before bringing it to his lips and placing a kiss on the back of it.

"I love you," he breathed.

"I love you, too."

Chapter Four

A lex wasn't sure how to feel once they reached the base above the bunker rather than returning 22to the city as expected. They came out the North tunnel and drove along the narrow road into the 22nd Wing of the Canadian Forces Base. The sun was already hanging low in the sky, the evening quickly approaching. The only downside to the Fall was how early the sun began to set. Judging by the cloud coverage slowly moving in from the north, they may be in for their first snowfall that night. The drop in temperature while they were underground was a good indicator of the change in weather in only a few short hours.

"It's going to be a bad one," Lucas noted as they pulled up to the medical building behind the other armoured vehicles. "I guess we are spending the night."

"Isn't that why you rented us a suite?" Alex teased.

He watched with trepidation as the medics began unloading the gurney with the girl still unconscious on it. His hand rested on the door handle, about to pull it open and follow her into the complex but Lucas caught it and shook his head.

"We did our job," he reminded him. "Now we leave."

Alex blinked in surprise but let Lucas pull his hand away. "She's alone."

"Her aunt is with her. They'll put her back in statis and she'll be safe from the Shadow. So will the rest of the city. You did exactly as you were asked to." Seeing the doubt in Alex's face, he smiled softly at him. "I promise."

Alex hesitated then finally let go of the handle.

"You're right," he conceded.

They had done what they had come to do, get the child safely out of the bunker. There wasn't really much more they could do. It wasn't as if the girl was his daughter and he had any say. The only connection they shared was the Celestial. He had to trust that her real family knew what was best for her, despite his misgivings. He didn't know them. They could be much nicer than he was allowing himself to believe. After all, discovering a long-lost niece who was fathered by an alien was enough to make anyone leery. Caldwell had done what she thought was best for the child and the Nation. Putting her back in statis was probably for the best. There was no telling how powerful she could become when she reached full maturity. She could be just as deadly or more-so than the Celestial had been, and that was a frightening thought.

They were driven back to the city to where their Jeep was parked, by which time the sky was dark, the clouds blocking out the last rays of sunlight, and the first flakes of snow began to fall.

James leaned out the driver side window as Lucas and Alex climbed out of the armoured vehicle and went to their own Jeep. "If you guys don't mind staying an extra day or two, we're going to have a debriefing in the morning and then perhaps put together another team to go back in the bunker...you know, make sure there isn't any hidden temple in the basement that no one bothered to tell us about. The government really wants to preserve it as a Heritage Centre but it's going to be worthless if it's festering with those Shadow things. Last thing we need is a sleeping Celestial waking up and ravaging the city."

"Indeed," Lucas agreed as he unlocked the Jeep. "And if there happens to be one? We can't simply destroy it without potential damage to the city."

James shrugged. "I don't know. We'll figure something out. Maybe seal whatever cavern it's in and cement it so nothing gets out."

Lucas nodded. "Makes sense. It's pretty much what the Ancients did to contain them for ten thousand years. Hopefully it works again."

"I'll call you at six and we'll get a team together."

"Sounds good."

Alex hesitated, wanting to go as well but not at the same time. He had had enough with temples, and certainly more than enough with Celestials, Shadow-beings, and Guardians. He bit his lower lip in sudden realization.

"There is no temple," he said more to himself than the other two men. "If there were, the Guardians would have already dealt with the Shadow. It would never have escaped the temple. It had to have some from somewhere else. Perhaps even attached itself to the host and got trapped in the bunker when he was killed."

Lucas regarded him for a moment. "There's no way to be certain without checking it out. Area 51 transported two temples from the oceans brick by brick and the Shadows and Guardians were still attached. They could have done the same here and not bother to tell anyone. All it takes is a few rogue scientists and soldiers willing to work for them, thinking they're about to make a big score and more money than the government pays them."

That was true. It was what had happened with Area 51. All it took was one con-man to convince the Generals that the ultimate weapon laid within the alien temples, and they invested everything they could to acquire the Dragon Triangle and Bermuda Triangle temples. They dismantled and transport port them to Area 51, reassembled and tried to use nuclear reactors to activate them. It ended killing almost everyone there, leaving a crater where the base once stood, and activating every Celestial temple around the world, freeing the Vaults or spaceships hidden within that launched into space. It caused world-wide destruction to monuments thousands of years old. Many countries were still recovering. Some countries no longer existed.

"Okay," Alex said after a moment. "We'll go down and check. Better to be safe than sorry, right?"

Lucas nodded. "Right."

Alex climbed into the passenger seat and waited until Lucas was seated next to him and the engine was started. "You know I hate this idea, right?"

"I know."

"We'll need to check the radiation level every floor. If there's a sudden spike, we'll have to gear up in hazmat suits."

"I know."

Alex slumped back in his seat. "I'm hating this idea even more now, thanks."

A smirk lifted Lucas's face. "I guess that's one more thing for me to make up for tonight."

He had almost forgotten Lucas's plan to woo him tonight. A grin tugged at his lips. "It better be good."

The truth was, it had been quite some time since they actually had sex. After being possessed by the Celestial, Alex had become afraid of intercourse. Not so much of having it as much as what he might do afterwards. The Celestial fed not only from sex but from literally ripping out its partner's heart and feasting on it almost at the exact time of their orgasm. It gave the creature some sort of power. It didn't technically need to feed during sex, a heart was a heart, but it gave the beast a strange sort euphoric high. After months of the creature inhabiting him, Alex became afraid that he may continue feeding off people once the creature left his body. He was afraid of hurting those he loved, of accidentally killing Lucas at the height of their love-making. The only way it worked was by being tied down. Alex enjoyed that, but sometimes an echo of the Celestial would rear its ugly head and he would struggle and fight, wanting the coppery taste of blood even though he no longer needed to feed. It was something from which he would take a long time to recover. Thankfully, Lucas was patient with him and never pushed him past his limits. If Alex said or signalled to stop, they stopped. Tonight, Alex wanted to push those limits.

Alex almost felt giddy as they pulled into the hotel's parking lot. The snow was beginning to fall heavily. Big fluffy flakes clung to their clothing as they hurried to grab their bags out of the back of the Jeep. There weren't very many cars in the lot which allowed them to park close to the building. This time of year, hotels weren't overly busy and Alex was happy for that. He hated crowds and long waits and was happy not to be faced with either as they stepped into the large lobby. Alex brushed off the snow and gave a little shiver as Lucas headed to the front desk. With luck, the snow would melt by tomorrow. He hated to think of the long drive back to Massey without proper snow tires on the Jeep. Those were still in storage in the garage. He made a mental note to book an appointment to have them installed as soon as they got home.

"Got our keys," Lucas announced, flashing two plastic cards for Alex to see. He grinned brightly as Alex took one. "Top floor with the best view in town."

Alex couldn't help but laugh. "You do know we're leaving before the sun even rises, right?"

Lucas's grin only grew. "I booked us for two days. Think of it as a second honeymoon."

"Oh...so if we do find another temple we have a place to hide?"

He shrugged. "Or fuck until the world ends. I'm happy either way."

"You're horrible!"

"Not when I'm between your legs."

Alex's face turned bright red. He really hoped the desk attendant had not heard that. Lucas was not shy about stating his intentions. He liked sex and he made sure everyone knew Alex was his, not caring in the least what homophobic people might think. Sometimes it was almost as if he was challenging people to say something. Alex both loved and feared that side of him. One day, someone might actually try something and while Lucas could hold his own in a fight, there could always be someone stronger than him that might want to cause trouble.

None of that concerned them now. Lucas wrapped an arm around Alex and led him toward the elevators on the far side of the lobby. He pressed the up button and a few moments later the double doors opened. No one else joined them in the car, and the moment the doors closed, Lucas dropped their bags, pushed Alex against the wall and began kissing him. It was as if they had not kissed in ages. Lucas's lips were hungry, not simply kissing but his teeth and tongue getting in on the action and trying to tease Alex's mouth open, which the younger man happily obliged. One of Lucas's hands slipped under Alex's coat to tug the zipper of his jeans down before delving inside to grasp his hardening length.

"What about the security cameras?" Alex breathed.

He honestly didn't care if they were caught. Lucas's hand felt cool from the chill outdoors but still make his blood race and pool in his groin with anticipation. What had gotten Lucas so worked up? They had made out in risky places before but never with this much passion.

"Fuck the security cameras," Lucas sneered in his ear. "I'm almost tempted to make you face this mirror while I yank down your pants and rail you until you can't walk anymore." He nipped the remains of Alex's scarred ear. His breath tickling the tender tissue and echoing through the hearing aid. "I wouldn't put anything past them jacking off to us."

Alex bit his lower lip. It was tempting. Almost as much as the time they had sex in the vineyard in the middle of the day. No one else was on the property at the time, but that could have quickly changed at any of their workers suddenly shown up. Having sex in an elevator could get them kicked out of the hotel before they even made it to their suite.

Thankfully, that decision was taking out of their hands as the elevator dinged on the next floor. They only had a split second to straighten their clothing before the doors opened, permitting an older couple in. Lucas nodded to them with a pleasant smile, as if he didn't have his hand down Alex's pants only a moment ago. Alex had to adjust his coat to hide the hard-on he now sported. Damn Lucas and his kinks. Now he was hot and bothered and really wanted to get to their suite so he could give a little pay-back.

Their suite was on the top floor and located at the far south-east corner, overlooking Lake Nipissing with the Manitou Islands off in the distance. The lights from the largest of the five islands was barely visible as the snow increased to almost white out conditions. If Alex didn't know it was out there, he would have barely noticed. His focus was elsewhere.

As per usual, Lucas had rented the most expensive suite in the entire hotel, far larger than they needed. However, it wasn't only luxurious, it was fully accessible and designed for someone with not only mobile difficulties but hearing as well. When they first began dating, Alex hated when Lucas rented these types of rooms. He hated having to admit to having a disability and being limited in what he could do. It took a long time for him to accept his limitations or the fact that Lucas cared enough to ensure his comfort and needs were addressed. Now he smiled whimsically as his gaze wondered about the room, noting the walk-in shower with bench seat, wide counters tall enough for a wheelchair to roll under, and wide entrance and space around the furniture. Alex rarely used a cane to walk with anymore, typically only when his right leg began to act up, but if he ever needed it, this pace was designed to let him move about with ease. He would likely need the cane by morning if the weather got any worse. His stump was already beginning to ache.

Nevertheless, that was the farthest thing from his mind as Lucas dumped their bags on the bench and began stripping off his clothing. Alex's face lit up in a large smile as he watched his beloved strip naked. Watching Lucas was always his favourite part. Lucas was a large man, tall and lean with a dusting of thick black hair on his chest that trailed down his toned stomach like an arrow to his groin. And, oh…was he happy to have Lucas alone in the suite.

"Are you going to strip or watch?" the larger man asked, a questioning brow raised.

Alex hummed softly as he eyed Lucas, then wetted his lips, his tongue lingering over his lower lip. "Honestly? I'm enjoying the show. What brought all this on? You haven't been this needy in a very long time."

Lucas rolled his shoulders in a lazy shrug. "I don't know…" he answered, his voice deep and silky. It was like a caress that moved over Alex and stirred his arousal even more. "Something about you caring for that child. You looked good…as if you were a father."

"And fathers turn you on?" That seemed like an odd kink. There were Daddy kinks, but this didn't seem to be the same thing.

"You being a father turns me on."

Alex's eyes widened slightly before he looked away. He wanted to be a father, he really did, but he was sterile and could never father a child. Even if he could, he was gay. He had absolutely no interest in women, despite experimenting in his youth and being forced to mate with women while possessed by the Celestial. Sure, he and Lucas could adopt, but the child would never truly be his. Not biologically.

Pursing his lips, he pushed that thought away before Lucas began worrying about him again.

"Well, I think you would be a great Dad. You would spoil a child so bad that I would get stuck being the bad guy having to discipline you both," he teased.

"Oh…I like that. How are you going to discipline me? Spank me?"

Alex bit his lower lip, his jeans feeling unbearably tight at the mere thought of Lucas bending over his knee and giving him a good, hard spanking. Normally, Lucas was the dominate one, but he'd be lying if he didn't enjoy the image of the round, firm globes of his ass turning bright red as his hand went across them.

Pulling off his coat, he removed his smartphone, placing it on the nightstand for safe-keeping, threw the coat onto the bench and began tugging off his sweater and under-shirt. In his rush, his arms seemed to get tangled. Lucas laughed before helping him, stripping him bare until all that was left was the prosthetic and his socks. They didn't remain on him long. Lucas pushed him onto the bed and quickly rid him of his assistive device. He rested it next to the bed, within reach, but Alex wouldn't need it until morning. Lucas would make sure of that. Alex cupped his cheek, his thumb rubbing small circles in Lucas's trimmed beard. For a moment all he could do was stare at the man he had come to love so much, to have committed his life to and marry. Lucas had given him so much. He had upended his life and moved from England to Canada to be with him and Alex didn't even ask him. If there was anyone Alex wanted to raise a family with, it would be Lucas. He would spoil them rotten.

"What are you thinking?" Lucas asked, his voice gruff with need but clearly curious.

Alex blinked away moisture from his eyes. "How much I love you."

Lucas smiled softly and kissed his forehead. "I love you too, sweetheart."

Alex closed his eyes as Lucas moved downward and kissed his eye lids then nose. His hands gripped the larger man's shoulders, unsure if he should ask to be tied up. He wanted this so bad it hurt. He wanted to hold Lucas to him while they made love but was also afraid of losing control and the echo of the Celestial lashing out and hurting Lucas, intentionally or not. If he was tied to the bed, it would be safer, and there was a certain thrill to having no control and giving it all to Lucas.

45

A moan escaped him as Lucas began kissing and nibbling the side of his neck. His lover knew exactly where all his sensitive spots were and attacked them with glee while his left hand moved to Alex's genitals, teasingly stroking his cock before grasping and rolling his testicles in his palm. Alex arched beneath him, his fingers digging into Lucas's muscular arms.

"Did…did you bring the toys?" he managed.

Not that he cared. Lucas could pin him down and ravage his body without toys. He felt as if he was going to burst already and this was merely foreplay.

Lucas nipped his ear and began stroking his aching cock. "Do you want me to stuff your cock with a 'sound' or the beads?"

Alex whimpered. They both sounded so good. "Surprise me."

A deep rumbling chuckle left Lucas. "Alright."

He pressed a kiss to Alex's lips before climbing out of the bed and retrieving one of the bags. Alex sat up as Lucas placed the bag on the bed. Inside were some of Lucas's favourite toys, sealed in a protective case. Lucas removed the case, surprising Alex that it was the smaller version of the one that was normally taken with them when they travelled. It was like an overnight bag for their toys with only two of the more than thirty "sounds" or "rods" Lucas owned, one string of urethra beads, one string of anal beads, two pairs of clamps, red furry cuffs, and a gag. Alex laughed. To many people, this would seem to be a lot, but it was rather mild for Lucas.

Alex pulled out the two pairs of red furry cuffs and playfully twirled them around one finger as he looked at the headboard to see where they could be attached. His face fell as he noticed the headboard as built into the wall and the bed frame itself was a platform with no legs and no place to attach the cuffs. One part of Alex was relieved – he didn't really like being tied down – but another was disappointed and fearful of Lucas's safety if he lost control. He looked to Lucas, wanting to proceed but unsure if it was safe. They could cuff his hands behind his back but as fun as that was, his shoulders suffered for it each time.

"I trust you," Lucas told him. He took the cuffs and placed them back in the case. "Just lay back and relax, I've got you."

Rubbing his face in growing anxiety, Alex took a deep breath before laying back. Lucas regarded him for a few moments before seemingly coming to a conclusion. He held up a silk scarf they used as a blindfold then shuffled up the length of the bed as Alex leaned on his elbows to give him unrestricted access to his head. He wrapped it around over his eyes then secured it at the back of his head. Alex lay back down, his fingers flexing as he waited for what Lucas would do next. He inhaled sharply as the clamps were attached to his nipples. They stung but in a good way. Lucas kissed them better before peppering kisses down his chest and over his taut belly, pausing to lap at his navel. Alex's hands tangled in the other man's short, dark hair, tugging at it in need the closer he got to his aching manhood. He was hard, so very, painfully hard. Lucas gave it a few firm pumps, his tongue licking over the dripping head before pulling away altogether. Alex whimpered at the loss of contact but it only lasted a moment.

"Oh God…" he breathed as he felt the tip of a well-oiled sound, press against the slit of his dick.

Lucas teasingly swirled stroked it over the slit before gently, expertly, pushing it inside. His movements were slow and precise, thrusting the metal rod in and out of Alex's length as if mimicking what he would soon be doing to his ass. Each thrust went in deeper until finally, the entire length of the sound was sheathed inside Alex with only the ring hanging out, capping the opening. It hurt and felt good all at the same time. Alex ached and thrust his hips upward, wanting more. His entire body was humming with unbridled desire.

Fingers teased the tight muscles of his ass. Judging by how hasty the movement was, Lucas was reaching the end of his patience for teasing. It had been quite some time since they were this intimate and they were both in a bit of a rush to finally join together. Despite that, Lucas did take his time stretching Alex's muscles, making sure he was loose enough to accept his massive length. When his cock finally did push into Alex, it was like welcoming it home. It was where it belonged and Alex gave a little whine when it withdrew, his hands automatically trying to find and grasp Lucas to back him go back inside. Large hands grasped his own as Lucas pushed back in while also pushing Alex's hands to either side of his head, effectively pinning him down while giving Lucas more leverage to thrust into him. Slow, measured thrusts grew in intensity. This thick, long length dragged tantalizingly over Alex's prostate with each withdrawal only to be stabbed almost painful on the inward thrust. Alex whined and whimpered, trying to move with Lucas only for the large man to shift his position so that he was kneeling between Alex's legs with the smaller man almost folded in half, his knees braced on Lucas's broad shoulders. In this position all Alex could do was take whatever Lucas gave him, and Lucas seemed intent on ruining him, ensuring he would feel it in the morning. His thrusts became so hard the platform of the bed began to creak and rock, thumbing against the wall with each hard, deep thrust. Alex's cries grew with it, his mind on the sensations filling him and unable to form coherent words to express his passion.

Being on the top floor with the bed on the outer wall had its benefits, but Alex was certain if anyone was in the next room, they could surely hear what was going on. He didn't care. He felt fantastic. The best he had in a very long time. In many ways, this was like the honeymoon they had been denied after the trauma they endured with the Celestial.

Music began playing, soft at first then steadily louder as his smartphone began to vibrate. Alex tried to ignore it and focus on Lucas, hoping it would go to voice mail. Lucas didn't stop thrusting and after a minute, the phone silenced and all that could be heard was the slapping of sweaty flesh, Lucas's grunts, and Alex's cries. Alex was close…so very close.

The music began playing again and Alex whined. He needed this. He needed Lucas to ravish him. He needed a mind-blowing orgasm. He was so close.

Lucas let go of one of his hands, but continued thrusting even as he answered the phone.

"Doctor Jackson's phone," he said, as if not perturbed by the interruption. "One moment."

He pulled off the blindfold then handed Alex the phone, surprising him as he continued thrusting as if talking on the phone during sex was normal. Alex gave him wide eyes, unsure what to do. Depending who was on the phone, it might be better to pause their activities, but Lucas went right back to what he was doing, uncaring of what others thought or heard. It was a silent challenge; to see if Alex could talk coherently while having his body slammed-into, repeatedly.

"Hello?" He bit back a moan as Lucas rolled his hips, purposedly taunting him. He gave his lover a dirty look.

"Alex? Are you busy?" James's voice came over the phone.

"You should put it on speaker," Lucas teased.

Alex's eyes narrowed before he bit his lip at the next thrust. That felt unbelievably good.

"Sort of. What's wrong?" he answered, trying to keep the quiver of pleasure out of his voice.

James must have heard it. "We...uh...have an issue with the girl."

Alex froze, his blood running cold. "What's wrong? Is she alright?"

"Physically...she's fine, but she woke up and is panicking. She won't let anyone near her again. She's been asking for you."

"Me? What about Caldwell...uh...oh God! Fuck!"

He covered the phone and glared at Lucas. The bastard had a smug look that clearly said he should hang up and focus on what they were doing. Alex's eyes rolled into the back of his head as Lucas focused entirely on hitting his prostate and stroking his hard length. His body felt as if it was on fire. He was so close....so very close.

"Alex...Alex are you okay?" James was yelling over the phone.

Alex tried not to laugh. "I…uh…hmm…stubbed my toe," he lied.

He didn't sound convinced. "Can you come?"

A grin lit Alex's face. "I will. Give me a few…minutes." He grunted as Lucas pushed his knees to his chest and came at him from a new angle. "I'll be there soon."

He hung up and dropped the phone next to him. "You're a bastard," he told Lucas before crying out.

Lucas was slamming into him now, hard and fast, each thrust meant to keep him in bed and from walking for the next day or two. Just as Alex thought he might lose his mind, Lucas pulled the clamps from his nipples. His cry was almost a scream as pain and pleasure warred with him. If the "sound" wasn't in him, he would have come, but he knew Lucas. That would not come out until they both reached their orgasms. Thankfully, he didn't have to wait long. James's call had triggered one of Lucas's kinks. He loved when other people heard them. It was as if by people hearing how much pleasure he gave his partner it showed his claim on that person, that no one else but him could do this to Alex. Alex wasn't as into it as Lucas but there was a certain thrill in knowing someone else could hear them, and no one, absolutely no one, could do the things to his body that Lucas could.

He had to cover his mouth as a scream tore through him when the "sound" was unceremoniously pulled from his cock. He came hard, spunk squirting from his length in thick white ropes. He could feel Lucas's seed filling him and that only heightened the pleasure he felt as his inner muscles milked his husband's hard length. His body shook with the force of his pleasure, his insides trembling as his vision bled white and mind went blank from euphoria. When it was over, he felt boneless, unable to lift his limbs or do more than lay there as Lucas flopped on the bed next to him. The older man pulled Alex to him, using his body to cushion Alex's.

"So, what did James want?" he asked as he traced the pattern of scars across Alex's back.

50

Alex hummed softly, snuggling into Lucas. "The girl woke up. Apparently, she's panicking again and asking for me."

"Oh."

Lucas fell silent and glanced toward the window. Alex followed his gaze, only then realizing that the curtains were open. If it wasn't for the fact that they were on the top floor and there were no other buildings between the hotel and the lake, anyone could have been watching them. He would have to keep a better eye on that. Regardless of that, it was snowing even heavier now. A full-out blizzard. It would be dangerous to go back to the base right now. Nonetheless, Alex had to. He knew he did. With Lucas no longer distracting him, he could feel the girl's fear just as he had before. She needed him, and despite the weather or how much his body now hurt, he had to go back to her.

Chapter Five

The drive back to the base was a nightmare. There was very little traffic on the highway, but the snow had increased, turning into a nasty snow-rain mix that made the roads slippery and dangerous to drive on. Lucas was forced to use four-wheel drive to keep the Jeep under control. The surface streets were the worst. Snowplows were focused on the highways where the speed limit was much higher than in the city. It was almost a blessing and a curse when they got stuck behind one midway between Highway 11 and Airport Road which led to NORAD, the air force base, and The Hole – the secondary entrance to the underground bunker. It slowed them down but gave their tires better grip. They followed it all the way along Airport Road until they reached the base. Plows were already working to clear the snow there as well. They pulled-up to the medical building as close as possible in hopes of being sheltered from the wind. The wind was whipping around the air base, slapping against them like sheets of ice.

Alex shivered as they hurried to the main door and shoved it open. "Why couldn't they have taken her to the hospital in town?" he grumbled, despite knowing the answer. It was safer for everyone to keep her on the base.

"It's supposed to warm up tomorrow," Lucas tried to sooth. "Hopefully you can calm her down and then we can get back to what we were doing."

"Or sleep," Alex countered.

He was exhausted, and his body ached. It was in a good way but it ached, nonetheless. He shook off the snow the best he could, the

52

dampness and cold clinging to him. The roads were going to be sloppy by morning, provided they weren't frozen over. He hated the mere thought of driving all the way back to Massey in these conditions.

James was waiting for them in the foyer. He had a smug grin on his face as he watched Alex limp in. "How's your foot?" he asked in a teasing manner.

"Uh?" Alex asked before remembering he had told his friend that he had stubbed his toe. James obviously knew the truth.

James's grin grew. "You must have hit it pretty hard."

"It's fine. My stump on the other hand...the weather is beginning to play havoc with it." He rolled his shoulders. "James, we're tired. Can you just take us to her?"

"Yeah, sure."

That grin never left his face. Normally something so small as such teasing wouldn't bother Alex, but while he had known James for well over a year, they weren't really friends, but work associates. The fact that he had overheard him and Lucas having sex was not something Alex had wanted. He was not happy that Lucas had done that. It would have been different if it was someone they knew well and was used to their antics – even then Alex would not have been overly happy about it. He'd get Lucas back. For now, he had to bear through the pain that was not only caused by rough sex, but also the deteriorating weather conditions. The fact he was walking at all was a miracle and had nothing to do with his and Lucas's rambunctious activities. Since losing the bottom half of his right leg, the weather tended to affect it. Bad weather like rain or winter storms caused the entire leg to pulse and ache, making it hard to put pressure on the stump. Alex had been able to ignore it at the beginning of the storm, his mind too busy focusing on other issues to register it, but now the pain made itself known and it was near impossible to think of much else. In order to keep his mind busy, he tried to focus on why they were there and the frightened child they were there to help. Her fear was seeping through the building just as strong as it had been in the bunker.

"What exactly happened when she woke up?" he asked, fighting the urge to limp.

A part of him wished he had brought one of his canes, but it had been years since he last had to use one and he'd much rather not do so unless absolutely necessary. There were enough people who judged him based on his appearance and disabilities, he did not need another reminded that he was missing half his right leg.

James shrugged. "One of the lab techs went to draw blood but broke the needle."

"In her arm?" Lucas said, aghast by the very idea.

"No, it wouldn't even go in. Her skin is too...tough...but it woke her up and she wasn't very happy being poked at."

Alex paused in confusion. "Caldwell drugged her. What gauge of needle did she use?"

The Interpol agent shook his head. "Something thicker. Whatever she used doesn't really matter. The kid won't let anyone near her...except you. Caldwell proposed gassing her. Knock her out, then put her back in a cryochamber and-"

"What?" Alex snapped, stopping in his tracks.

"Alex..." Lucas began. He reached out to Alex to calm him down but stopped just short, knowing better than to touch the younger man in such a state.

This explained the girl's fear. She knew what her aunt was planning.

"Where is she?" Alex demanded.

He hurried into the main building without James and Lucas. He didn't need them to tell him. He could feel the girl crying out to him, terrified, but for a new reason this time. The Shadow was still after her but for now, it wasn't the biggest threat to her. He followed that fear, moving through the building with ease. He passed lab technicians and doctors, many of which seemed frustrated and even angry, no doubt having hoped for a chance to study a Celestial-human hybrid. It was a look he was familiar with after being freed from the Celestial. Anyone who knew about his possession wanted to study him to learn how his body may have changed while under the creature's control, as well as how it had healed and changed Lucas. Even if Lucas did not want to admit it, they were still tied to the Celestial and by extension, this child. Alex was not about to let them put her back into a cryochamber, let alone drain her of blood just to figure out her DNA. This was going to stop now.

He stormed down the long corridor. The medical building was far smaller than any hospital and the layout was rather basic. It didn't take long to find the room in which the child was being held. It was glassed-in, meant to observed whatever or whomever was inside. He glanced inside. It was sparsely furnished, a simple hospital bed on wheels, and chair. The room was brightly lit with only a monitor installed on the outside with the screen facing inward. Currently, it was off. This was not a place meant for healing. The child sat on the floor in the middle of the room, hugging her knees and looking just as frightened as she had before.

Caldwell stood next to a glass door, looking just as frustrated as the technicians had. She spoke rather loudly to what appeared to be a doctor, clearly not happy. Neither was Alex.

"Are you insane?" he demanded, storming toward her with no care of her rank. "You're planning to gas her?"

She turned toward him, clearly startled by his sudden appearance but her face hardened.

"Doctor Jackson, shouldn't you be at the hotel?" she countered, as if not hearing what he had said.

He gave a curt nod. "Yeah, then I got a call that she was in trouble. Are you seriously planning to gas her?"

She gave him a hard glare but said nothing in response. Instead, she glanced past him toward James as he and Lucas hurried to catch up.

"You called them back here," she accused, accurately figuring out who had contacted Alex.

James shrugged as he removed his coat. "The kid wanted him. Considering she won't let anyone in that room, I thought Alex might be able to get through to her again. It's that or let the kid starve. She hasn't eaten anything since waking up and I highly doubt she ate anything in the bunker." He glanced toward the frightened girl. "She's likes Alex, was even asking for him. Who knows, maybe he can find a better way to deal with her than putting her back on ice. You know, help you create that family you promised to give her."

The woman's nostrils flared in anger, as if she had been hoping they would forget what she had said that morning. Alex met her glare. She had lied. She had no intention on caring for the child as her own. Were they even related or was that a lie as well? She looked from James to Alex to Lucas then back to Alex.

"She's too dangerous. We don't even know what she eats. The Celestial *ate people*. She may be the same," she argued.

"And what if she doesn't?" Alex countered, not deterred. "She doesn't feel like it did."

"And what if you're wrong? What if she kills you, hmm?"

Silence filled the space in between for several long seconds, but it was the next question that shook Alex and it didn't even come from Caldwell.

"What if she possesses you like the Celestial did?" Lucas asked. He placed a hand on Alex's arm to draw his attention away from the General. "She's right, Alex. We don't know the extent of her power. We need to think this over. She may look like a little girl but she's older than I am. Her mind may be as well. If so, she can manipulate us. We really don't know what we're dealing with."

"Stop," Alex said sternly. His gaze met Lucas's. "Stop and listen. You can feel her just like I can. She's not like the Celestial. Just listen…please."

With a sigh, Lucas did as he requested. He closed his eyes and shut out everything else around him and listened, simply listened for the small voice that spoke no words that anyone else could hear, anyone but for he and Alex. Their connection to the Celestial allowing them to hear the child. Alex knew that Lucas could hear her as well, not as loudly as he could, but still an echo of her thoughts and fears. The moment Lucas's face softened, proved that he connected to her.

Lucas opened his eyes and let his breath out slowly. His dark brown eyes gazed into the glassed room and child beyond with a new warmth.

"Alright," he conceded. "She didn't hurt you in the bunker. I don't think she will now."

"You're going to trust your gut and not the fact she's not human?" Caldwell exclaimed, flabbergasted by Lucas's reaction. "Because you can 'hear her'?"

"These two know more about the Celestials than anyone else," James reminded her. "If they think she's safe, then she's safe. Let them in."

She gave a snort. "You think I have the key? She locked us out. If you want in, you need to ask her." She turned back to the doctor she had been talking to. "Leave her alone, but I want guards posted around the cube. No one goes in or out except those two. The girl is not allowed to leave, regardless of the circumstances."

"Yes, ma'am."

Alex watched the woman hurry off as Caldwell turned back to them.

"I'm serious, Jackson. You try to leave here with her and you'll spend the rest of your natural life in a jail cell for treason, *without* him." She nodded toward Lucas but didn't continue her threat. It was clear she would not let anyone get in her way for what she had planned for the child.

Alex's blood boiled at the sheer audacity of it all.

"She's full of hot air," James assured the moment the General was out of earshot. "She'd have a hard time keeping you locked up for more than a few hours before we have you out again."

"A few hours is all she needs," Lucas noted. "She seems desperate to put the kid back on ice which means she's hiding something she doesn't want us to find." He glanced at the child then to Alex. "You might be right. There's probably a temple hidden under the bunker. I can't see any other reason for her to be acting like this."

Alex hated to admit it but Lucas was probably right. "What do you want to do?"

Lucas pressed his lips into a thin line as he considered their options. "Does Interpol have access to the bunker...without military escort?" he asked James.

The agent nodded. "We're our own military," he said with a sly grin. "And according to your Prime Minister and the Department of Defense, the bunker is wide open to us. You really think NORAD is hiding a temple?"

"Yeah, I do," Lucas answered. He folded his arms across his chest and turned back to the little girl. "And we're going to find it before the Shadow finds her and destroys it. James, can you put a team together? I don't want you going back down with me. I need someone I trust to stay here with Alex." He glanced in the direction Caldwell had gone. "I don't like what's going on here, and I certainly don't trust Caldwell and her people."

"Yeah, of course," James answered.

He pulled out his cell phone and called the team leader while Lucas looked over the glass room, inspecting the structure and sturdiness. There was a small air vent on the top left wall, another on the right. Both were equipped with small sliding doors that covered and locked them tightly. What was disconcerting was the hose attached to the bottom of the right wall and the strange looking metal box it was attached to. Lucas's hands balled into fists. He glared at it for several long moments before coming to a decision. He yanked the hose out of the wall and device it was attached to.

"Lucas!" Alex objected, a mix of surprise and relief filling him.

He wasn't sure what exactly what it was for, but Caldwell had talked about gassing her and the unit the hose had been attached to no doubt had something to do with it.

"I'm taking this with me," Lucas stated, holding the hose in one hand. He showed it to James. "Make sure no one attaches a new hose. Alex, are you sure you'll be alright with her?"

As soon as Caldwell left, the girl had gotten up and come to the door. Alex watched her but she didn't make any attempt to open the door or escape. She simply stood by the glass wall and stared up at Alex with those pale-pale mesmerizing eyes full of hope.

"Yeah, we'll be fine," Alex promised, placing one hand over the child's.

Lucas placed a hand on the small of his back then leaned in and placed a chaste kiss on his lips. "Okay, we'll be back in a few hours. Just be careful."

"I will." He smiled into the kiss. "Just promise me you're not going to try hunting down a Celestial. Find the temple, destroy it, and come back to me."

That brought a rumbled chuckle from Lucas before he pulled away. He waited long enough for Alex to enter the chamber with the girl, making sure he was safe, then gave the girl a small smile. "You take good care of him for me, alright?"

She looked surprised before giving a small nod. She stepped back as the door slid open, no longer locked, and Alex stepped in. It promptly closed and locked behind him, just as if had with the decontamination chamber. Alex glanced back at Lucas and raised his hand in goodbye, praying his husband would be safe in the bunker. They knew of one Shadow being but there was no telling how many others there may be down there, especially if there was a temple. There could be an entire army and all that might be holding them back were the Guardians…if the Guardians still existed.

Alex glanced around the glass room. It offered no privacy. Even the small bathroom was visible to everyone. It looked more like a prison than a hospital room. No wonder the girl was scared. Waking up in such a place would frighten anyone as strange men and women walked by, some ignoring the glass room, others staring in with open curiosity. The only plus side was the vast amount of light flooding the room. It was almost blinding. No Shadows would make it inside, but it would be next to impossible to sleep. Not only was it unbearably bright, but it was also cool, the floor hard concrete covered in tile. They didn't put the child in here to protect her. They put her in here to imprison her. It wasn't right.

"James, can you get her some food? Maybe soup?" he asked the other man just outside the room. "And a few blankets. Its too cold in here for her."

"Sure. I'll get you a cot as well. You look beat." Thankfully, he didn't make another joke about rough sex, probably because of the child. He gave orders to one of the guards then took his place.

Alex took a deep breath. "Thanks."

He waited until James left before turning his full attention to the girl. She stood a few feet away, watching as the guard retreated down the hall. She seemed more relaxed, her entire posture more at ease now that it was just the two of them, as if the other guards did not exist. There were cameras stationed in the corners of the room but either the child didn't realize what they were or didn't care. She climbed back on her bed and pulled the thin sheet over herself, seemingly going back into her shell again. That was odd. Celestials tended to be more social, wanting to feed and seduce potential victims. Either Alex wasn't her ideal victim or she simply held no interest in feeding. Alex was almost certain it was her age, but why would she call for him if she planned to ignore him?

"I'm sorry about what happened earlier," he began as he moved toward the bed. He sat on the far edge, giving her space but showing he meant no harm like before. "Do you remember me?"

She nodded. "Doctor Jackson."

He smiled softly. "Yes. I'm not the same type of doctor as they have here. I'm not going to run tests on you."

She eyed him for a long moment, absorbing his words then slowly bobbed her head in understanding.

"What's your name?"

She was silent for a moment then looked around, as if afraid of anyone else hearing her name. She crawled out from under the sheet toward him then stopped just out of reach and again looked around.

"My name is Kyra," she whispered. She bit her lower lip and looked toward James then back at Alex. "I want my Mommy."

"Oh... Uhm...honey, I'm sure how to tell you this but..."

A shimmer of tears dotted the edges of her eyes.

"She's dead," she told him, already knowing.

Alex swallowed the lump in his throat and nodded. "I'm so sorry, Kyra."

The tears rolled down her cheeks but she said nothing more, instead curling up on the bed and pulling the sheet over her. Alex bit his lower lip, unsure what to do. He gently patted her leg and let her be. He was probably the first person she had ever spoken to. Letting someone know her name and acknowledging her mother was dead was likely more than someone so young could handle, especially while imprisoned. Nonetheless, Alex had no intention on leaving her now. He'd stay with her, regardless what Caldwell had planned for her. His heart ached for her as her little body began to tremble, soft sobs barely audible. He wanted to hold her and comfort her, promise that no one would ever hurt her again, but he couldn't. Caldwell would stop him, may even kill him to keep her. Of that he had no doubt. It didn't matter. He wasn't going to leave her. He'd find a way to protect her from the Shadows, and stop Caldwell from putting her back into a cryo-sleep.

When the guard returned, Kyra utterly ignored him, as well as the other soldiers who were kind enough to bring food and drink for her and Alex. Coffee for him with cream and sugar on the side and milk for her. She left the door unlocked this time, trusting Alex to protect her from the doctors and lab technicians and their needles. The food was placed on a small table on wheels close to the bed while two other soldiers brought in a cot and extra blankets.

"Damn, it is cold in here," one of them remarked before promptly going back out. "I'll see if I can find a heater on something for you."

"Thanks," Alex called after the guard.

He stayed with Kyra as the cot was set up and folded blanket laid on top, unsure how she would react around so many people. She barely moved under the sheet, her small body still trembling, either in fright or sorrow, perhaps both. It wasn't until everyone left that he reached for one of the bowls of food. Steam wafted off them, swirling in the cool air. At first, he thought it was soup but one look told him it was a thick stew instead, which was probably a good thing. Soup would help warm Kyra up but a good thick stew would help fill her empty belly. He hoped it wasn't too rich for her. It was unlikely she had ever eaten proper food before. And as much as he hated to think it, he didn't trust Caldwell. The food could be poisoned or drugged. There was no way to tell for certain but to taste the food himself and pray that it wasn't.

He inhaled deeply, taking in the scent of stew. It smelt heavenly, nothing out of the ordinary. Dipping the spoon into the bowl, he took a little bit and tried it. It tasted fine, nothing coppery or sour, although truth be told, he had no idea what poison might taste like. He hummed softly in thought and waited to see if there would be any strange effects. Nothing happened. His vision was still clear and while he felt tired, it had nothing to do with the stew. He took that as a good sign.

"Kyra, can you sit up? I want you to eat, honey," he said, gently patting her leg. "This will help warm you up."

The was a small sniffle before the child pulled down the sheet and looked at what he was holding. She looked confused for a moment before taking a deep breath through her nose, inhaling the rich smell of the stew. Curiosity filled her as she climbed out from under the sheet and crawled the short distance to him.

"What is it?" she asked softly.

"It's food."

Her head tilted to one side as she stared into the bowl. She bit her lower lip before finally sitting down next to him and reaching for the other bowl.

"Whoa…it's hot, honey."

He placed the bowl back on the table, then carefully pulled it close so that the table-top went over the bed and between them. Then he leaned forward a little and blew into the bowl on Kyra's side. She watched him for several moments before doing the same. Alex smiled as he watched her. Despite her pale complexion and somewhat alien appearance, she was just like any other kid. She paused when she noticed him watching her, blinked in surprise, then smiled and went back to blowing on her stew.

"Do you think it's cool enough?" Alex asked in a fatherly tone.

Her face seemed to pinch in deep thought, then she nodded.

Alex took the spoon from his bowl and lifted it up for her to see. "Do you know what this is?"

She shook her head.

"Well, this is a spoon. You hold it like this." He demonstrated. "Then dip it into the bowl and take out a little bit of the stew and put it in your mouth."

He showed her how to do that as well then popped the spoonful in his mouth and hummed softly. It really did taste good, and with how cold the room was, it didn't take long for the stew to cool down. He grinned as Kyra copied him. Her eyes widened in surprise when she tasted the stew. Delight filled her face as she dug into her food, obviously not used to actual food but having much better coordination that someone who allegedly grew up in a cryochamber. He kept that thought to himself. With every passing moment, his doubts about Caldwell and her intentions with the girl grew. NORAD was definitely hiding something much bigger than a little hybrid girl. He only hoped Lucas and Interpol discovered their secret without getting themselves killed, otherwise the only ally he had to protect the child was James. With the raging storm growing outside…whether in the glass room or not, they were trapped. If Caldwell decided to take Kyra, there was very little he could do to stop her. She had an army. He had James. It wasn't going to be a fair fight if it came to that.

For now, he pushed back those nagging thoughts and focused on Kyra and how normal her actions were. He could feel as well as see the happiness a simple meal gave her. He sipped at his coffee, already lukewarm, and watched her eat and drink contentedly. It wasn't much, but it meant everything to her. He wished there was a way he could make her feel this safe and secure all the time. If Caldwell didn't try taking her between now and the morning, he could convince Lucas or James to go into town and purchase her some proper clothing and a doll. At least then she would be a little warmer and have something to play with. This room was no place for any child to be forced to stay in. It was horrible for anyone.

His gaze moved toward the all-too-visible toilet and sink. He certainly hoped neither of them needed to go to the bathroom overnight. That was a little too much of an invasion of privacy and far too similar to how people were treated in prison. It was not how an innocent child should be treated, no matter who or what she was.

Chapter Six

G etting back into the bunker proved more of a challenge than Lucas initially thought it would. While Interpol still had permission to go into the Hole, finding someone with the access code at that time of night turned out to be another challenge completely. Caldwell had them, but wasn't in the sharing mood. She, like many of those spending the night on the base, retired to the barracks, her anger and worry getting the best of her. Lucas felt for her. Being the only living member of her family and then discovering a long-lost niece who just happened to be half alien, was enough to shake anyone. Thankfully she wasn't the only one with security access to the bunker. One of her lieutenants accompanied the hastily-put-together task force to the huge iron doors and into the tunnels. It wasn't easy to access with the growing blizzard. The snow was building up. It was wet and slushy, making snow tires a must. One wrong turn and a vehicle could land in a ditch or worse. There was a considerable drop from the road to the entrance of the tunnel. The turn to it was tight, unlike the one from the city. They had to drive slowly or risk a potentially fatal accident.

It was almost a blessing once they were in the tunnels. The brutal wind ended, as did the cold. The floodlights on the vehicles lit up, illuminating the tunnels, and chasing away the shadows. It was just as still as it had been before. Lucas studied the layout of the bunker on Alex's tablet, thankful it had still been in their jeep. Alex had all the blueprints, including 3D models. They offered an in-depth look at the old NORAD facility but there was nothing that suggested anything below it or a way to go under the base. Of course, the same had been true about Area 51 yet there had clearly been a huge cavern under that bunker that housed two huge temples. It could be the same here.

He tapped the edge of the tablet thoughtfully. He had never seen Alex react to someone like he had this child. Sure, she was a hybrid and there would always be a part of Alex that was tied to the Celestial. It had possessed him and taken control of his body, making him do things he normally never would. Alex had seduced people and killed them. He had eaten human hearts while still warm and dripping blood, the bodies to which they belonged still in the throes of death. It had made Alex do horrible things. Lucas still worried about the effects it had on him. Especially now. Alex's connection to the child meant he was still attached to the Celestials and that was a bad thing. She may look innocent, which was likely the Celestial's plan in creating the hybrids, but a child's hunger could be unsatiable. Alex was strong though; he could handle her.

He swiped a finger over the screen to access the file icon. He didn't mind going through the files, he and Alex shared the tablets they owned since both had a bad habit of misplacing them, but he would not try accessing Alex's email. They were each entitled to their privacy and he knew there was probably nothing in the emails Alex would hide from him anyway. They didn't keep secrets from each other. Not anymore. He was searching for a possible file about the girl that James may have sent Alex. If there was, it had to still be in Alex's email.

Humming softly, he tried to think of how to find the files he desired. The computers in the bunker were old. He doubted they would be useful to him, however, they were likely too old and files potentially corrupted with age. However, hardcopy files could still be in the labs or even the archives. He turned back to the blueprints. There was an archive room. With luck, the files contained within haven't been moved to Winnipeg yet. He needed those files. It was the best way to figure out who and what exactly this child was. Caldwell was lying to them which meant either the child was more of a threat than she was telling them, or the government had plans for her that they didn't want anyone knowing about. Either way, Alex could be in danger staying with her, but Lucas would not be able to change his mind; he would protect her with his life. It was Lucas's job to protect Alex's life.

It wasn't long before they were back inside the bunker. Interpol agents exited the armored vehicles, weapons drawn with high-powered lights connected to them. Lucas slipped the tablet in a large inner pocket of vest, shielding it under Kevlar in case they did come up against Shadows of any other creature that may be hiding within the decommissioned bunker. He would need it later the find the archive.

He took the lead, turning on the powerful light before pressing the butt of the semi-automatic rifle to his shoulder. Glancing through the view-finder, he made sure it was lined properly. Bullets would have no affect on the creature should they come across it, but that wasn't the point. He needed the sight to launch the flash grenades attached to the rifle. Each member of their team was equipped with the grenades. They would vaporize any Shadow-being they encountered, at least in theory. They had yet to be tested against one of the creatures. If anything, the weapons could buy them enough time to escape if they were ambushed. To protect their eyes, they also wore tinted goggles that allowed them to pick up heat signatures. Not quite night-vision goggles, but the premise was the same. In this case, to protect them from the blinding light of the flash grenades as well as the intense light already filling the bunker.

"Stay close," he told the team as they moved forward. "No one go off on their own. These creatures will possess anyone they see as vulnerable."

There was a murmured response of the agents around him but he didn't have to ask if they understood. Many have fought next to him against the Celestials before and were accustomed to taking his orders in such situations. Aside of Alex, he was the most knowledgeable of the Celestials and Shadow creatures, even the Guardians. He knew what beings were safe and would help them, and which would tear them apart and feast upon them simply because they could. The inner bunker may be well lit but once they found the staircase that led them to the next level, it likely wouldn't be. They would have to use the stairs to get to each floor and search them. That was three floors of the main figure-eight like section, before they even made it down to any possible chamber hidden beneath the bunker. There was no telling if there was still power to the lower floors until they reached the stairs. They were going straight to the bottom and working their way up. Lucas didn't care so much about finding the Shadow. Even with the flash grenades, it could escape. Finding and destroying the temple and Vault were the only things that would truly kill it. It was possible a portal was open inside the temple, allowing the Shadow to enter their realm. The Celestials tended to use portals to move about the planet and other worlds. Normally they kept the portals closed, opening them only when necessary.

They swept through the first floor as a unit, making it to the stairwell without incident. Lucas paused just outside the door as the team began making their descent and looked toward a large vent that was blowing in fresh cold air. The bunker was uncomfortably warm due to being so far underground and fresh air needed to be brought in from the surface and circulated through each floor. Despite being so deep underground, he could hear the wind howling on the surface as the storm grew increasing worse.

"Pierce, where does that come out?" he asked.

Pierce was a young woman, who was new to Interpol but had served five years in the Canadian Armed forces. She was in charge of intel and had been in charge of doing an in-depth study of NORAD long before any of them came to the bunker the first time.

"By the radio tower," she reported. "Why?"

"Is there any way to block it off?"

Her brows furrowed in confusion. "Not unless you plan on people suffocating or passing out from heatstroke. We're six hundred feet underground and about to go deeper. It can get hot in here pretty fast."

She was right, but Lucas had a bad feeling that if the Shadow found it, it would be a direct route to Alex. It didn't take a genius to know that there was no light in that shaft. It would be a haven for the creature. Strolling to the shaft, he grasped one of the flash grenades, pulled the pin, then threw it in the shaft. It bounced around inside, traveling down it several dozen feet.

"Live blast!" he yelled to the rest of the team. A moment later there was a loud bang that echoed throughout the large chamber.

"Sir?" Pierce asked in surprise.

Lucas shrugged as he rejoined the group. "Sneaky bastards hide everywhere. If it was in there, it should be gone now."

As long as it didn't try running topside. He would kick himself in the ass later if it did.

"Pierce, radio to James and instruct him to have someone drop a few flash grenades from above every five to ten minutes. That should keep it from escaping that way," he told her.

She shook her head as she radioed in the order. "I certainly hope you know what you're doing," she remarked afterwards.

"You and me both," he agreed with a curt nod.

They slowly moved down to the lower levels, checking every nook and cranny to make certain there were no shadow-beings hiding under the steps and in the corners. The sound of pops could be heard as flash bombs were periodically set off in the vents, echoing loudly at times as they passed by a vent. The sulfuric smell of them wafted in with the circulating air flow. It was nauseating but necessary. When they reached the bottom of the steps, the large metal door opened to the third level of the underground complex and went no further. It was the same as the upper levels. Nonetheless, Lucas urged his team forward to search the entire level, certain there was another door or access to an underground chamber. He checked the elevators they passed, including the freight elevators, expecting to find additional buttons that would take the car deeper underground. He found no such thing. Each elevator ended on the level they were on and there were no additional staircases going down, only back up. He didn't give up though. They were six hundred feet underground. The bunker could have been built next to the temple cavern. There would likely be panels that opened to large viewing windows. He had the team search every room, on every floor, trying to local any sort of panel on the outside wall that may hide a window…but again, they found no such thing. No one questioned his orders but after almost two hours of finding nothing connecting NORAD to the Celestial temples, members of the team were obviously starting to question his mental state. Usually, it was Alex obsessing over the temples, not Lucas.

Eventually, Lucas had to admit defeat. There was no temple and if the Shadow was still in the bunker, it had made no attempt on anyone. It was time to turn his focus back to the question of the hybrid child and who she truly was, which meant finding the Archives. The team followed reluctantly behind him, each member tired or bored from their failed search and ready to retire to what little of the night remained.

Pulling the tablet out of his vest, he began following the blueprint back down to the second floor.

"You've got to be kidding me," Pierce grumbled.

The Vault was huge, much larger than even Lucas was expecting, with a huge fireproof iron door. Once it was pulled open, it was like walking into a massive library with rows upon rows of metal shelves that rolled and locked into one another to create more space.

"Well," Lucas began. "It was built during the Cold War. Canada needed some place to store it's vast knowledge."

"Why would they keep the hybrid's file down here instead of in the lab?" Pierce asked as they step inside.

"My guess…because she's been here so long that the original scientists that found her only left a briefing of her case for whoever took over and kept a more in-depth file here."

"This is going to take hours."

He stopped and looked at her and then the rest of the team.

"Do you have somewhere better to be?" he asked, directing the question to everyone there. No one answered. "The faster we find the file, the faster we can get out of here. Look for anything marked temple, hybrid, Celestial, or unknown specimen. I highly doubt they would file her under Alien or UFO. There's no computer to help us so spread out in teams of two and search every shelf. And remember, the Shadow may still be here. If you see anything out of the ordinary, shout."

He turned back to the rows upon rows of shelves. The was going to take hours to sort through, maybe even days or weeks. They didn't have that sort of time to spare. He only hoped that the titles he gave the agents were enough to go by. This was going to be a long night.

The space heater did little to actually warm the glass room and even with the extra blankets, Alex could feel the cold. He did his best to get some sleep, despite the cold and harsh lights still flooding the room, even burrowing his head under the covers. Kyra had done much the same. She craved the light but found it hard to sleep in the cold. Alex couldn't help but make a mental list of things a child needed to stay warm in such conditions. In the morning, he would head to the nearest clothing store and purchase some warmer clothing for her such as proper pajamas and socks, maybe a beanie and gloves to help stave off the cold if she was going to be stuck in such a horrible place. Once those thoughts entered his mind, he began thinking of other clothing she may need like undergarments and sweaters and pants, unsure what little girls preferred to wear. Anything had to be better than that flimsy nightgown she was wearing that did nothing to protect her from the elements. Elizabeth would likely know better. Despite not wanting children of her own, she did have nieces and nephews so knew more about kids than he did. He knew the basics, food, clothing, and shelter. Maybe toys. He knew kids were into electronics. Heck, he had a challenge some days getting his students to pay attention rather than play on their phones. He doubted Kyra would understand what a phone was and perhaps that was a good thing. Cell phones were highly addictive.

If it wasn't the cold keeping him up, it was his brain working overtime trying to figure out how to make Kyra's life a little more pleasant. He knew she didn't like it here but wasn't sure how to fix that for her. He had no say on where she lived, he wasn't related to her in any way. If anything, she was a ward of the government, which meant sooner or later he would have to leave and she would be alone. He hated that idea. Hated the fact that no matter what he did, she would likely end up back in one of those tubes. It wasn't right, but he had no say on the matter.

He stifled a surprised gasped as the blanket covering him was suddenly pulled aside and Kyra stared down at him questioningly.

"You're noisy," she whispered, as if not wanting to be caught out of bed.

Alex stared up at her curiously. "What do you mean?" he whispered back.

"You think too loud."

"Oh? I'm sorry."

The wind howled outside the building, causing the windows to rattle. She looked toward them and shivered.

"It's cold," she remarked.

"I know, honey. Get back under the covers before you get sick," he told her, climbing off the cot to tuck her back into bed.

"Can I sleep with you?" she asked, surprising him.

He stared at her for a long moment, unsure if that was wise or appropriate. The child was shivering, obviously cold, and body heat was supposed to be the best way to warm a person. He bit his lower lip before grabbing the blankets and pillow off her bed and piling them on the floor next to his cot to make the sleep area a little larger.

"Alright, you get on the cot and I'll sleep here," he suggested.

This way they had enough room to sleep beside each other without one of them being shoved off the low cot. It wasn't the most comfortable thing to sleep on, better than the floor, but they would make do. He tucked her in then got under the covers as well, close enough to share heat without anyone making any sort of accusation against him.

"Do you always think so much?" Kyra asked as she snuggled as close to him as she could get.

Alex laughed softly. "Sometimes. Lucas says I overthink everything."

She stared at him thoughtfully for a moment before closing her eyes. "I like your thoughts. They're pretty, like you."

His mouth fell open at the compliment. He wasn't used to anyone calling him "pretty", if anything, he thought the opposite. His body was scarred from head to toe, the worst of which was on his right side with his ruined ear, raised burn marks, and missing lower-half of his leg. There were days when he still questioned what Lucas saw in him. For this child to call him "pretty", well that just took his breath away. He blinked away tears that threatened to fall and smiled at her instead.

"Thank you."

She nodded sleepily and gave a big yawn. Alex watched her for a long time before finally closing his eyes and trying to drift to sleep. He froze when he felt a small hand stroke across the right side of his face, the side that was scarred, then tangled gently in his hair. He dared a peek at Kyra but her eyes were closed and breathing even. She was sound asleep. It felt weird having her fingers clasping his hair but he didn't try moving her hand. Gripping his hair seemed to bring her comfort and if that was the case then he was happy to let her to do so. He fell asleep like that, Kyra's hand in his hair and the wind howling outside. At least they were warmer now.

He wasn't sure how long they slept. It could have been hours or only a few minutes but a loud boom seemed to rock the complex, startling them awake. Alex placed a comforting hand on the child's hip as he stuck his head out from under their cocoon of blankets. It was pitch black, the power knocked out in the storm. It lasted a few long seconds before a hum filled the building and the backup generated kicked on. The lights flickered back on, but not as brightly as before.

"James?" he called, staying next to Kyra.

"I'm here," James called from his post next to the glass room. "It looks like a transformer blew, but the generator will keep everything running until it's fixed."

"What about the bunker?"

"It has its own generator. Don't worry, Alex. Lucas will fine. How's the kid?"

Alex looked back at her. She had already fallen back asleep.

"Sleeping," he responded.

He yawned and slid back under the blankets. He was exhausted. How James managed to stay awake was beyond him. If he could get a solid hour's worth of sleep, he would feel much better. Another sudden bang startled him before he could dose off. This time it was followed by a panic cry not from them. A coldness that had nothing to do with the small room filled him, as did the familiar prickle at the back of his neck. Energy seemed to move around him, like electricity running through him, causing his right hand to itch and pulse.

"It's here," Kyra whispered, now wide awake.

Alex nodded. He glanced around. With only the generator providing electricity, the lights were dim. Only the most necessary ones were on, casting the rest of the complex in pockets of darkness and shadow. The creature could move around freely now. Had the transformer actually blown or did the creature somehow disable it?

"James, we need to get out of here," Alex whispered.

"No," the agent answered, looking just as worried. "The storm's getting worse."

"What about the floodlights? Do we have any portable ones?"

"Yeah…yeah, okay…uh…go gather what floodlights you can and bring them here," he instructed two of the guards.

They glanced toward Alex and Kyra as they got to their feet but the one on the right shook his head. "The power's out. We need to stay at our stations. If you want the floodlights, then you're going to have to get them yourself."

Alex bite back a retort and wrapped Kyra in one of the blankets to keep her warm. The pulsing on his hand was beginning to sting intensely, the sigil burned on the palm making it hard to focus on anything else. It had been a long since it hurt this badly. It was as if he was inside a temple, about to open one of the Celestial's portals, the sigil being the key to the alien computer shaped like an altar.

Kyra pressed herself against his side, fear rocking her tiny body.

"We need to go," she pleaded, her hand wrapping around his. She pulled him toward the door, displaying surprising strength. "We can't stay here."

"Kyra, we can't," he tried to explain. He knelt before her and gently took her arms. "We're safe here. These people are here to protect us."

She shook her head, a shimmer of tears in her eyes. "They're already dead."

He inhaled deeply, wanting to assure her that wasn't true, but screams interrupted that thought. He turned toward where they came from. Gunfire erupted, followed by more screams and flash bombs that lit up one end of the building for several moments.

"Oh god," he breathed. "James, we need to go."

"You're safer in there," one of the soldiers retorted, bringing their weapon up the bear against their attacker. "It's bullet proof. Shield your eyes."

Alex lifted Kyra into his arms and adjusted the blanket around her so that it covered her head and face. "There's going to be a bunch of loud noises and bright lights. Don't look at them, alright? It'll hurt your eyes."

He turned her away from the gunfire, hoping to shield her from what was to come. There was no way to stop the Shadow, not when it could hide everywhere and move through anything. He hoped his tie to the Celestial was enough to stop it, but there was no telling what would happen once it reached them.

Darkness swept into the vast room that Cube was housed in. The soldiers tried firing into it with no affect. Flash bombs caused it to retreat but only for a few moments. They couldn't stay there, but with the power out there was no place safe for them to go.

One of the soldiers screamed as dark tendrils grasped him, tearing him apart. The sickening sound of flesh being ripped from flesh. Alex backed to the far corner of the Cube with Kyra as another soldier was plucked from his position and slaughtered.

"Kyra, unlock the door," he whispered, trying to hide the quiver in his voice.

They had no choice but to make a run for it. If they stayed in the glass room, they were sitting ducks.

The door slid open and James grabbed his arm, pulling him and Kyra out of the room, just as the Shadow was about to descend upon them. Without thinking, Alex raised his right hand to ward off the creature. What happened next left him dazed and confused. A shock ran through him and all but shot out of his hand into the Shadow like a flash of light. It sent him and Kyra flying backwards and slamming into a far wall some twenty feet away while also sending the Shadow reeling back. It gave a pain filled shriek before retreating.

"Alex!" James yelled, rushing to his side.

Alex sat on the floor, leaning against the wall, and breathing heavily, but otherwise unhurt. Same with Kyra. He stared at James with wide eyes, unsure what had just happened but whatever it was, it had been exhilarating and frightening all at once. Nothing like that had ever happened before. Whatever he had done had bought them precious minutes as the soldiers pursued the creature. He grasped James's hand when he offered it and let him help him to his feet.

"I have a Hummer with floodlights just outside. We can take shelter in there," James told him, taking a defensive position in front of Alex. He nodded toward the exit. "Go, I'll cover you."

"You can't face off against that thing," Alex argued.

James threw him the keys. "I'll be right behind you. Get her in there and turn on all the lights. It'll buy us a few minutes."

Alex caught the keys in one hand. Kyra turned to look in the direction the Shadow, but Alex didn't give her time to see what was going on. He held her tightly as he darted toward the front of the building and the nearest exit. Not in the mood to try figuring out which Hummer was James's, he pressed the alarm button, causing the vehicle to begin honking, then ran through the blistering cold wind toward it. The cold was even worse without his coat. The snow hit his face, feeling like sharp shards of glass cutting into his face. It hurt but he focussed on getting to the vehicle. Hitting the unlock button before he reached it, he grasped the backseat door, yanked it open and put Kyra inside, quickly buckling her in. He hurried around to the driver side and climbed in, turning on the engine. It roared to life and a few presses of buttons had the interior lights on and floodlights outside. He felt slightly better with them on and turned to check on Kyra who was staring out the rear passenger window in a mix of fear and awe. This was likely the first time she had ever seen snow. It was not exactly the way he would have wanted her to see it.

James showed up a few moments later, yanking open the passenger door and climbing in. "Now what?" he asked, panting.

Alex shook his head. He didn't know what to do. He didn't even know how he managed to stop the Shadow even if only temporarily. His gaze traveled in the direction of the Hole. Lucas was still in the bunker. Lord only knew if he and his team had encountered the Shadow or found a temple. His hands gripped the steering wheel tightly. He was torn in two. He needed to protect Kyra and keep her as far from the Shadow as possible, but Lucas was his husband and best friend. He couldn't leave without him. The Jeep was still parked in front of the medical bay. At least Lucas could get home. They would be safe at their home.

Setting the Hummer into gear, he backed away by the medical complex. The Hummer had studded tires and dug into the snow and ice with ease. Within minutes, they were off the base and on Airport Road, headed toward the highway. They needed to get onto Highway 17 and head home. With luck the Shadow would follow them, giving Lucas and the others a chance to escape without suffering the same fate as the others.

"Send Lucas a text and tell him what's going on," he instructed James. "Have some of your agents meet us at the house. We need to fight this thing somewhere far from the city."

"What about your neighbours?" James asked as he typed on his phone.

Alex nodded to himself. "By the time we get there it'll be morning. They'll be safe. So will we."

He glanced into the rear-view mirror at Kyra as she stared out the window. The power was out in the entire city, the only light coming from the floodlight on top of the Hummer. He would have to turn them off, but not until they were far enough from the base for Alex to feel safe enough to do so. Being pulled over by the police was the least of his worries. They were in a clearly marked government vehicle. It was unlikely anyone would stop them until the power came back on.

Chapter Seven

When the power went out, chaos broke out in the bunker. The teams initially thought it was the Shadow and began throwing flash grenades, some going as far as to shoot into the darkness, narrowly missing their teammates as Lucas yelled for everyone to stow their weapons. Bullets had no affect on the creatures and they were wasting ammunition. I-int lasted only a few seconds before the generator kicked-in, but despite their high-powered flashlights, everyone was spooked. Lucas slipped the files into his vest with the tablet, needing his hands free in case the Shadow did attack. His gaze took in their surroundings. The lights were not as bright as before, the generator only powering the most vital of areas within the bunker. If the Shadow attacked, it could come from anywhere.

Thankfully, no such attack came. They made their way back to the first floor then to the waiting vehicles and turned them around, hurrying back into the tunnels and out into the raging storm. The snow had built up against the heavy steel door, making it hard to push open and even harder to drive through. It hid the ice beneath. Their vehicles slid on it, having trouble making the ascent to the road above, forcing them to stop once more to place chain on the tires. The temperature was steadily dropping, the winds whipping around them. Lucas worked diligently with the rest of the team to get the chains on so they could get back on the road and to the base. His fingers stung from the cold by the time the last tire was covered. He flexed them, absently wishing he was somewhere much warmer. He never liked the cold. Winter was the best time to be on vacation and Hawaii was starting to look like a good place to retreat until spring.

Exhaustion filled him by the time they reached the base. It was late in the morning, still hours before sunrise, but a time he was normally waking up. Right now, all he wanted was rest. He wanted to gather Alex and take him back to the hotel, get some proper sleep in a nice warm suite after a hot, steaming shower. He instinctively knew that wasn't going to happen, that Alex was more concerned for the child than his own comfort, but Lucas was hoping to convince him to come with him. They needed someplace private to read the files. Once Caldwell learned he had them, she'd demand them back. He needed to buy time to either read them or take photos of each page so that he could study them later. He needed to know what they were dealing with and what exactly this child was. Was she a born hybrid or something else? There were a lot of unanswered questions but he was beginning to think Alex may be right; Caldwell wasn't telling them everything.

He ran his hands through his hair and yawned as he followed Pierce and the other agents into the medical bay. He didn't care if he had to sleep in the glass room, he felt ready to fall to the floor, claim a small spot as his own, even if only for a few minutes just to get a little rest. It was nearing twenty-four hours since he last slept. Of course, that thought quickly left him when he took in the state of the medical bay and the bodies that lay torn to pieces on the floor. Survivors, many of which were badly injured, moved about checking the bodies to see if they were indeed dead and not merely knocked unconscious. There appeared to be an awful lot that were dead.

"Alex…" Lucas breathed, rushing to the glass room.

He didn't need to enter it to know it was empty. He looked around frantically, hoping to see his lover amongst the survivors but he was nowhere in sight. Terror began to seep into Lucas's soul as he looked toward the bodies, fearful one may belong to Alex.

"He's gone," Caldwell told him. She limped toward him having suffered obvious injuries. "That Shadow thing attacked us and Alex booked it. Took the Asset with him."

"Asset?" Lucas repeated, utterly confused. It took a moment for realization to hit him in amongst all the chaos. "The girl? He took her with him?" Anger quickly followed but he wasn't quite sure where it was directed but in that moment Caldwell was a convenient target. "She's a child not an asset, regardless what she is!"

She didn't seem phased by the outburst and met his glare, clearly as angry with the situation as he was, even if for different reasons. He took a deep breath and tried to calm himself. He had seen their Jeep when his team pulled in which meant Alex was in another vehicle, likely one that was better equipped for the icy road conditions. If the Shadow was chasing them then he wouldn't head for the city, he'd go to the only place he felt safe and was outfitted to combat Celestial creatures. He'd go home. Lucas didn't voice that out loud though. If Caldwell knew where Alex was then she'd likely taken an entire airbase to their front door which in turn would lead the Shadow to him and the child. For now, he needed to buy Alex time. He only hoped the kid wasn't a threat and that Alex could handle her on his own.

"Dr. Griffith," Caldwell said, her voice softening almost to what it was when they first met. "We need to find her. She's only been awake a few hours but you have no idea of her power. We need to put her back in stasis for the good of all humanity. Alex has no idea what he's dealing with."

Lucas shook his head in bemusement. "No, General. You have no idea what Alex is capable of. He's dealt with far worse. If anyone can keep her powers in check, it will be him. Take care of your wounded, I'll find out where Alex is and we'll go from there."

He turned to leave, debating if he should chase after Alex or give him a little space to figure out what he wanted to do. If he raced after him right now, he would be leading Caldwell and her people directly to Alex and his gut told him that was a bad idea. Instead, he went to the Jeep and drove slowly back to his hotel. He would be of no use to anyone on the base. There was nothing he could do to help them and he needed to focus on what trouble Alex may have gotten himself into with the child. Despite how much he wanted to call him right that moment, he waited. Alex was only an hour out, but with the road conditions, his focus needed to be fully on the road, not fumbling around to answer his cell phone. Lucas would simply have to wait and pray that Alex knew what he was doing and was safe. Perhaps he would call Elizabeth to check in on him. She was the only other person he trusted to have Alex's back.

Once he was back at the hotel, he dialled Elizabeth's phone number.

"Hey Beth," he said as soon as she picked up.

"Lucas?" a tired voice mumbled on the other end.

He could hear the sleep still in her voice. He sighed softly. He hated to wake her so early.

"Yeah, sorry, hun," he apologized. "Look, I hate to ask but are you heading back to Sudbury today?"

The was a grumble in the background that was not Elizabeth. Guilt hit Lucas even more. She was with someone.

"Not until this evening. Why?"

He bit his lower lip. He should just head home and not involve her in this, but he was exhausted. There was no way he could drive in this weather and safely make it to Massey. Not without snow tires. And driving in his state of mind mixed with the weather would only lead to an accident. He wasn't accustomed to driving in a blizzard, not like Alex and Elizabeth, and it was not something he would ask of either of them. Nonetheless, Elizabeth was closer to the vineyard than he was.

"Lucas, what's wrong?" Elizabeth pressed.

"How bad is the weather there?"

"One sec." There was a groan and more grumbling as she got out of bed to check the weather outside. A moment later he could hear her inhale deeply before yawning. "A little snow but it's clearing up."

Relief filled Lucas and he let out his breath slowly. "Thank God. Alex is on his way home. There's a blizzard here and I'm worried about him driving in this."

"Did you two have a fight?" She sounded more awake now, worry filling her voice.

He couldn't help but laugh. "No...no, nothing like that. We..." He leaned back in his seat and stared out the windshield at the hotel in front of him. "I'm in North Bay. We were asked to come here for a job. Something happened and Alex had to leave. He has a young girl with him. She's...uh...he's looking after her."

"Who is she?"

That was a question he had no idea how to answer. If he told Elizabeth the truth she would panic and race off to protect Alex, if he lied, she would blame him if anything happened to Alex. "There are people searching for her. I don't think their intentions are good though."

"What about her parents?"

"Both dead."

"Damn."

"Remember when everyone seemed to be after Alex? It's the same with this child...for similar reasons."

She was silent for a long moment before taking a deep breath. "Lucas...damn it...alright. Let me get things organized here and I'll head out. I just have a few things to finish with my parents."

"Thank you."

He felt a bit better now. There weren't very many people he trusted to protect Alex but it there was anyone who would make sure he was safe at all times, it was Elizabeth. She and Alex had known each other most of their lives and in many ways were like siblings, even if she harbored romantic feelings for him, feelings he didn't return. She never left him though. She would always protect him.

They bid each other farewell and hung up. Lucas leaned his head against the headrest and took slow, deep breaths, trying to ease his racing heart. If the weather was good in Sault Ste. Marie then perhaps the storm was moving eastward and would blow over soon. With luck, Alex was out of it and on dry highway by now, or would be soon. It was hard to tell for certain. The closer Alex got to Lake Huron the more the weather would change as the lake effect took over.

Feeling guilty for not chasing after Alex, yet knowing he would only be endangering them both if he did, he headed into the hotel. He paid for an additional night, even though he planned to leave by noon, then headed to his room. He was beyond exhausted now. Before he climbed into bed, he sent Alex a text, assuring him that he was alright and asking him to text back as soon as it was safe to do so. Laying his phone on the nightstand, he removed his coat and went to remove the vest beneath only to remember the files and tablet hidden in it. He took them out and placed them on the bed. He should sleep but the archeologist side of him won out.

Kicking off his boots and shrugging off his coat and vest, he climbed into bed, sat against the headboard with the pillows stacked to cushion his spine. Then he pulled the two folders onto his lap and began reading. He only paused to take pictures of each page to make sure he had a copy of each files so he can forward them to Alex. Each page only served to create more questions than answers, but the story they painted of what was really going on with the child was enough to create a horror story. Everything Caldwell had told them was a lie.

The sun was rising to the east as they neared the turnoff to Espanola. The blizzard had slowed into light snowfall, eventually ending as they passed Sudbury. Alex's stress level began to ease with it and he slowly began to relax. Plows were working endlessly to clean up the highway, but it looked as if everything west of Naughton was spared the winter storm. There was snow, and a lot of it, but not to the degree North Bay had been hit.

He glanced in the rear-view mirror at Kyra. She was sound asleep in the backseat, her small cheek pressed against the cool glass, the sun beaming down on her like a halo. She look incredibly small. Far too small to be sitting back there without a booster seat. He absently added it to the list of items she would need.

"I need to make a stop," he told James as the entered the town.

"It's kind of early," the other man pointed out, gesturing to the clock on the dashboard.

"I know…but she needs more than that blanket and gown. She needs proper clothing."

James was right, but there was one store that was open and they had to pass it to get to the back road that led to the vineyard. The parking lot only had a few vehicles. Alex found an empty spot close enough to the store for him to get in and out quickly. He paused before climbing out to check his cell phone. Relief flooded him at the sight of Lucas's message. He was okay. The Shadow had not gotten him. He had made it out of the bunker in time and was now at the hotel.

He sent a quick text in response, letting Lucas know he'd be home in a half-hour and that Kyra was alright. He didn't go into detail about what happened. He would have plenty of time to do that once he got home.

"If she wakes up, tell her I'll be right back. I won't be long," he told James then paused. "What size do you think she wears?"

"I'm not sure. Maybe a size seven?"

Alex hummed softly. Kyra looked to be the same age as one of Elizabeth's nieces. Perhaps she could help. He found her name on his contact list and pressed it. It dialed while he walked into the store and grabbed a cart.

"Alex!" Elizabeth all but yelled over the phone.

He pulled the device away from his ear and shook his head. "Hey," he answered a moment later, unsure why she sounded so relieved. "I've got a question for you."

"And I have about a dozen for you, starting with…where are you?"

Alex raised a surprised brow. "Espanola."

"Thank God!"

"Okay…so about that question. What size is Kelly?"

She was silent for a moment as if having to think about it. "A size six, I believe. I tell you what, how about we facetime and I can help you. Maybe show me who it's for?"

He hesitated, almost tempted to go back to the Hummer and show her Kyra, but that would only serve to wake the child and Kyra was far too tired for such a thing. "She's asleep in the truck."

"You left her alone?"

"James is with her."

"Oh…okay, approximately how tall is she?"

"To my stomach," he answered without having to think too hard on it. "Small build. It's sort of hard to tell her age though. It's a long story."

She made a small clicking noise. "Alright, switch to facetime and let's go shopping. Anything you miss I can pick up on my way home."

His shoulders fell as the tension eased out of them. He knew he could count on her to help him. It wasn't exactly easy to push a cart, hold a phone, and shop all at once, but having Elizabeth see what he was seeing made things much easier. She would call out clothing she thought would be best for Kyra and tell him the size, going through a checklist of necessities before picking out outfits she thought was cute. By the time he reached the cashier, the cart was full of every possible thing Kyra could need, from undergarments to pants and shirts to winter boots, mitts, coat, and hat. Even the booster seat. He grabbed extra milk and juice, things they didn't typically keep a lot of at home.

He also grabbed crayons and colouring books, trying to think of things in which a child may be interested.

The total ended up being several hundred dollars, but it didn't matter. He placed it on his credit card, ignoring the strange looks several people who knew him were giving. He taught at one of the local high schools, meaning many people in town knew him and Lucas and the fact that they did not have children. Yet no one asked any questions, for which he was thankful. He wasn't sure how to explain Kyra or if he even should. After all, there was no telling how long she would be staying with them.

The clothing was bagged and placed back in the cart. He took them out to the Hummer, which had gained a few curious onlookers. Thankfully, it was high off the ground and the back windows heavily tinted. Alex piled the bags into the back of the vehicle before climbing back into the driver's seat. Kyra was still asleep in the back, not at all bothered by the stop. Alex smiled at her then pulled out of the parking lot. They had another twenty-minute drive before they were home.

That proved to be uneventful with next to no snow to interfere with the drive. Alex was grateful for that. When snow storms happened in the valley, snowdrifts would wash across the fields making it impossible to see where the road was, the snow building so high that even the ditches were hidden. The roads were currently snow packed but not icy. They made it home in remarkable time. The Hummer made short work of the snow in the driveway as he pulled in front of the house, next to the silver sedan he and Lucas used as a secondary vehicle. James gathered the bags from the back while Alex carefully lifted Kyra out of the back seat, ensuring she was still bundled in the thick blanket before carrying her across the snow-covered walkway to the front door. He took her directly to the guest room and tucked her into bed; a proper bed with proper covers that was warm rather than ice cold. She barely stirred, far too exhausted to even acknowledge the change in location. She would be hungry when she woke up. Alex wasn't sure if he should try to get a few hours sleep while she was out cold or if he should prepare for when she awoke. He had a lot to do. The snow and cold may have damaged the grapes. Yes, he liked making ice wine, but this may have proven to be too much for them.

When he went out to the living room, James had already removed his boots and coat and was laying on the sofa, the bags sitting next to the armchair. He looked just as exhausted as Alex felt. Alex patted him on the shoulder then took the bags to put the food away and sort through the clothing. He also had to figure out where to put it. There was a dresser in the guest room. Elizabeth usually used it when she came to visit for a few days. It might as well become Kyra's while she stayed with them. He managed to put the clothing away without waking her.

After that, he went about his normal morning routine, checking on the dogs and making sure they had enough food and water, despite having placed several days worth of food in the heated dog house the day before. He also checked the grape vines, worried the grapes he had set aside for making ice wine may have been damaged in the storm. They weren't too bad but they would need to be picked today and be processed, but he would wait until later in the day for that. The rush of adrenaline that had made him flee with Kyra and James was beginning to wear off and exhaustion was creeping in. He glanced at his watch as he headed back to the house. Lucas was likely still asleep but he wanted to hear his voice, assure him that he was alright. He was a little surprised that Lucas had gone after him, but also thankful. The roads had been awful leaving North Bay and there had been a few times when the Hummer had slid on ice and he had to fight to keep control of the large vehicle, despite it have snow tires. The Jeep would never have made it and he never would have forgiven himself if something happened to Lucas for chasing after him.

He waited until he was inside before calling him, placing the phone on speaker while he made a pot of coffee.

"Hey babe," he said cheerfully when Lucas answered. Yep, he was overtired now and getting to that giddy stage. It meant he would not be able to fall asleep for at least another hour until he came down from it.

"You are far way happy after being up all night," Lucas muttered, sleep evident in his voice.

Alex couldn't help but laugh at that. "I haven't even had coffee yet...working on that right now."

He placed the filter in the coffee maker then scooped some ground coffee into it. Lucas usually complained about that, preferring to freshly grind the coffee, but when people were sleeping, grinding coffee was not ideal. It was far too noisy and both Kyra and James needed their sleep.

Lucas gave a small laugh. "When you finally crash it'll be next to impossible to wake you up."

"Probably," Alex agreed. He wasn't planning on drinking any coffee right away, just have it ready for when James woke up. "How are you feeling?"

"Tired. It took a while to get out of the bunker when the power went out. The hill to the Hole was covered with snow, we had to put the chains on the tires."

Alex hesitated before asking his next question, his stomach churning with fear and guilt. He turned the coffee on then took a seat at the table. "How bad were things at the base?"

"Bad. Caldwell believes you stole their 'asset.' If it wasn't for the number of injuries and dead, she probably would have gone after you. I don't know if you're safe at the house or should find another location to keep the kid until things blow over."

Alex frowned and glanced outside to the hills in the distance. "Then I *would be* kidnapping her. Caldwell knows where we live. She can come here. Staying so close to the city is too dangerous. Even here there are too many people but there's more distance between us, less chance of death." He pressed two fingers to his left temple. "James called Interpol on the way here. There should be a few agents here shortly to guard us. If Caldwell wants to pick a fight then let her."

"Alex..." Lucas sighed.

There was a long moment of silence and for a moment Alex feared Lucas was angry with him, thinking he was acting too impulsive and judgement was clouded by his need to protect Kyra. Perhaps it was. Alex had never felt the need to protect someone so much in his life. He hoped Lucas understood. He waited, afraid to break to silence in case Lucas was upset.

"I need you to go to the office and log in your laptop. I found Kyra's file and...I think we have bigger problems than Kyra's parentage," Lucas finally said.

Alex glanced toward James but the Interpol agent was still asleep. "Okay, I'll put you on speaker so I can..."

"No, put your ear buds in. I like James, but I don't know how much he actually knows. If the government was hiding this file in their archives then it's safe to say that either Interpol is in on it or it was hidden from them as well. Until we know which, keep this between us."

"Alright," he agreed.

He felt a little off about that. However, if Lucas said to keep what he found only between them then it had to be important. He went to the office and shut the door behind him, engaging the rarely used lock to ensure privacy. Hopefully, Kyra would sleep a little longer so he could read whatever Lucas was sending him. His laptop booted up quickly as he placed a small ear bud in his left ear, the right currently containing his hearing aid, then logged into his account. There was one new email from Lucas with a PDF file attached. Opening it, he read the first paragraph while Lucas waited patiently.

"Wait...the mother was possessed by the Celestial not the father?" he asked in confusion.

"Every adult that was in a cryochamber had been possessed. The child's DNA only matches the mother's. Not just that but they managed to capture her and took the baby from her, not back in the seventies but seven years ago. Kyra hasn't aged slowly, they kept her in an incubator. She was their science experiment," Lucas explained, getting to the point. "Alex...they purposely mated the Celestial with a human male to produce Kyra then killed the host. They couldn't control the Celestial so produced a hybrid that they could. Kyra's a living weapon. The only reason she was in that cryochamber was to be moved to a new laboratory, not the new NORAD base. She's been awake this entire time believing one of the scientists is her mother."

Alex scanned through the file, trying to keep up with what Lucas was telling him. "So where is she?"

"I don't know. It looks like she tucked Kyra in the chamber then took off. She's probably waiting at this new lab."

He sat back and sighed. "Fuck. Lucas, this means everything Caldwell told us was a lie. They used us because of my tie to the Celestials." He wet his lips and glanced at the file once more before closing the laptop. "I don't think James is in on this. He wouldn't have helped me bring her here if he was, or called in for backup. He would have made us stay in North Bay. What if this is some sort of Black Ops, like what happened in the US with Area 51? Perhaps the Canadian government doesn't even know about this?"

Lucas was silent for a moment or two before sighing. "Perhaps. Alex, what did we get into?"

"I don't know, babe."

Seven years. That was before the temple in British Columbia was discovered, which meant their government may have known about the Celestials much longer than they were letting on. Or at least someone in the government did. Lucas was right; they didn't know who they could trust, but James was the only back-up Alex had until Lucas got home. He had no choice but to rely on Interpol, as they had for the last few years, to help him protect Kyra.

"When are you coming home?" he asked.

"A few hours. I want to snoop around more, see if I can find anything more about the Shadow. There's no temple here so it had to come from somewhere." Lucas paused as if in thought. "Uh...Alex, there's a few things I forgot to mention about Kyra."

"Okay?"

"They really were experimenting on her. Her reproductive organs have been removed and they were tinkering with her brain. I think they were trying to find a way to control her but it didn't work. Everything they tried failed. She's scheduled for surgery in two weeks. It doesn't say for what exactly, only that they wanted to study her neocortex and pain receptors. Brain surgery. It's what killed one of the male hosts, not Caldwell."

Alex felt sick. How could someone do this to a child? It wouldn't be the first time something like this happened. There were cases of old Residential Schools allowing scientists to visit and perform such experiments on Indigenous children. There were some places that still sterilized Indigenous people without their permission. It wasn't such a far stretch to believe they would do the same to someone they thought of as "sub-human."

He closed his eyes and took a deep breath. "That file didn't happen to tell you what she likes to eat, did it?"

For a moment Lucas seemed confused, then gave a small laugh. "Sorry, no."

Alex gave a small laugh. "I'll figure it out. She probably has more experience with regular food than they let on."

"Most likely."

"Come home soon," he told Lucas as he closed the file and began to shut down his laptop. "I love you."

"I love you, too. Be safe."

"I'll do my best. Give me a call when you leave."

"Will do. Bye."

"Bye."

Running his fingers through his hair, Alex tried to think of what to do. He was tired but he doubted he would be able to sleep more than an hour or two if he was lucky, but he had to try. With a long sigh, he left the office and went to ensure the security system was working and doors were locked. The dogs would alert him if anyone came onto the property. Hopefully, the rest of the Interpol agents would arrive shortly. Once Lucas got home they could figure out their next move.

Chapter Eight

A lex didn't get any rest until after the Interpol agents arrived, but even then, it wasn't for long as he pondered everything Lucas had told him. He had read over Kyra's file twice and both times he felt nothing but rage on the child's behalf. For years he had tried to make himself believe that the Canadian government had learned from their mistakes and the way they had treated people, but it had been a foolish thought. They were no better now than they had been in the past only now they were not experimenting on the Indigenous, but aliens. It was almost laughable. People feared alien abduction and experimentation when it was their own government doing that to those aliens that visited Earth. He knew that was an unfair assessment. After all, the Celestials had come to Earth hundreds of thousands of years ago, colonizing the planet and changing the human race to what they were today. He just wanted to think that they were better than that. It seemed he was wrong.

He pushed those thoughts out of his mind when Kyra awoke. She padded through the house with eyes wide with awe. Everything was new to her, and Alex took a few moments to watch her look through the cupboards and fridge as he made them a late lunch. It was simple, just macaroni and cheese. Lucas would certainly complain if he saw it. He called it "lazy man's food", but it tasted amazing and Alex knew from experience that it was the go-to food for most children. And he highly doubted Kyra had ever eaten anything fancy like what Lucas preferred. He filled two bowls and placed them on the table. He would have made enough for James, but the agent had gone out to brief the other agents and would likely eat with them as he normally did. That meant he and Kyra were alone together for the very first time with no one eavesdropping on their conversation.

Of course, starting a conversation with a child while they were eating was not always the easiest thing to do. Alex had so many questions, he wasn't sure where to begin.

"So...can you tell me a little about what life what like in the bunker?" he asked, thinking that was as good of a place as any.

She didn't answer, instead digging into her food hungrily. Alex raised a brow. She didn't normally ignore him.

"Kyra?"

She swallowed what was in her mouth, licked her lips, then looked up curiously.

"Did you hear me?" he asked.

She pursed her lips before pressing them into a thin line, looking a little confused. "Mommy says it's rude to talk with your mouth full," she answered in way of explanation.

His mouth made a surprised "O" shape as embarrassment filled him. "Oh...I'm sorry. You're right. We can talk after. Would you like some milk?"

Obviously relieved to not be in trouble, she nodded then began eating again. Alex chuckled softly to himself as he went to the fridge and grabbed the milk pitcher. He filled two glasses – silently wishing he had a plastic one for Kyra, then placed them on the table before their respective places. He watched her as they ate in silence, noting exactly how accustomed she was used to eating and using utensils, proving once and for all that she had not spent her life in the cryochamber.

When they were done, he washed the dishes and pot, then placed then on the rack to dry. He wiped his hand on the dish towel while he thought of ways to entertain Kyra.

"How about we get you into some nice new clothing while you tell me about yourself?" he offered. "Then we can go outside. Have you ever played in the snow before?"

She shook her head but seemed excited by the notion. Judging by her reaction to the snow when they were racing away from the air base, she had never seen snow before let alone played in it. He was thankful he had the foresight to buy her winter gear.

Taking her hand, he led her into the guest room and showed her the clothing he had bought for her. He stepped aside as she began looking through the drawers, her eyes wide with wonder. He pointed out the different items she needed but let her pick out what she wanted to wear. She needed a little help putting some of it on, not quite used to wearing pants, but she chose a cute pair of warm track pants and long baggy sweater. She needed help with the socks, but again proved she was used to getting dressed. It took a little longer to get her hair brushed out. Alex struggled with it, fearful of pulling her hair as he worked out the knots. Her hair was so thin and pale, it seemed almost fragile. It was the opposite. It was strong, strands not breaking or snapping as he ran the brush through it. Once it was brushed, he divided it into two bunches and began braiding each side into long plaits. Once he was done, he held up a mirror for her to inspect herself.

"What do you think?"

She touched one braid than moved her fingers across one cheek, as if seeing herself for the first time. It was impossible to decipher the emotions that raced across her face. For a moment she looked excited and then sad, but he wasn't sure why, she merely gave a whimsical smile, as if none of what was happening was real and merely a dream. Alex knew that look, had experienced it before when he was freed from the Celestial yet not quite believing it was all over.

"They'll come for me," she murmured. "Mama's not going to happy I'm gone."

"Tell me about her," Alex encouraged, hoping that by opening up, Kyra would feel a little safer.

She didn't continue. Instead, she headed back into the kitchen, wanting to go outside and not understanding she still had to put her snowsuit and boots on. Alex caught her as she was opening the back door and managed to coax her back inside to finish getting dressed before she stepped into the cold snow.

He lifted her up and sat her on the table.

"Alright, we don't need to talk about her," he promised. "We don't need to talk about the lab or anything like that, but you do need to dress properly for the outdoors. We didn't get as much out here as North Bay, but it is cold and wet, and I have a big property to tend to. So, snowsuit, boots, toque, and mitts. Yes?"

"Okay," she answered, seemingly relieved to not have to talk about her past.

He gave a curt nod and helped her into the snow pants then boots. He made sure the laces were double knotted and snow pants snug at the ankles to keep the snow from getting inside. Then he got her coat on her, did it up right to her chin, and helped her slip the mitts over her hands. Lastly, he placed her toque over her head, making sure that it covered her ears and back of her neck. He picked her up and stood her on the ground while he grabbed his coat.

"Why don't you have snow pants?" she asked as he opened the patio door.

He had put on his boots and gloves, even a toque, but he had not worn snow pants in many years. There was no reason for them. Once harvest season was over there was very little for him to do outside over the winter. The building that housed the winery was fully heated and maybe fifty feet from the back of the house and the path was always plowed when they did the driveway. Right now, there was a few inches of snow but not enough to warrant him wearing snow pants. For a moment, he wondered if perhaps he was going overboard making Kyra wear them, but she was a child who had never experienced winter or the cold. She needed the extra protection.

"When you're a grown up, you won't need them as often. Unless you get into winter sports, then I just have a really good pair like what you're wearing now," he explained as they stepped outside.

For a brief moment, her face fell and sadness reflected in her eyes, but it was gone just as fast as it appeared as she stepped into the snow. Her small feet left little footprints as she descended the back steps. Alex watched with a small smile as she began bouncing and running through the snow, completely enchanted by it. The Interpol agents nearby watched as well with small smiles of amusement. Many had children of their own and had surely experienced this with their own child. Alex introduced Kyra to the agents, not wanting her to be afraid of them. If something happened, these would be the people that would protect her. She seemed to charm them, no one questioning her strange appearance or pale skin. Alex watched her, unsure if they were truly accepting or if her Celestial side was somehow manipulating them. There was no way to tell for certain. He could feel her power, but it didn't feel as if she was using it, at least not consciously. Perhaps she was just very charismatic. Lucas was similar. He could charm just about anyone. Well…almost. It took him longer to charm Alex, but when he did fall for Lucas, he fell hard, and he had no complaints whatsoever about it.

He took Kyra to inspect the vineyard and last bit of grapes as the workers picked them. Lucas had hired them to help run the vineyard. They hurried to fill the baskets with the frozen grapes. They would need to get them into the processor soon to extract the juice and begin making the wine. It would ferment over the winter and by spring be ready for bottling. It was a long process but well worth it. He absently popped by one the plump grapes in his mouth, savoring the sweet taste that only came after the frost which was why he liked Ice Wine so much. They grew longer but the taste was unlike any other wine.

He let Kyra try one of the frozen grapes as well as he told her about the grapes and making wine and how he had come to the decision to start the vineyard because of his father's dream to have his own upon retirement. Sadly, his father had died. Kyra didn't need to know about how he was murdered, as was their entire research team. Alex didn't want to think about that. The memory of that horrible day was imprinted on his memory for the rest of his life. Kyra did not have to relive that with him. So, he told her the good things, what an amazing man and professor Alexander Jackson Senior was and how he had inspired hundreds of students and anthropologists across Canada. It felt good talking about his father. Over the years he had tried to hide from the past, fearful of flashbacks from the attack haunting him as they had for many years. He still had them, but not nearly as bad as they used to be.

"I like Owen," Kyra said as they walked back toward the house hand-in-hand. "He's funny."

Alex stumbled in surprise. "Excuse me?" he asked.

There was a lump in his throat and the corners of his eyes prickled with the threat of tears. He blinked them away, not wanting to concern the girl.

Kyra glanced up at him with curiosity before staring off her right side, as if someone else was walking beside her. Alex followed her gaze, trying to see what she was seeing. Was there really someone there? Was Owen there? He had died almost four years ago saving him and Lucas, another person who had given his life for him. The very idea that Owen's ghost may be there had guilt eating at Alex all over again. Had Owen and Lucas not gotten mixed up with him then Owen would still be alive. Yet, as odd as it sounded, had it not been for Owen, he and Lucas would never have been together. Owen had saved him when terrorists attacked his team. Had gotten him help. He was a hero.

Whether his spirit was with them there now or not, Alex wasn't sure. He often felt as if Owen was watching over him but until now, he thought that was only wishful thinking.

After a moment or two, Kyra shrugged, as if nothing had happened, and gave his hand a little tug. "Can I play with the dogs?"

He stared at her for a moment or two then nodded. "Sure, just don't grab them or try hugging them. They're not used to kids and I don't want them nipping you, okay?"

She nodded before running off. Alex watched her for a moment before glancing back to where she had seemingly been talking to someone.

"If you're here, Owen," he began, feeling slightly choked up. "I miss you. Lucas misses you."

Even though they had only known each other a short time, Owen had come to mean a lot to Alex. He had never fallen in love with two men at once before, but he had loved the brothers with all his heart. He often wondered what life would have been like if Owen had survived. Would the three of them be living here together? Would he have married Lucas?

He wiped at his eyes. It was best not to think of what may have been. He loved Lucas and wouldn't want to change anything about their lives. They were survivors. When Lucas got home, he was going to remind him just how much he loved him.

He headed to the winery, making sure that everything was running smoothly before the staff headed home for the evening, then called Kyra to come inside the house with him. She was giggling as the dogs crowded around her, sniffing, and licking her face, something that they never did with anyone else. She was a charmer, that was for certain. It seemed she could charm anyone.

Her snowsuit was damp when they took it off her, but her clothing underneath was still dry. He hung the snowsuit over the heater next to the door to dry then hung his coat next to it. Their boots were flipped upside-down on a special dry rack to make sure the insides stayed dried and warm. The sun was slowly setting on the horizon, the sky taking on a shade of indigo. It was going to warm up overnight. That meant the highways were likely clear with wet spots and Lucas would be on his way home soon.

"Alrighty, it's a little early to make dinner, and we ate not that long ago," he began as they walked into the living room. "So, how about you play in here while I check in with Lucas?"

"Is he coming home?" Kyra asked.

She sat in front of the coffee table as Alex placed a pack of crayons and a few colouring books on it. He sat in the armchair across from her and took the doll he had bought out of its packaging before handing it to her. Her eyes were wide as she took it. She gave it a big hug before setting it next to her to watch as she began flipping through the colouring books, looking for a picture she liked, then emptying the box of crayons on the table and sorting through them. Again, these were actions of someone who had done these things many times before.

Alex watched her for several long moments before deciding to call Lucas and check in on him. With luck, he was already driving home. If he was, Alex wanted to know how far away he was and if he should start dinner or wait. He left Kyra in the living room and moved to the kitchen as he dialled Lucas's number. It rang twice before being picked up.

"Hello, my love," Lucas answered cheerfully.

"Something good must have happened," Alex teased, glad to hear his husband in such a good mood.

Lucas hummed. "You could say that. I told Caldwell I was heading home and she didn't seem to care. Apparently, she's in a bit of hot water for not telling the whole truth about Kyra. I forwarded the files to my contact at the head of the new Earth Defence Command, and they weren't too happy to find out NORAD was hiding Kyra there and knew about the Celestials before the whole issue with the temples. Had they informed the United Nations, they could have saved hundreds of lives and we would have been better prepared not only against the Celestials, but also the terrorists."

Alex bit his lower lip, not sure how true that would have been. Even if they had known about the Celestials and temples in advance, it didn't mean the terrorists wouldn't have been after them. After all, they attacked right after each temple was discovered. They knew about the temples and who was looking for them. They had tapped phones and hacked emails. The technology and skill used were on par to that of high-level government agencies. There was no telling if the Canadian government already knew or if the people at NORAD had kept it secret. They could have even been working with the terrorists.

His mind was a whirl with all the possibilities, but he kept those thoughts to himself. "What are they planning to do with Kyra?" he asked instead.

"They didn't say," Lucas answered, still cheerful. "I guess she's staying with us for now."

That was a relief. Alex hated the idea of her going back to live in a lab. It was no place for a child. Any child.

"So, did you start dinner yet?" Lucas asked after a pause.

"No, we had a late lunch, and I wanted to wait for you."

Lucas hummed, obviously expecting as much. "Look, I'm just entering Sudbury now. How about I pick up some Sushi? Then tonight, after Kyra's sound asleep, we can pick up where we left off last night."

Had it been only one night since they made love at the hotel? It felt much longer…days even. So much had happened in such a short amount of time. He glanced back toward Kyra, but she was focused entirely on colouring.

"Oh? I don't know…we get pretty loud. I don't want to wake her up," he teased, his voice low and sultry, only for Lucas's ears.

"I may have to gag you."

"May have to lock the bedroom door."

"Hmm…I've got the toys…we could always play in the dungeon."

Alex laughed at that. "I don't think that's such a good idea, at least not for a few days. I don't want her wandering into the basement searching for us and stumbling into *that* room. Besides, the old well only has a wooden cover. It's too dangerous."

"You're right," Lucas sighed, the flirting momentarily broken.

"You know what...I'd much rather tie you down and..." He lowered his voice as Kyra looked up and glanced toward him. He turned away from her. "Ride you while you have one of your precious rods pushed all the way into your urethra. Better yet, the beads. A nice long set..."

He paused when he heard the dogs barking. Were the agents changing guard? It was only quarter past six, far too early for a shift change.

"Alex, I'm driving, can you save the dirty talk until I'm home," Lucas said, drawing his attention back to the cell phone in his hand. "I swear, I'm going to take you over my knee and spank you tonight."

That sent a thrill through Alex that ran the length of his body and shot straight into his cock, making it swell with need. He didn't exactly like being spanked but there was something about being dominated that always made him needy.

A yelp made him pull the phone away from his ear and walk over to the patio door. Was that one of his dogs? He pulled the door open and looked around. At first he saw nothing but then he spotted Sasha, one of the female German Shepherds laying in the snow twenty feet from the house. Not far from her was the body of one of the agents. He inhaled sharply then looked around quickly, fearful of finding another body. He didn't make any other sound, didn't call out to any of the other agents. Instead, he stepped back inside, closed, and locked the door, then moved to the front door and made sure it was locked as well.

"Lucas, someone's here," he said as calmly as possible as he took Kyra's hand and pulled her to her feet. The girl grabbed her doll and brought it with her. He grabbed their coats then took her with him to the office to retrieve the Browning 9mm handgun from the safe. "They killed one of the dogs and an agent, maybe more."

"Did you see anyone?" Lucas asked, his mind immediately switching gears.

"No, I saw their bodies."

"Can you get to the car?"

Alex kept the light off and went to the window, hoping to catch a glance of who may be on their property and attacking the Interpol agents. His gut twisted as he thought of Caldwell possibly betraying them and having summoned an attack on the vineyard to get Kyra back.

"Not directly. The Hummer is parked next to the cellar. It's locked from the inside. We'll go out that way."

He could almost see Lucas nod in agreement.

"It's armoured. You should be safe in it."

Lucas was right, Alex just didn't like the idea of a high-speed chase on the backroads. He knew them like the back of his hand, but there was only so much road before they ended up at one of the many channels that led to Lake Huron. They would have to head to the highway but that would only endanger more people. He wasn't sure what to do but he had to think fast.

"When I reach the Hummer, we're going to head toward Sudbury. Meet us in Worthington. Get an evacuation team to meet us there. I'll let you know where when we reach Nairn Centre."

He helped Kyra put on her coat, boots, and hat but left the mitts and snow pants, both of which were still wet. He managed to shrug his own coat on before he heard someone trying to open the front door.

"Alex, I don't like this," Lucas said.

"Neither do I. I'll see you in Worthington."

He hung up, knowing there was nothing else he could say to Lucas. There wasn't any time. He needed to get Kyra to safety and right now, he was hoping they could get through the cellar unnoticed. They went down into the unfinished basement. There was no lock on the door, not that it would have mattered. Whoever was attacking the house would kick it in, but it would have bought them a few extra seconds. He picked Kyra up mid-way down the steps when it looked as if she would trip. There were very few places to hide in the basement. It was primarily open and mostly unfinished which was why Lucas jokingly called it the dungeon. It did feature two rooms, one of which was finished and used for Alex's and Lucas's more intense sexual activities. The other was a wine cellar that housed their personal collection. The sound of the cellar doors shaking made Alex rethink of going out that way. They would have to wait until whoever was there had left, provided they didn't break the lock and come in that way. They needed to find a place to hide which left one of two rooms, and Alex was not taking Kyra into his and Lucas's "play-room".

They rounded the old well and washer and dryer as they made it to the wood pile not far from the large woodstove that heated the house. The cellar doors were usually used to chuck chopped wood down. Two cords were currently stacked against the far wall, next to the cellar steps. He wondered if there was a way to use that. The thumping of heavy footsteps above made him forget that and head to the cool room instead. There were racks upon racks of wine twenty feet deep. Alex carried Kyra to the back and set her down before going back to the front of the room where a second weapons cabinet was located. He unlocked it and pulled out a rifle and box of bullets. He loaded the weapon then poured the rest of the bullets in a coat pocket for easy access. Lastly, he locked the door. He wished he had something heavy to shove in front of the door but all he had aside from the rifle was the wine, a lighter, and some old rags used to dust the wine bottles and other bottles of alcohol. They had a few dozen bottles of Vodka, Rum, and Bourbon. Wine didn't naturally burn but the rest of the alcohol did. That meant possibly turning the alcohol into weapons, Molotov Cocktails. It was a last resort and Lucas would hate him for even considering it, but Alex didn't know what else to do. With luck, it won't come to that.

He turned off the light then carefully removed the bulb, using the flashlight from his smartphone to guide into the back and Kyra.

"Okay, we need to stay very quiet," he said as he knelt in front of her.

He carefully set the rifle on the rack and aimed it toward the door, ready to fire the moment someone opened it. Kyra curled up against his side, hugging her doll tightly in her arms. Her small body was trembling. It was understandable. The girl had been hiding from the Shadow-being by staying within the light and now she was in utter darkness, the Shadow's domain, hiding from people who should have been protecting her. There was no doubt in Alex's mind that they were dealing with Caldwell's people. He wasn't certain if they were on official government orders to reclaim Kyra or if they were working outside government regulation. Either way, Alex was not giving her up without a fight. Not now. They had killed at least one of his dogs and an Interpol agent. They would likely kill more to get to her. They hadn't even tried knocking at the door with a warrant. They were out for blood and Alex would return it in kind.

He pumped the rifle and took aim, listening carefully at the growing number of thumping footsteps above as the invaders moved through each room, tearing the house apart in search of them. His gaze followed the sound, tracking them as the moved toward the basement stairs. Soon enough, they were moving into the basement. He counted the number of different footsteps, trying to gauge how many people were in the basement. Four...no five. They spoke in hushed voices as they searched the basement. A small, silent laugh escaped him as he heard someone curse about the "play-room". He would have loved to see their face at the sight of some of the toys stored in there. Lucas had some interesting kinks that would make some people go pale at the sight. It was why they were locked away in the basement and not where people would normally see them. The sheer disgust and horror in the person's voice made Alex's day. Not everyone could appreciate kink.

"Stay down," he whispered to Kyra as the footsteps neared the cool room.

He slid down and laid on his belly with Kyra next to him, the rifle lined perfectly with the door. There were no windows to the room meaning no chance of light giving away their position. They were in utter darkness. The door handle jingled as someone on the other side turned it. Alex wrapped his pointer finger around the trigger or the rifle, pulling the butt of it against his shoulder as he lined up the sight, his eyes already adjusted to the darkness. A few moments later the jingling turned to pounding then to someone slamming something against the door until finally someone tried to kick it in. The door was made of solid oak which meant it would take a while before they broke through. He waited, unsure if he should fire or allow whoever was on the other side to break in. With how dark it was, they would either have to search each row or have an extremely powerful light to spot them. If he fired, there was a ninety percent chance they would fire back, depending on if they were there to retrieve Kyra or terminate her. The last thing he wanted was them to come in; he and Kyra would be trapped. He had to make a decision. One he didn't like.

He pulled the trigger.

There was a cry from the other side of the door as a small hole was blown open. Alex watched the shapes move about through it, trying to determine where their attackers were. Certain where to fire, he inhaled deeply before firing once more. Another hole, another cry, but this time people fired back. Alex placed a hand on Kyra's back, slightly instructing her to stay down. He waited, counting the shots then fired in between, striking another person. That was three so far and someone was still firing into the room. Bottles shattered all around, glass and wine raining down on them. Kyra was gasping out sobs, trying to stay quiet while becoming increasingly frightened by what was going on. Whoever was firing at them was bolder than the rest. He kicked the door in, attempting to charge the room. Alex didn't give him a chance. He managed to hit him in the chest, knocking him back.

For several long moments there was no sound from outside the remains of the door other than moaning from those that were injured. Alex wasn't certain if he had killed them all or merely injured them. He waited and listened, keeping him and Kyra laying on the floor.

They waited in silence until he heard the survivors retreat, clearing the entrance for them. Alex waited a few minutes longer, not willing to take a chance until he began to smell smoke. His eyes widened in surprise. Did they set the house on fire to smoke them out? If that was the case…they were in the worst spot for an open flame. They needed to get outside, but that was what the enemy wanted.

That was proven when he led Kyra to the ruined door and peaked outside. The cellar door was wide open, the outside inviting as smoke seeped through the basement from the "play-room".

"Son of bitch," he grumbled to himself as he watched smoke billow out the room.

The extinguisher that normally hung by the dryer was gone, as was the hose that was stored under the large wash basin. They made sure he couldn't put the fire out. He pursed his lips and glanced toward the open cellar doors. It was tempting but he knew the moment they stepped outside they would be shot. They had to go back upstairs and try to escape through the back door. The forested hills were five acres from the back door. It was a long distance for them to run but they could use the vineyard to their advantage and duck behind the hay bales his neighbours had yet to move onto their property. Once they reached the forest, they could hike through them to one of the distant side-roads. There were several abandoned old farms back there that would throw their attackers off their track for a while. Lucas would know where to find them.

He slung the rifle over one shoulder and pulled the Browning 9mm from the back of his jeans, making sure there was a bullet already in the chamber.

"Stay close to me," he told Kyra.

She grabbed the back of his coat as they moved back to the stairs, staying far from the open cellar doors. He took her hand as the made the way up the stairs, keeping her behind him in case someone attacked from the top. He should have been prepared for them to come at them from both sides.

Alex turned as soldiers stormed in from the cellar door, stepping in front of Kyra and pushing her against the wall in hopes of protecting her. A bullet hit his right shoulder, causing him to drop the gun and stumble back into her. She gave a frightened cry but Alex couldn't comfort her as more men appeared at the top of the stairs, weapons drawn and aimed at his head. There was smoke behind them. The main floor was also on fire. Alex stared past them in horror. Not only were these people going to kill them, but they were also going to make sure no one found their bodies. He could hear Kyra sobbing behind him and feel her terror. He shared in it but they were trapped. There was nothing more he could do.

He reached back and squeezed her hand and glared defiantly at their attackers. He expected to be executed, waited for it as the smoke grew thicker, eating up his home. Instead, the lead soldier lowered his assault rifle and turned it in his hand. Before realization clicked in, the butt of the weapon smashed into his face. Kyra screamed. For a moment, Alex's world went black as he tumbled over the edge of the steps and slammed onto the wood covering the old well, his thoughts being of how he should have re-installed the rail that used to be on that side of the stairs. He hit the thin wood hard. It was meant to cover the well but not actually seal it, they were going to have a professional come in and cement it.

Why hadn't they done that yet, he wondered as the wood cracked under his weight. Moments later, it gave and he fell through, tumbling into the darkness and ice-cold water far below. The last sound he heard was Kyra's scream as the soldiers began firing into the well in hopes of finishing him off once and for all. Pain consumed Alex as he sunk deeper into the water, and then darkness as his consciousness slipped away.

Alex wasn't sure how he managed to remain conscious. He could feel the bullets hit the water all around him, slicing through it with ease yet somehow missing him. Nonetheless, he held his breath, grasping the metal ladder on the side of the well to help keep him deep underwater so that those firing at him could not pinpoint his location. Time seemed to drag on before they finally gave up, believing he was dead. A bright spotlight flashed down into the well but could not penetrate the depths in which he was hidden. The well was old and narrow. It was easy for a body to get trapped inside and never float to the surface. Evidently, they must have assumed the same. Soon the light turned off, replaced by the flicker of flame. The fire had reached the basement, or the basement had also been set on fire. There was enough alcohol for it.

He moved slowly to the surface, his gaze skyward, ready for another possible attack. He made barely a ripple as he surfaced, just enough to inhale a deep breath of air and listen. There was no sound of anyone left in the house, only the creaking and crackling of flames as the entire house was slowly engulfed. The house was about to come down around him. He couldn't stay in the well. He had to get out. He had to find Kyra.

His only body ached as he struggled to climb up the ladder. He was lucky to not have lost his prosthetic in the fall, but his right arm barely worked and could not hold his weight. His wet clothing weighed him down, forcing him to ditch his winter coat to lighten his load. He huffed and puffed as he made the seemingly long trek back to the basement, until, finally, he pulled himself over the edge and tumbled onto the basement floor. Exhaustion filled him. For a moment all he could do was lay there and stare up at the wooden beams above him as flames licked along them, reminding him he could not stay there. With a pain-filled groan, he stumbled to his feet and looked around. There were bodies on the floor, the people he had managed to kill, but Kyra was nowhere to be seen. There was only one way out, and whether there was a firing squad waiting for him or not, he had to go through it.

His body was battered and bruised, making it hard to move. He stumbled and limped his way to the cellar doors, dragging himself more than walking. He all but crawled up the stairs and outside, slumping into the snow next to the Hummer. A groan escaped him when he noticed that it, too, was on fire. He needed to get away from it. It took all his strength to get back to his feet. He headed to the back of the house, fearful of being spotted in the front where the attackers were no doubt parked.

The whirling of a motor caught his attention, the sound of a helicopter. When the hell did a helicopter land on the property? He staggered toward it, rage feeling him. The bastards that had torched his home were escaping and they had Kyra. He may not have any weapons but he sure as hell was not about to let them take off with the girl. He'd stop them even if he had to throw rocks at the copter's blades.

It hurt to run but he made himself do so. He rounded the house only to find the winery also in flames. All the out-building were burning, including the dog house. The dogs were all dead, lying in the snow alongside the Interpol agents. The helicopter was taking off not far from the winery. Alex hurried toward it as it took to the air.

"No!" he yelled, spotting Kyra's small face pressed against the window. She struggled against someone, but it was impossible to tell who. Soon it disappeared into the night sky, leaving Alex alone amongst the dead bodies. The rest of the attackers were gone, but despite being unable to see the markings on the helicopter, he knew it was government issued.

The sound of sirens could be heard in the distance, but Alex ignored them as he stared at his burning home. He barely paid attention as fire trucks pulled into his driveway, along with the local Provincial Police.

"Get down!" an officer yelled.

Guns were drawn and aimed at him as they rushed into the yard and saw the bodies with only him alive. Alex didn't look at them. He placed his hands on the back of his head and fell to his knees, surrendering to them without a fuss. Twenty people were dead, as were five dogs, and everything he owned was now burning to ash. He had no fight left in him.

Chapter Nine

Elizabeth pulled to the side of the road as police cars raced past her. It was rare to see so many police vehicles on this stretch of back road. Her gut twisted in worry as she waited for all of them and two firetrucks to pass her. Once the road was cleared, she began following them. It didn't take long to see what the issue was. Alex and Lucas's house was in flames, as were the outbuildings. That made no sense. How could they all be on fire? She pulled up as close as she could to the house then hurried out of the car, leaving it running in her haste, and rushed up the driveway to the open gate and into the back yard. Bodies lay scattered everywhere and in the center of the chaos knelt Alex. Two officers manhandled him, forcing cuffs on his wrists before dragging him to his feet and toward her and the cars waiting in front of the house.

"Alex!" she cried, rushing to him.

An officer caught her, forcing her to keep her distance. She tried to pull away but another caught her arm.

"What happened here?" she demanded before turning her focus to Alex.

He looked utterly crushed and obviously injured, but he met her gaze. "They attacked us and took Kyra. Tell Lucas they took Kyra!"

"Who? Alex!" She pulled away from the officers as Alex was loaded into a cruiser and whisked away toward Espanola. She turned on them. "He didn't do this! He wouldn't have!"

"Ma'am, we were called about a shooting. When we arrived, the whole place was in flames and he's the only survivor," one officer explained as she pulled out a notepad. "Can you tell us about the suspect?"

"Suspect? Alex isn't a suspect. He was protecting a child. Look at those bodies, they're Interpol agents. They were here to protect him and the child. Do you really think one man could take out all these agents, kill his own dogs, and destroy his life's work, then remain to be caught, without a gun or opening fire on you and your people?" She rubbed her hands over her face. "Good God, you do!"

"Ma'am, we're only following orders..."

Her hands balled into fists. "Fuck your orders. Call Chief Tenzyn and let him know you just arrested Doctor Alexander Jackson. You can also tell him I'm on my way to the station. My name is Doctor Elizabeth Monroe. He'll know who you're talking about."

She stormed away, knowing full well that they could arrest her as well if they wanted to. They didn't. They were too busy dealing with the fire and bodies. She got back in her car and raced after the cruiser with Alex, careful of the road conditions. They may be clear but the temperature was dropping and it didn't take much for ice to build up on the back roads. She wasn't sure what she could do. Yes, she knew the police chief for the local Ontario Provincial Police, but that didn't mean he could help her. Right now, Alex was facing arson charges, multiple murders, and possibly kidnapping depending, if he had been reported for taking the hybrid child. Her hands gripped the steering wheel tightly.

She pressed a button on the steering wheel. "Call Lucas," she snapped on the onboard computer.

"Elizabeth?" Lucas's voice came over the speaker.

"Alex has been arrested," she said quickly. "I'm not sure if they're taking him to Espanola or McKerrow. Which one deals with Massey?"

"McKerrow," Lucas answered. "They'll take him straight to McKerrow. Was he injured?"

"I think so, but given what happened, I don't see them making a pit stop to the hospital. Lucas, what's going on?"

"I'm not sure. Someone attacked the house. I have it recorded." He fell silent for a moment. "And I have back up. We'll have him out of there within the hour."

She almost missed the next turn, taking it a little too sharply. The tires gripped the pavement and kept her from sliding into the ditch. "How?"

"It'll take too long to explain. I'll be there in twenty minutes."

She nodded to herself. "Alright. Drive safe."

"You, too." The phone went dead a moment later.

Elizabeth inhaled deeply and slowly counted backwards from ten. She needed to calm down and think. Driving like a maniac wouldn't help Alex, it would only get her killed. If Lucas had someone that could help prove Alex's innocence, then she had to trust him to do just that. Whatever had happened at the vineyard had not been Alex's doing. She had known him most of her life and this was not like him. He had put his heart and soul into the vineyard and winery, he would not have killed a bunch of agents then torch everything he worked for to cover it up. Something else was going on and she wanted to know what. Perhaps she needed to make a few calls of her own. She only hoped Melissa's plane had not yet arrived in Sault Ste Marie.

She told the computer to dial Melissa and gave her a quick summary of the situation. There was very little she could do other than contact Interpol and tell them what had happened. Right now, they needed Interpol fully-informed of the attack. Alex had security cameras throughout the vineyard and winery. It fed directly to his and Lucas's smartphones. There may be no footage of what had happened in the house but there was sure to be plenty of what happened outside.

It may be exactly what they needed to keep Alex from being charged with murder.

When she reached Espanola, she took Highway 6 to McKerrow. It was a tiny town on Highway 17, only five minutes from the heart of Espanola. She turned went to turn West but paused in astonishment when she noticed military vehicles lined up along the highway in front of the OPP station. The markings on them were a mix of the Canadian Armed Forces Wing 22 and Interpol. How they had managed to catch up to Lucas would be a mystery she would save for another day. There was just enough space for her to turn into the station where she spotted Lucas's Jeep along side two armored vehicles. Okay, this was not what she was expecting when Lucas said he had back up. There was just enough room for her to pull in. Along with the police and military vehicles, there was an ambulance.

Elizabeth's heart dropped as she rushed to the entrance. She pressed the buzzer and waited to be let in. The officer at the desk didn't seem too surprised to see her. If anything, she looked exasperated, as if the line up of people coming into the station was becoming a little much for her. She didn't even ask Elizabeth her name, seeming to have been expecting her. Considering Lucas had made in to the station before her – likely speeding as soon as he had back up – he would have made sure the officers knew she was on her way.

She met with him in a small lobby section and all but threw herself at him.

"What is going on?" she demanded as he held her tightly.

He rubbed his cheek against the side of her head. "It's a long story. They have a paramedic looking at him right now."

"Why would anyone attack the vineyard? Who is this girl? I know she's a hybrid but why is she so important? Why would someone kill all those agents to get to her?"

He pulled away and held her by her shoulders. "I don't know."

"Did you give them the security footage from your phone?"

115

He nodded. "I gave them everything. We just have to wait and see if the General and Major will back us up. Right now, they're not happy about Alex leaving with Kyra. He may still have to face kidnapping charges."

"Kidnapping? He saved her from the Shadow. He kept the creature from attacking the city."

"I know...but it's up to Caldwell whether or not he'll be charged. Legally, Kyra is a ward of the Canadian Government. She's not even classified as human. She's their property."

She ran her fingers through her hair as she began pacing. She couldn't believe this was happening again. Alex wasn't possessed by a Celestial this time but had been harbouring a half-breed one and was now paying for it. Why couldn't he stay away from them? Why did he have to play hero? This time he had lost everything, just as he had when the terrorists killed his father and research them. It was happening all over again. Alex could have died, and for what?

Because he was devoted to protecting someone who could not protect herself.

Her hands fell to her sides. He had done it to protect someone like him, and despite how mad it made her, she couldn't blame him. Perhaps he had not gone about it in the right manner but he had done what he thought was right.

"Do we need to get him a lawyer?" she asked.

"I already called one," Lucas assured. That meant it was probably a very expensive one already on Lucas's payroll.

"Okay." She took a deep breath, tears prickling the corners of her eyes. She shook her head. "It's gone. It's all gone. The house, the winery...everything."

Anguish filled Lucas's face but he only gave a curt nod. It was something they would deal with later.

"He has a gun shot wound to his right shoulder and at least two broken ribs," Caldwell reported as she stepped into the lobby. "The paramedics are patching him up and then he's being transferred into my custody."

Elizabeth looked to Lucas who seemed just as confused as she was. "And you are?" she asked.

"General Caldwell. Kyra was in my custody. Whoever attacked them, knew where Alex was, that people protecting them, and how to dispatch them with ease," she answered, all business. "It was too well-orchestrated."

"Were there any survivors?" Lucas asked, glancing anxiously at the metal door behind her that led to the prison cells.

The middle-aged woman nodded. "James. They found him not far from the house. It looks like someone gave him quite a beating. I suspect he was the first one taken out since he wasn't shot. Looks like they only began shooting people once they realized the exact number of agents there were."

"Who would do this?" Elizabeth asked.

"It could be anyone. It was a military operation. Alex has managed to piss off more than one nation because of these creatures. It could be Russia, it could even be the Americans, or Terrorists, or even another cult. Whoever it was, had inside information, either one of mine or Interpol, or…" Her words trailed off as she met Lucas's gaze.

His face hardened. "I'm going to pretend you didn't just imply I attempted to have my own husband murdered."

Her mouth opened to object, but it could not erase what she had said. She didn't get a chance to say anything more as Alex came out of the back, escorted by two officers. He looked toward Lucas and Elizabeth but didn't say anything, obviously still in shock and angry by what happened. He stopped at the Sergeant's desk and signed several forms before being released into Caldwell's custody.

"Let's get out of here," he grumbled, stumping pass them and outside. He paused at the door to look back at the OPP officers. "If you're looking for me, I'll be next door."

"Next door?" Elizabeth asked, looking at Lucas.

"Caldwell rented out the motel next door as our base camp, and to keep the OPP from thinking he was being whisked away rather than facing any possible charges. Tenzyn's on his way. He'll be joining us for a briefing along with the Fire Chief...as soon as the fire is under control."

He held the door open for her as Alex headed toward the motel, crossing the grass between it and the station. Elizabeth was tempted to run after him but she had to move her car to the other parking lot, which meant getting back on the highway and going around. At least a coffee shop and fast-food restaurant were within walking distance. They wouldn't have to go too far to get some descent coffee and food.

"You go after him," she told Lucas. "I'll move my car and come back for the Jeep. You take care of him."

He smiled softly at her and placed a hand on her shoulder. "Thank you," he breathed before darting off after his husband.

Elizabeth watched them as she slowly walked toward her car. Alex was injured and walking slowly; it didn't take Lucas very long to catch up to him. When he did, the younger man broke down. Lucas had to catch him as his knees gave out and he knelt in the snow. Lucas knelt next to him and let him cry in his arms. Her heart went out to them but she didn't interfere. She did as she promised Lucas, fetching her vehicle, and then following the military vehicles as they pulled onto the highway and made their way the short distance to the motel.

By the time she found a space for her car, Lucas had Alex and were entering the office of the motel. Lucas stopped long enough to throw her his keys before going inside. Thankfully the snow wasn't too deep and she was able to jog back to the station to get the Jeep, but rather than hurrying to the motel, she decided to get some food and coffee, certain that both men were in desperate need of something in their stomachs. She went with basic ham and cheese sandwiches and their favourite coffee mixes. Normally Lucas would drink tea at this time in the evening but given their current situation, coffee seemed to be the better choice.

She wasn't the only one getting food. Members of Wing 22 and Interpol were also placing food orders, preparing for a long night, and wanting to get food before the restaurants closed for the night. They nodded to her in greeting, likely not realizing she was with Lucas and Alex. She returned it, nervousness filling her stomach. They were in for a long night, and while Alex was free right now, he could wind up in a military prison before the night was out unless they could figure out who attacked the vineyard and what they wanted with the child. Given what had happened when they were stuck in the United States over a year ago, she didn't trust the military, regardless what branch they were from. Even if they now worked for Interpol, they were not protected from their own government if they decided Alex and this child posed some sort of danger. She was tempted to tell Lucas to take Alex and run, leave Canada, and never come back. Alex had been betrayed enough times by their government and the university for which he once worked. He didn't need to continue going through this, and without the vineyard, there was nothing left to tie him down.

It was time for him to go someplace where no one knew him or his past. It was time for him and Lucas to start a new life. Even if that life no longer included her.

She took a deep breath and pushed that though into the back of her mind. She would talk to them about it later, after they figured out what was going on and who had attacked the vineyard just to get to the mysterious hybrid. She knew Alex; he would not rest until he found the girl and knew she was safe. Elizabeth only hoped that he accepted the fact that Kyra would have to go back with Caldwell and not stay with him.

Chapter Ten

Lucas frowned as he leaned against the wall and watched Alex pace the room. His limp was more pronounced, the stress on his body being displayed by the way he walked. His prosthetic probably needed to be adjusted on his stump, but at the moment, Alex didn't seem to care. The younger man was cursing, his fingers curling and uncurling into fists. There was an energy coming off him that everyone could feel even if most could not understand where it was coming from. Lucas wanted to go to him, to hold him, and assure him everything was going to be alright, but that wasn't what Alex needed right now. He was angry and hurt and needed to vent. If he bottled it up, things were only become worse, which would trigger the new energy he possessed. Alex tried to hide it, but Lucas knew he still possessed some of the Celestial's power. They had yet to see what that power was capable of, and Lucas would rather not have it on full display. Especially in front of Caldwell.

"She was safe," Alex fumed as he passed the General. "We got the Shadow away from North Bay and it didn't catch her. All you had to do was wait a few days, let me protect her, and I would have brought her back. You could have called! Why attack?"

"We didn't," Caldwell objected, but Alex would have none of it.

"My home! My business! You destroyed everything! And now the police think I murdered twenty agents! Twenty! My dogs…" He pulled at his hair as he turned on his heel and began walking in the opposite direction. "Everything's gone. She's gone." He looked at Caldwell. "Why?"

For the first time, Caldwell looked sympathetic. "It wasn't my people. Dr. Jackson, we arrived in Sudbury minutes before Dr. Griffith called. Whoever attacked knew we were in the air on our way here."

Lucas nodded. "She's telling the truth, Alex. We met off the Highway 144 bypass."

Alex shook his head in disbelief. "Then she sent a team ahead of her. These people were military trained. What? Am I supposed to believe it was the US military? Olivia's mercenaries? Tell me who did this! Tell me…"

He stopped and leaned against a table, his chest heaving as he blinked away tears. Lucas's heart went out to him, but he kept his distance. Alex still needed his space. Lucas had yet to see what remained of their home and he was afraid to. In the morning, once the fire was fully extinguished and the police had been able to conduct some of their investigation, he could check it out. For now, he needed to stay away from it and focus on Alex. The idea that it was all gone was only that at the moment. It didn't seem real. It wouldn't until he saw it for himself.

"I wish I could," Caldwell said in an almost soothing motherly voice. "Kyra is very important to us. Whoever took her took a powerful asset…"

Alex glared at her, energy rippling through him enough to make the hairs on Lucas's arms rise.

"Alex," he said, hoping to calm him.

The younger man glanced at him then shook his head. "We need to find her. These guys see her as an asset, lord knows what the people who took her think she is."

Lucas nodded in agreement. "We'll find her."

He glanced past Alex to the main entrance as Elizabeth came in balancing a tray of coffees and paper bag of food. He gave her a small nod, both thankful she was there and worried of her reaction to Alex's outbursts. She was Alex's best friend, the closest thing to family he

121

had left. Alex's mother lived outside Toronto and had very rarely visited due to her work schedule. That left Alex with only Lucas and Elizabeth. Right now, he needed both.

Lucas made a small gesture for Elizabeth to keep back as Alex fought to control his temper and the energy he was producing.

"Okay, what do we know?" he asked Alex, hoping to get him focused.

As an anthropologist, Alex was able to pinpoint even the most minute detail. His husband stared at him for a moment before folding his arms across his chest and glaring at the wooden floor. "They wore masks. Their faces were completely covered. And they were in military fatigues, carrying fully automatic rifles. They knew where the agents were and killed them so quietly and with such ease that if the dogs didn't start barking we wouldn't have had time to react."

"Any markings on the fatigues?" Caldwell asked. "Anything that would mark who they were or where they came from?"

Alex's lips pressed into a thin line. His face pinched in anguish as he shook his head. "No. Nothing. By the time I managed to get out of the house, it was in flames and everyone was gone except a helicopter that took off from behind the winery. It must have arrived in the middle of all the chaos. I never heard it land."

He ran his fingers over his ruined right ear where his hearing aid should be. It was missing which would explain why he could not have heard the helicopter above everything that had happened. It wouldn't have mattered if he had heard it. There was nothing more he could have done. He had nearly died trying to protect Kyra, had nearly drowned in the well, and escaped their burning home before it came crashing down on him. Had he not surrendered to the police, he could have been killed by them, suspected of murdering the agents. They already suspected he was somehow at fault, and by taking Kyra, in many ways he was, at least in the eyes of the Armed Forces.

Lucas sighed. "Okay, it's not much to go on, but there was a helicopter which means there has to be some sort of report about it.

Most of the helicopters that fly around here are either OPP, Search and Rescue, or Emergency Medical Transport. They all need to communicate with the OPP which means they would have a record. If not..." He glanced to Chief Tenzyn who had so far remained quiet and been observing Alex. "Either they registered under a false name or have an inside person at one of the stations."

Tenzyn raised a brush black brow. "I don't like what you're implying, Griffith."

"I'm not implying anything, I'm stating a fact," Lucas pointed out. "Not one can fly through here and land without radioing it in. Where we are is still rural, not completely urban. We have a few crop dusters and private planes, but they still need to radio in when they leave and return. Any low-flying aircraft does. So, either they posed as Search and Rescue, which would explain why the OPP and Fire Department got there so fast, or they have someone on the inside that gave them the time they needed to get in and out."

Tenzyn stood and faced off against Lucas. "And this could have been an insurance scam under the guise of a terrorist attack," he snapped. "My people would not align ourselves with anyone who would attack civilians, let alone in our community. Dr. Griffith...Lucas...we've known each other for a few years now. I've known Alex since he began teaching at the high school. I know you're good people, but whatever you're into...the attack on your home wasn't just on you, it was on everyone who lived on your road. You had members of Interpol on your property. A child that neither one of you are the father of, that was essentially kidnapped from a military base. Alex could be facing a long jail sentence if either the General or Interpol decided to press charges."

He looked to Caldwell but she shook her head. His eyes narrowed but when he turned to the Interpol representative, Agent Michaels, he received another shake of the head. No one was pressing charges against Alex.

Lucas gave a small sigh or relief. One less worry for them. He went to Alex and took his hand, bringing it to his lips to kiss the knuckles. They were bruised and scratched, turning a horrible purple.

Once they were alone, he would have to strip him down and see just how hurt he was. The paramedics had patched him up, but since it was while he was in an interrogation room, it was just a quick look over. There would be a lot more damage hidden under his clothing that even Alex would be unaware of. Right now, he was still in shock, but it would wear off soon and the enormity of the situation would hit him like a jackhammer to the gut. When it did, Lucas had to make sure he was somewhere safe and not alone.

"Are you hungry? Elizabeth got us some food and coffee," he told Alex. He ducked down slightly to catch Alex's gaze. He could feel the slight tremor in his hand, the shock working its way through him. "We can go to bed after that, get some rest then figure out how to find her after."

"She was so scared, Lucas. I couldn't do anything. I lost consciousness in the well. I should have died, but I didn't. I got out and I still couldn't save her. I couldn't save any of them." His words were coming out as more of a babble than coherent, exhaustion getting to him.

"Honey, there was nothing you could have done. If you hadn't fallen into the well, you would have been killed along with them. You survived so that we can find and save Kyra. And we will, I promise." He gently squeezed Alex's hand, careful of the bruises and injuries. "How about we find our room and relax. I'll run you a bath and we'll find you some clean clothing. I'm sure Elizabeth wouldn't mind running into town to get you some." He glanced toward the woman who nodded in agreement.

Alex shook his head. "No…I need to find her."

"I know, but she needs you to be strong for her. Come on. The rest of this meeting can wait until morning."

He wrapped an arm around Alex's waist, looked to Caldwell and Tenzyn, then took two of the key cards on the table, throwing one to Elizabeth to ensure their rooms were next to one another. No one objected to them leaving, and for that, he was grateful. Alex needed time to recover and to be properly tended. He wasn't kidding about the hot bath either. Alex's clothing was still wet and ice cold. He hadn't even been given a blanket or change of clothing while in the police station. He wasn't in there long enough to even have a cup of coffee before Caldwell stormed the place and demanded his release.

The room they were in was small compared to what Lucas would normally rent for them. It didn't matter though. It wasn't about comfort this time around; it was a place to sleep until they could figure out what to do. Lucas realised that they were now homeless.

Homeless.

Lucas had never endured that before, not even when his father disowned him, or when he was dishonourably discharged from the British Army. He had always had a home to go back to. He couldn't think about that now. So far, Alex had kept himself together. He sat on the Queen-size bed as Lucas filled the tub. It wasn't as large as the one they had at home – used to have – but it would do the job. He helped Alex undress and remove his prosthetic, then get into the warm water before he undressed as well. He slid into the tub behind Alex and wrapped his arms around him, pulling him back against his chest. Alex was smaller than him, with narrow shoulders and a slim waist. A swimmer's body compared his Lucas's much broader build. They fit together perfectly.

Alex leaned his head back against Lucas's shoulder. He didn't say anything as he turned his face toward Lucas's neck and pressed it against warm flesh, but Lucas could feel his tears and the gentle shaking of his body as he began to sob. Lucas leaned his head against Alex's and rubbed his arms. He didn't say anything or made promises he couldn't keep. None of that would help Alex. All he could do was let Alex express his emotions and hold him as the events of the evening took their toll. Everything else they could deal with in the morning. For now, they sat in the water together, Alex clinging to him as he sobbed, mourning the loss of their home, their dogs, the people they worked with, and a child they barely had a chance to know, but one they both determined to find and protect.

"I'm an idiot," Lucas suddenly announced, causing Alex to look up questioningly.

The younger man sniffled as he turned in his arms. "Why?"

"I still have your overnight bag in the Jeep. Elizabeth didn't need to go shopping."

Alex studied him for a long moment before laying against him. "You're an idiot," he agreed.

Lucas hugged him to his chest. Well, at least they could agree on something, and he almost got a smirk out of Alex. It was a step toward healing. They stayed curled up together in the tub until the water got cold, then Lucas lifted Alex out of the tub, wrapped him in the largest towel he could find, and carried him to the bed. They snuggled under the covers together until Alex fell into a sound sleep. Lucas, however, lay wide awake, staring at the ceiling in deep thought. It still didn't feel real to him, and it wouldn't even after he viewed the damage for himself, that much he knew. It wouldn't truly kick in until they began going through the rubble of the life they made together. He was just grateful Alex was alive and so was James. He would have to talk to the agent and find out how someone managed to get the drop on a group of highly trained Interpol agents without alerting anyone. Someone had to have seen something. The neighbours…someone.

The knock at the door startled him out of his thoughts. He glanced at Alex, but he was out cold. Nothing would wake him now. Lucas carefully untangled himself from his lover and made sure he was tucked in before grabbing his slacks and pulling them on, minus the underwear. He looked through the peephole, not wanting to have to deal with Caldwell or Tenzyn, and was thankful to see Elizabeth on the other side with a bag of clothing and the coffee and food.

"I hope your room has a microwave," she said by way of greeting when he let her in. "Everything's ice cold."

"Yes, it's on the dresser," he told her, stepping aside. He closed the door and locked it then gestured to the small table near the window and back door. "Thanks again for getting all this. I'm such an idiot. I had his overnight bag in the Jeep. I completely forgot it."

She shrugged her jacket, her gaze on Alex's sleeping form. "Given what happened today…it's only natural. Besides, whatever is in the Jeep is probably all the belongings either of you have now. You'll both need more clothing soon enough."

"I suppose."

He sat in one of the chairs at the table and pulled out a sandwich from the bag. It didn't matter that it was cold. He had not eaten since noon and was famished. Ham and Cheese was not one of his favourites but it was better than nothing.

Elizabeth went about putting removing the lids of two coffees then put them in the microwave to reheat. He made a face at that but was not about to ask her to go back out and buy him a fresh one. Nor was he about to make a pot. It was still early in the evening but he wanted to save the motel provided coffee until morning. They were going to need it.

"How's he doing?" she asked. She set the coffees on the table and sat across from Lucas.

He shook his head. "It took a while for the shock to wear off enough for him to process what happened. I don't think it'll completely set in until we inspect what's left tomorrow."

She nodded in understanding. "From what I saw, it was a war zone. There was nothing that could be saved. I'm so sorry, Lucas. I'm just so happy he managed to make it out."

"Me too."

She wrapped her hands around her coffee cup and blew on the steaming hot liquid. "What's the deal with this kid? You told a bit and so did he. I mean, I spent part of the morning shopping with him over the phone. He spent a small fortune just getting her clothing and the essentials, including a booster seat. All of which, I might add, just burned up in the fire. Is she really a Celestial-Human hybrid?"

Lucas licked his lips as he put the sandwich on the table. He used one of the paper napkins to wipe his mouth before answering.

"Her mother was a Celestial host. The lab techs at NORAD bred her in order to produce Kyra. She was supposed to be a walking weapon. No one was supposed to know about her. She was raised in the Bunker and when NORAD moved to Winnipeg, she was put into a cryochamber to be moved along with the rest of the lab equipment. She has never been treated as a child…just some science experiment. When her chamber was somehow breached – likely by the Shadow – she hid in the only place she knew was safe, a decontamination chamber with the brightest lighting in the entire facility. Alex was called in to coax her out…"

"Because he had been a host and bore the same marking as the woman that birthed her," she finished.

He nodded and rubbed the back of his neck. "Exactly. They knew he would bond with her but rather than let them remain together, Caldwell wanted to put her back in a capsule and ship her off. The Shadow attacked before she could do that and Alex acted on instinct, taking her to the one place he thought she would be safe. That didn't go as planned."

"No." She sipped her coffee. "Do you think Caldwell sent a team ahead of her to retrieve the girl? Maybe tried to get rid of anyone who knew her. It wouldn't be the first General to try and get rid of witnesses in order to continue getting government funding for their experiments. She may have come here to ensure you and Alex are dealt with."

He had thought about that. She could have had Alex released to her custody in order to kill him herself, but now there were too many witnesses. Or they could be overthinking this and she really was trying to do what she thought was best. Either way, Lucas didn't trust her. Caldwell was still lying to them, of that he was certain. If she didn't know where Kyra was taken, she would likely know how to find out. And if she was somehow involved in all this, then she may want Alex alive. He would be no good to her for breeding. He was no longer possessed by a Celestial and even if he was, he could not have children. He was sterile. Alex would never have biological children of his own.

Lucas had more questions than answers. It was the first time he actually wished the Celestial still had possession of Alex. It was mysterious and murderous with an unquenchable hunger for sex and human flesh. Lucas would give it all it desired if only to get the answers to his questions. He would give anything to ensure Alex's safety. It was the one thing he and the Celestial had in common.

"I wish we could talk to James," he said absently searching through the paper bag for a donut. He hated donuts with a passion. Far too much sugar in his opinion, yet he was suddenly craving one. Hell, soda would even do. Something with a high level of sugar. "He may be able to give us a little more insight on who attacked them...provided he survives the night."

"The injuries were supposed to me minor...minor-ish," Elizabeth reminded him. She handed him a blueberry muffin from another bag. "You don't think someone will go in the hospital and finish him, do you? There must be all sorts of security protecting him."

He shrugged. "I don't know. I don't know about anything anymore."

She reached over and grasped his hand, her fingers curling around his. "Can you promise me something?"

He raised a brow, curious by the sense of dread he felt coming from her. "Of course."

"When this is over, regardless if you find this child or not, you'll take Alex as far from here as possible. Take him somewhere that the government won't easily find him. Somewhere that people won't actively hunt him down. I don't care if it's England or Australia, or the ends of the Earth. Get him away from all this and help him have a normal life."

His mouth opened and closed but no words came out. After a moment, he nodded. He had no idea where to take Alex that would be out of reach, but he knew it was not something easy to accomplish either. Alex loved his life here, loved teaching. None of that mattered anymore. Elizabeth was right. The only way Alex was ever going to be truly safe was to be somewhere no-one could find him. He wasn't sure where to start looking for such a place. Another country made sense but which one? England was not an option.

He sighed and sat back. He didn't want to leave. He had come to love this area and the beautiful life he and Alex had created. They could start from scratch, rebuild it all. Even if the insurance didn't cover the damages, he had enough money banked to get them started. Was it worth it though? Should they rebuild here or start new somewhere else? Anywhere else?

His mind was whirling but he was to full of nervous energy to sleep. He offered Elizabeth his spot next to Alex, fearful that she may be attacked in the middle of the night now that she was part of this. She declined, pointing out that it was still early and that her own anxiety would not let her rest either. They sat together at the table. Lucas shared everything he knew about Kyra with her and how she reacted to Alex. She listened intently, as she always did, the scientist in her just as curious as it was in Alex. She wanted to know everything and Lucas did his best to answer. One question began to form in their minds. If Kyra's mother was a host to a Celestial then what temple did it come from? Celestials didn't normally leave the general region of their temple unless it was destroyed. When Alex was possessed, the Arctic temple from which the Celestial emerged had been destroyed by Lucas and a joint team of Interpol agents and Canadian Armed Forces. It had been actively searching for other temples but never met up with other hosts. For a long time, Lucas thought it was the only one of its kind until the Vaults – large alien ships hidden within their temples – suddenly broke free and flew into space. Thousands of them from all around the world fled the planet, proving that the Celestials did indeed exist and that there were far more than anyone ever anticipated. Many took their hosts with them. Others killed them, but each had been mating...creating a new breed of human...Celestial-Human hybrids. They had yet to be found until Kyra, at least so Lucas had thought. Now he no longer knew. Even if they could find the temple Kyra's mother's Celestial had come from, the Vault was likely gone, and with it any answers it may have contained.

Canada was a large country. If the temple still existed, it could be anywhere. They didn't have enough time to search an entire country, especially one this large in winter. There may not be a lot of snow here yet but further north would have much more and could even be covered in ice.

That would have to wait. His first priority was Alex, after that, he would figure out a way to find Kyra.

Chapter Eleven

D aylight brought with it the utter devastation caused by the fire. Their house was nothing but rubble, burned to the ground with nothing more than a few timbers left to show the skeleton of the structure. The winery faired slightly better. It was a wide building with few things that were truly flammable inside. The firefighters had been able to get control of it more easily than they did the house. Lucas walked along the perimeter of the destruction, unable to search the rubble as firefighters continued searching for and putting-out hot-spots. The only things that weren't destroyed were the vineyard and greenhouse, not that it mattered. All the grapes had been picked and were in the winery at the time of the fire. Their entire stock was gone, all the wine they had made and presold. Tens of thousands of dollars worth. That seemed minor though. Their insurance would cover it and reimburse their buyers. Almost everything that was lost could be replaced…except those who died, including the dogs.

He tried to think of the positives, that Alex was alive and that they could rebuild. They walked together, taking it all in, trying to figure out their next move. Elizabeth was off to the side, speaking with Caldwell, hoping to find something that would identify who attacked them.

He squeezed Alex's hand as they made their way back to the driveway. "We'll rebuild. It'll be bigger. More grapes, more flavours of wine. We can turn this into a huge business for the local community."

"Yeah," Alex murmured, but it was easy to see his heart wasn't interested in it. At least, not right now.

Lucas took no offense to that. He was trying to get Alex's mind off Kyra, but inspecting their home was not the best way to go about it. He wasn't sure what was. Everywhere they went people looked at them questioningly or asked if they were alright. No one knew what truly happened and assumed it was either an accident or arson. The local reporters had been calling them all morning, asking for details, despite the police running interference. It was not what they needed right now. Alex needed to get away from all this, but until Tenzyn and Caldwell came to an agreement on whether or not Alex would be charged, they had to stay close to home…or what was left of it. Lucas was at a loss at what to do. It wasn't just the loss of their home that dwelled on Alex's mind, but the child; where she may be, what may be happening to her, and whether she was still alive.

The night before, Lucas had promised they would find her. He wasn't sure it that was possible. He wanted to believe it was and that the people who took her were someone they had already dealt with, such as the mercenaries that had attacked Alex and his research team in British Columbia when they discovered one of the many underground temples. Or perhaps the Russian Cult that had used Alex to unlock the Arctic temple. Even the members of Area 51, that officially no longer existed after the whole base caved into the vast underground chamber it was built over when the two Vaults hidden in the twin temples launched into space. He and Alex had gained a lot of enemies after the temple discoveries, a lot of people who still viewed Alex as some sort of key due to the scars on his hand created by an artifact that was, in fact, a key to the temple Vaults. All of them. If it had been one of those groups, they would have kidnapped Alex as well, not just the girl. The attack made no sense. Only Caldwell's people knew where she was. Only they would have reason to attack and take her by force.

A speck of silver caught Lucas's attention as they paced where the fireplace still stood, one of the few remaining parts of the house. It was charred a dark smoky grey and black, but on the hearth below, mixed with other burnt items, was a silver lid, covered in soot, several broken frames and half burnt photographs, and an overturned urn.

"Oh…" he breathed. "Stay here."

He let go of Alex's hand and carefully picked his way through the rubble – the floor not safe to walk on – until he reached the fireplace. Thankful for his heavy winter gloves, he picked through the debris. The photographs were damaged beyond repair, the glass melded to the frame on one side and photopaper curled and blackened by the fire. They were photos of Alex's father and former research team, as well as Lucas's older brother Owen. Even the British flag that had been safely placed in a hard wood and glass case was unsalvageable. All the remained that he could possibly take was the urn with most of Owen's ashes. The rest were in much smaller urns that had been fashioned in necklaces that he, Alex, and Elizabeth wore in remembrance. The metal was twisted and melted, the majority of the ashes spilt on what remained of the floor, mixing with the ashes of the house. There was little difference between one type of ash from another. His shoulders fell as he lifted the damaged urn and lid. He tried fitting them back together but both were warped due to the intense heat.

A shaky sob escaped him as he hugged it to his chest. It was the only thing of his brother's he had left. Now there was barely enough of Owen left to fill a teaspoon. He felt tears stream down his cheeks. It had been a long time since he cried over Owen. He missed him. His brother had always protected him, had stood by his side through thick and thin, had given his life to save him and Alex.

Wiping his tears, he stood and did something he had promised to do long ago but had never been able to bring himself to do; he dumped what little ashes remained, letting the cool early winter breeze carry them away. His gaze met Alex's, who's eyes shimmered with the same grief Lucas felt. They had both lost so much because of the temples and Celestials. Lucas couldn't imagine losing anyone else.

Alex's fear for Kyra made more sense now. Even if she was a hybrid, she was perhaps the closest person like him. To Alex, it must have felt like he lost a part of himself when they took her. Lucas wanted to take away that pain and promise Alex they would find her, they just needed a clue as to where to look.

His attention diverted from Alex to a van pulling up in front of the house. It was one of the local taxis from Espanola. He gestured with his head toward it to draw Alex's attention to the newcomer as he exited the vehicle. It took a moment to realize who it was, but a sense of relief filled him as James limped toward them. His left arm was in a sling and he used a cane to help him walk.

"James!" Alex called out, darting toward him. "Shit! I thought we lost you!"

James gave a small laugh as Alex embraced him. "No…no…I'm fine. A little sore but fine."

Lucas hurried over to him as well and clapped him on the shoulder. "We were told you were shot. You should still be in the hospital."

James gave a small shrug. "I'm just happy they're a crappy shot. It grazed my hip and then I was hit in the head. Next thing I know, I'm waking up in the hospital and a nurse was telling me your house burned down. Do we know who attacked us?"

Alex's face fell. "No."

"It was military or a mercenary group. We haven't learned who yet," Lucas through in.

James looked around. "They destroyed everything? God, I'm so sorry."

"You and Alex are alive, that's all that matters. The rest can be rebuilt." He sighed, realizing how cold that must have sounded. "We'll find who did this…and Kyra."

James gave a nod. "Of course, we will. We have the best people on it." He placed a hand on Alex's shoulder. "Hey, listen, she's a strong kid. She managed to survive everything in that lab and escape the Shadow. I'm sure she can handle whoever snatched her."

Alex shook his head. "She's only seven. She wasn't born in the 1970s. She's just a child. Whatever gifts she has, haven't

135

manifested yet. We don't know when they will, or if they will. And we don't know what will happen when they do."

"Can't you just connect with her like you did before?"

Alex stared at James as if he had grown a second head.

"No...I..."

His eyes widened as he looked to Lucas for support.

Lucas tapped his tongue on the inside top of his mouth in thought as he studied Alex. In all the chaos, Alex had not mentioned being able to connect with Kyra. He doubted their connection had been severed. No, it was due to the stress and the thousands of thoughts that must be running through his mind since the attack. If he was about to take a deep breath and calm down, perhaps he could reach out to her once more. She may not be able to tell him where she was but perhaps her memories of being taken could help them locate her. The key was getting Alex to calm down enough to be able to focus on her. That was not going to be easy. He was still rippling with nervous energy, it wasn't as bad as the night before, but enough to keep most people at a safe distance. Standing just feet from what used to be their home was not a good place to relax. Neither was the motel but they had few other options.

"Do you want to leave?" Lucas asked, changing the subject. "There's nothing we can do here. The police need to investigate the scene. We might as well go out for breakfast."

Alex shook his head. "I don't think I can handle another person asking if we're okay." He nervously wrung his hands as he looked toward Elizabeth who was still speaking to Caldwell. "I just..." He let out a big buff of air. "I don't know what I want."

"Okay, let's go back to the motel. We can order room service or have something delivered."

"Yeah, that sounds good," Alex agreed. He leaned in Lucas as his husband wrapped an arm around him. "I'm starving. A Spanish Omelet would be amazing."

Lucas made a face. "Darling, I have no idea how you can eat that, Eggs Benedict is much better for you."

Alex's love for spicy food was interesting to watch, but not at breakfast. A Spanish Omelet was loaded with peppers, red onions, tomatoes, ham, and cheese, topped with salsa and sour cream. Alex swore it was the most delicious food one of the local restaurants made for breakfast. To Lucas, it was just a little too much for an omelet and did not look appealing, not to mention how it left Alex's breath afterwards. However, if that's what Alex wanted, then that's what he would get. He'll place the order and have a delivery service to pick up the food once they got to the motel.

"Did Elizabeth bring her own car?" James asked, looking toward the vehicles lined up along the road.

Lucas nodded toward the small blue sedan toward the back of the line up. "Yes, she wanted to handle things for us today, especially with Caldwell. Have you spoken to Michaels?"

"He's trying to track where the helicopter went. Given the description Alex gave him, there's only a few likely places. Either way, they would have changed to another vehicle to wherever they're took her. They would know we're looking for the helicopter." He gave a small shrug. "You guys head out, I'll catch a ride with Beth."

He gave Alex's arm a squeeze before passing him to hobble to Elizabeth, who seemed just as excited as they were to see him, as he were to see her. She threw her arms around James in greeting.

Lucas waved to her, signalling that he and Alex were leaving, then headed to their Jeep. The drive back into Espanola was filled with an uneasy silence. Both were processing what they had seen, the loss of their home and what few belongings they had of those they had lost. He absently touched the small canister that contained some of Owen's ashes. What he, Alex, and Elizabeth held were all that were left of him now. It was more than what Alex had of his father, but at the same time, it was not enough.

"She saw him," Alex suddenly said, surprising Lucas.

"Uh?"

"Owen…Kyra saw him. She said he was there, looking over us," Alex clarified.

Lucas took a deep breath and let it out slowly. "She probably saw his picture and decided to make him her invisible friend."

A sigh left Alex. "I don't know. Maybe. The energy felt strange when she began talking about him. She knew his name. I never told it to her."

It was getting hard to focus on the road. Lucas's eyes burned with unshed tears. When they first bought the vineyard, Alex used to say he felt Owen, that he was there with them. He would spend hours in the vineyard, talking to someone that wasn't there. Then he stopped. Lucas didn't know why. He assumed that whatever part of his psyche that had been damaged by the death of his father and team, then Owen, had healed. For a time, he was even willing to consider the temple Guardians had latched onto Alex and were protecting him. They were the souls of the men and women who had died protecting the temple and trying to keep the Celestials from returning to their realm. They had stopped communing with Alex after he was possessed by one of the Celestials. Nonetheless, he refused to believe Owen's ghost had been hanging around their home for all these years. He would have known. He would have felt him.

"James must have told her."

"I suppose," Alex sighed.

He looked out his window, his mouth pulled down in a frown. For a while, neither one of them spoke, that uneasy silence filling the space once more as the entered Espanola and made their way to the highway to go to the motel in McKerrow. Lucas placed the food order as the crossed the bridge leading out of Espanola. He should have done it before the entered the town but his mind was on Owen and the possibly that maybe…just maybe…Kyra had seen him and was able to speak with him. What did it mean, especially now that their home was gone and his ashes with it?

Once they reached the motel, Alex went straight to the bed, kicked off his boots, and sat on it cross legged. He didn't say anything, his face taking on it's usual mask when he was deep in thought or unhappy. To anyone who didn't know him, he would look bored when in fact there was anger boiling under the surface. Lucas knew that look but waited until after the food was delivered to address it. He placed it on the table when it arrived and tipped the delivery driver.

"If you're going to yell, you might as well do it now instead of bottling it up," he told Alex as he set the table. "Just tell me what's on your mind."

Alex didn't move from his spot for a long time. A sigh puffed past his lips as he stood. "You believe I can connect with Kyra through this connection we have, yet you refuse to believe she can commune with spirits...with Owen."

Lucas held back a groan. "No...it's not that. I was taken by surprise, and you know me, I need to find a logical explanation before accepting the fantastical. The idea of Kyra speaking to Owen...it would be as if she claimed to speak to your father. You'd want some sort of proof, wouldn't you?"

His face pinched in thought, took a deep breath then let it out slowly. "You're right."

"I'm not saying she wasn't talking to him, its just a little hard for me to accept it," Lucas explained. He rolled his shoulders, fighting back his emotions. "I just like to think that if his spirit was still with us, he would have let me know...somehow."

He sat at the table and leaned on one elbow, fingering the tiny silver urn hanging from the chain around his neck, grief filling him once more. It felt like he had lost Owen all over again.

Alex's mouth opened in surprise as understanding dawned on him. "Oh...oh geez, Lucas...I'm sorry. I didn't even think how that might affect you." He crossed the room to him and slid onto his lap, his arms wrapping around his husband's neck. "I shouldn't have said anything. Seeing you dump what was left of his ashes...it made it seem final, that he was really gone when only yesterday Kyra swore he was speaking to her."

Lucas pulled him into a tight embrace. "It's alright. With everything going on...it's just beginning to sink in. Losing his ashes..."

He hugged Alex a little tighter, fighting back the sobs that threatened to consume him. He didn't want to cry. He had done enough of that. Right now, they needed to focus on their next move, in more ways than one. They needed to decide where they would live, deal with the insurance agency, and find Kyra. For all of that, they needed to be calm and able to think.

He gently turned Alex's face towards his and placed a small kiss on his lips. "We should eat before it gets cold, love. Then we need to figure out how to re-establish your mental connection to Kyra. It's the only way we're going to find her."

"I take it you'll deal with the insurance company?" Alex asked, slipping off his lap to sit at the other end of the table.

Lucas nodded. "Of course. Explaining our home was attacked may take some work, but I think we have even evidence to support it."

"Thankfully."

"I guess all we need now is a crash course on meditation."

A hollow laugh came from Alex as he unwrapped his plastic utensils. Lucas grimaced at the sound of the crackling plastic wrapper. They needed proper utensils. Plastic was not cutlery, but for now it was all they had.

It turned out, meditating was not as easy as movies and books made it seem. After breakfast, Alex sat in the middle of the bed, trying to calm his thoughts and focus on Kyra. Lucas watched him, which only served to make him self-conscious, as if his every movement of facial expression was being scrutinized. They tried meditation music and even chants, but that only made Alex feel even more anxious than he already was. Every sound got on his nerves. The passing cars on the highway. The hum of the mini fridge. The way Lucas would sip his coffee, although barely audible, to Alex it suddenly sounded like loud slurping. After a while, he had no choice but to ask Lucas to leave the room in hopes of shutting himself off from the rest of the world. That worked for only a few minutes before the outside noise creeped back it, sounding ten times louder than before.

He flopped back on the bed and covered his eyes with one arm. It was dark in the room. He had shut curtains and turned off the lights when Lucas left in hopes that it would help, with no success. His mind continued to wander to other things, the loss of their home, their business, Owen, and yes, Kyra, but he could not put his full focus on her like he wanted. He felt like a failure, as if everything he touched died. All because of finding the temple in the Rocky Mountains. Had they left when his father wanted them to, none of this would have happened. His father and friends would still be alive. He never would have joined Lucas in the search for more which meant Owen would still be alive. The Celestial never have possessed him, meaning the dozens upon dozens of people it fed on would still be alive, and Kyra...would still be hunted by the Shadow but the people who came after her would not have slaughtered those Interpol agents because Alex would probably still be in Sudbury, blissfully unaware of it all.

His fingers knotted in his hair. He couldn't change the past, and, right now, he couldn't even imagine the future. Lucas said they could rebuild but what was the point if someone was going to attack them and burn it all down? It just didn't make sense to invest all that time and money again.

A knock at the door startled him. Rubbing his face, he sighed. He might as well answer it, his concentration was blown anyway, not that he had much to begin with. He padded across the room and unlocked the outside door. He expected it to be Lucas, asking if it was safe to come back in, or maybe Elizabeth checking up on him. Instead, if was James with a rather perturbed look on his face.

"Do you have a minute?" the Interpol agent asked. He leaned heavy on his cane, looking worn out. Given his night, Alex could sympathize.

"Yeah, sure, come on in. Lucas is out for a bit."

Alex moved aside to let the other man in and gestured to one of the chairs at the table.

"Thanks," James mumbled. He leaned against the dresser instead of sitting down. He rubbed his left arm, a frown marring his appearance. "I was just talking to Michaels…they may have a lead on where Kyra was taken." He looked up and met Alex's gaze. "You're not going to like it."

Alex raised a brow as he shut the door. "Alright. Where do they think she's been taken?"

James picked nervously at the sling around his arm. "You might want to sit down for this."

"Just tell me, James," Alex said firmly. He folded his arms across his chest and leaned his lip against the door. He wasn't in the mood for guessing games.

"Okay…well, back when your research team discovered that temple in BC, it seems that after the terrorist attack, someone bought the property. I thought it was the government so never looked into it but it seems someone else might have," James began.

Alex's brows furrowed in confusion. "What are you talking about? That land was bought by Laurentian University and used for anthropology and archeology research. It was then seized by the Canadian government as a protected historic site. No one could dig there."

"Yeah, well, it looks like someone has. It's not our people, and it's not military; at least, it doesn't appear to be," James said, his voice taking a harsh edge. "Michaels is supposed to be discussing it with Caldwell. It might turn into a turf war over who gets the site and which faction is going after whoever took the kid. So far, it's turning into a shit-show."

Alex felt a little light headed by the news. He took a seat and stared absently throughout the room. "I don't understand. Why there? The temple was destroyed. The Vault…it should be gone. Even if it is still there, she can't open it. I don't think she can open it." He turned to James. "I need to get there…right now."

"Alex…"

He shook his head. "No, James, you don't understand. I need to get to her. If the Vault is still there and they try to get into it…they could wittingly unleash an army of Celestials. The Shadows are

like their attack dogs. They'll come first, kill, or possess whoever they need to, but the Celestials will be right behind them. If they come back in force…there may be no stopping them this time."

"That's a three-day drive," James tried to reason. "And that's when the roads are clear. "It's winter in the Prairies. We'd have to fly there. Michaels isn't going to sign off on that without more information and evidence that they took her there. Not only that…but we have the Armed Forces to deal with. Kyra is still technically Caldwell's ward. They have first dibs at going after the people who took her. We have to follow her move."

"And what of the agents that were killed? Doesn't Interpol have a right to seek justice for them?"

James sighed. "We do. Look, I'll talk to Michaels. I'll see what we can do. I just thought you deserved to know what's going on." He pushed himself away from the dresser and headed back to the door, pausing to place a hand on Alex's shoulder. "I didn't want to upset you, I just wanted you to know what's going on. Now that we have a location, we just need to wait for the higher ups to come to a decision. Then we'll know what we're doing. We're not abandoning her."

Alex nodded. "I know. Thank you."

Nonetheless, it didn't make Alex feel any better. If anything, it made him feel worse. As if his mind hadn't been dwelling on what happened in the Rocky Mountains already, now it was even more so. He had so many questions and wanted to demand answers for them. Why would someone build a base there of all places? Did they build directly over the temple as several other places had? Did they even know what it was? Were they a part of the government or one of the cults seeking the Celestials power? Why did they take Kyra? Did they know what she was? Did they care? How did they know she was with him and that Interpol was protecting them? All these thoughts swirled in Alex's mind. One thing was clear though, he had to go to her and get her away from them and what remained of the temple. Even if no one was willing to help him. Even if that included Lucas.

Chapter Twelve

lex sat silently as Caldwell and Michaels explained their findings to those that were still present. A number of soldiers were already heading back to North Bay while agents were enroute to British Columbia. Those that remained were there to protect Alex and Lucas, and by extension, Elizabeth. Due to Alex's history with the temple discovered in the Rocky Mountains, Interpol wanted to keep him as far from it as possible. Lucas, despite claiming to support Alex and wanting to save Kyra, agreed that Alex should not go to the old temple site. The risk of how it may affect Alex was too high, which was seconded by Elizabeth. Alex bit back the arguments that piled in the back of his subconscious. He wasn't sure how he would get to British Columbia. It would take at least three days to drive, and even if he drove to the city and caught a flight there, it would take the better part of the day to get on a plane, fly to Vancouver, and then another six hours to drive to the site. It was worth it though if he could reach Kyra before anything bad happened to her. Hopefully, she was alright. He still couldn't connect with her.

He wasn't the only one not happy with the decision. James stood off to the left of Alex, his lips in a thin line that echoed the anger they both felt. With James's injuries, he was also not allowed to go on the rescue mission. He was to head back to Ottawa in the morning and had objected loudly to it. Kyra had been taken on his watch. His team had been murdered. Alex and Lucas's home had been destroyed. He wanted payback but was not in any condition to do so. He was effectively grounded and on leave until he healed. For James, that was like a slap in the face and he was not going to take it laying down. However, objecting or making a scene would only put him on administrative leave for longer, and James was like Alex; he would find a way around things. He was still Alex's best chance at reaching Kyra.

They shared a look. One way or another, they would find a way to get to her.

"Maybe we should consider house hunting," Lucas said offhandedly as they headed to their room. He unlocked the door and held it open for Alex. "Even if we have to rent for a short time until the insurance agency decides if they're helping us rebuild or purchase a new vineyard."

Alex bit his lower lip, wanting to yell at him. Finding a new house was the least of their worries.

"Yeah," he answered. He took a deep breath and let it out slowly to hide his anger.

Lucas closed the door and locked it. "Look, I know I promised we would find her, but Michaels is right...we don't know how going back there would affect you. The last thing we need is you having a panic attack while on the mission. A lot happened there. You nearly died, people you loved were killed. For your own well-being, it's safer for you to stay here."

Alex's entire body tensed at those words. It sounded almost as if Lucas was gaslighting him in order to justify why they shouldn't be there. Yes, he had lost just about everything when his team discovered the underground temple. He will bear those scars for the rest of his life, but this wasn't about him. It was about Kyra and saving her from whatever fate awaited her there.

He drew a deep breath through his nose and slowly counted to ten before releasing it. He didn't want to fight. He wanted to yell and scream but he couldn't do that either. He was tired of people treating him as if he was some fragile porcelain doll. He wanted to fight, and oddly enough, he wanted to fuck. He wanted it deep and fast and so hard that it would hurt to sit or walk. His mind had a weird way of working when he was mad, but sex was better than punching a wall.

He made sure the back door was locked before pulling off his shirt and throwing it on one of the chairs.

"What are you doing?" Lucas asked, surprised.

Alex gave him a pointed look before crossing the room. He placed his hands on Lucas's broad chest, feeling his toned pecs. "You want to house hunt, I want sex, so how about you help me work off this pent-up energy before I do something stupid and take the Jeep on a cross country drive."

"Alex…" Lucas breathed.

His whole body was tense but in a good way. Lucas liked sex. It was his favourite way to release stress. His body nearly vibrated with the need for it and it was easy to see he had been holding back in fear of upsetting Alex. Now that Alex expressed his own needs, Lucas was more than willing to accommodate him. His large hands grasped Alex's hips and drew him close, their bodies pressing together. The younger man hummed softly as he felt Lucas's hard length press against his lower stomach. He always felt safe with Lucas. It could have been the height difference. Lucas was several inches taller than him with broader shoulders and wide chest. He was able to almost wrap himself around Alex. Alex raised his face for a kiss and smiled into it as Lucas obliged.

It was slow and gentle and Alex almost wanted to cry into it. He loved Lucas with all his heart but he couldn't shake the feeling of betrayal he felt at his husband not fighting for them to be involved in Kyra's rescue and ultimately siding with Caldwell and Michaels. He pushed that thought aside and instead focused on Lucas's lips and how perfectly they fit against his, the taste of his tongue darting into his mouth and licking the inner walls, his large hands gripping his hips hard as his groin ground insistently against Alex's. When they broke apart, they were both panting.

"Do you want me to tie you down?" Lucas asked. He looked toward the bed which, unlike the one in North Bay, actually had a headboard they could use cuffs or rope with.

Alex hummed softly as he studied it. "No...but I would love to tie you down." He glanced back up at Lucas. "I want to play with you."

Perhaps it had something to do with being possessed by a Celestial, but he wasn't as timid as he used to be when it came to sex. Lucas was a dominant while Alex a sub, but the Celestial had made Alex express his more dominant side and he and Lucas had been experimenting with it. The only problem was, Alex needed to set aside his emotions so to not hurt Lucas. It would probably be better to let Lucas dominate him but that wasn't what Alex needed.

Lucas ran his fingers along his cheek. "Are you sure?"

Alex nodded. "Yeah."

"Do you know what toys you want to use?"

His mind went blank for a moment. Normally, he knew exactly what he wanted, but he had forgotten what Lucas had packed when they went to North Bay. They had the cuffs, rods, and clamps, did they have the beads? It didn't matter, they had enough toys to play with, and they were ready to use. Lucas was meticulous when it came to cleaning them.

Lucas pressed a kiss to his brow before stepping back and stripping off his clothing. This was Alex's favourite part, even after so many years together. His gaze roamed over Lucas's muscular body, following the trail of dark, curly hair from the larger man's chest to dust over his stomach like an arrow to his groin and semi-erect manhood. The hair was trimmed perfectly, Lucas intent on manscaping almost everyday, even if Alex thought it was rather silly. He was beautiful though and Alex enjoyed admiring him whenever he could. In his mind, Lucas was built like what he imagined a god would be. Not like a chiselled Greek God, but still perfectly toned, with a swimmer's body with a small fatty patch in his lower stomach. The scars he had were barely visible, unlike Alex's, and for one brief moment, he wondered once again what Lucas saw in him that kept them together. Lucas had all his limbs and was breathtakingly beautiful while Alex was scarred and missing the lower half of this right leg, part of his right ear and was half deaf. They were the polar opposites yet Lucas loved him with all his heart.

Alex hated how self-conscious he became when he watched Lucas undress. After so long, he would have thought he worked through it, but it was not as easy as some thought and moments like this had a nasty habit of popping up when he least expected them. It took even longer to banish them.

Lucas was crawling onto the bed when he noticed Alex's sudden downturned look. He paused what he was doing and sat on the edge of the bed instead.

"Hey," he said gently. He reached out for Alex and pulled him over so that the younger man saddled his lap. "Take a deep breath, babe, clear your head."

Alex shook his head. "I'm okay, just being silly."

Lucas caught his chin in his thumb and forefinger. "Never. The last couple of days have been hell. We don't need to do this. We can just cuddle if you want."

"I need this," Alex insisted.

He stood and undid his jeans, letting them slide off his narrow hips to pile on the ground. His boxers followed a moment later. Lucas touched his right side. It had taken the worst of the damage when Alex had accidentally stepped on a landmine. It had ripped off part of his lower calf and thrown him several dozen feet, breaking bones, and tearing flesh. Even with Owen finding him, it was a miracle he had survived.

He knelt between Lucas's legs, his hands on his husband's inner thighs to push them apart just a little more. A small smile lit his face as Lucas cupped his cheek. He pressed his cheek against it, knowing that it was Lucas's silently way of reminding him he didn't have to do this and that the older man would be happy to switch roles. Lucas seemed happier taking care of Alex's needs than having Alex care for his. He appreciated that.

149

The fingers of his left hand grasped Lucas's balls and kneaded them slowly as his right hand began stroking his thick, long cock. Lucas's cock was large, with a nice bulbous head. Alex ran his tongue over the tip as he pulled back the foreskin. Lucas was not completely erect yet, when he was, his length was almost monstrous in size. Like everything about him, he was above average in Alex's eyes, and it reflected in everything about him, especially his beautiful cock. Alex kept eye contact with Lucas as he licked and kissed that wonderful appendage, teasing him and daring him to not lose control. It was why he wanted to tie Lucas down. He loved when the usually calm and collected man lost control and manhandled him, possessing Alex's body, and slamming into him as if to remind him to whom he belonged. A delightful shiver ran through Alex at that very thought. His tongue delved into Lucas's slit, tasting the salty-sweet pre-cum that was steadily leaking from it. A sharp inhale from Lucas told him all he needed to know about the enjoyment it brought him. Alex gave a small chuckle and left the slit to lick and kiss up and down the length, nipping at bulging veins, and playfully tugging at the foreskin with his teeth before returning the head. He wanted to stuff the urethra with a string of beads, but they were still in the overnight bag in the closet. It was only a few feet away but even that short distance seemed too far. Instead, he wiggled the pinky of one hand into the small opening.

Lucas hissed but did not object. His hand moved from Alex's cheek to card through his hair, letting his young lover do what he wanted. The teasing lasted only a few minutes, only long enough to get Lucas panting and whining with need. It wasn't something that happened often. Lucas was always so calm and collected that it was amusing to break him now and then. Nonetheless, Alex withdrew that pinky and licked it, running his tongue seductively over the digit and glistening juices it had gathered. Lucas watched intently, his mouth practically watering. Alex grinned then dipped his head, taking the head of that dripping cock in his mouth.

The sound that escaped Lucas was like music. He leaned back on the bed, one arm holding him up while the hand that was carding through Alex's hair gripped his auburn locks, not quite focusing Alex to take more, but keeping him in place. It gave Alex a rush of power as he took more into his mouth. His tongue ran over the underside before swallowing Lucas's length, slowly, inch by inch, taking the meaty flesh into his throat. It was hard to do. Lucas was so large that it was almost impossible not to gag on it, but Alex was used to giving him head. His gag reflex was all but gone. He bobbed his head, withdrawing almost all the way, sucking, and licking, even raking his teeth over the tender flesh before swallowing it again. All the while, he continued to massage Lucas's balls, alternating between rolling them between his fingers and squeezing them tightly, as if milking them.

"Alex…" Lucas breathed.

His grip on Alex's hair tightened painfully, as if fighting the urge to pull him off. His legs were beginning to shake as an orgasm edged ever closer.

As much as Alex wanted Lucas to spill his seed in his mouth, he didn't want it at the same time. He pulled off the wonderful length with a resounding "pop." Lucas's grip on his hair relaxed at the same time, allowing him to get up off his knees and climb onto the bed. Slowly, seductively, he crawled up the length of Lucas's body, not once breaking eye contact with Lucas. The older man's eyes glazed over with lust, the pupils blown out, turning the normally rich brown almost completely black with need. It made him look vulnerable and that part of Alex that still held a tiny part of the Celestial growled with hunger. He didn't waste time kissing or making out with Lucas any further. Instead, he mounted his beloved, Lucas's thick length already slick with his saliva. Lube would have been much better, as would have taking the time to properly prepare himself. A desperate need he had not felt in a long time filled him. It pushed all those things into the background, like a noise scratching at the back of his mind. That wonderful cock penetrated his opening with a mix of exquisite pain and pleasure.

A groan puffed from Lucas's lips, his body arching underneath Alex. He grasped Alex's hips once more as his own hips thrust upward, pushing himself deeper into the younger man, until every last inch filled him. Without proper lube, it took work, a mix of pushing and rocking on both their ends, but soon enough, they were there, joined together in the most intimate way. They took a moment to catch their breath. Alex leaned forward to press a kiss to Lucas's lips while the other man stroked his hips, side and back, his long fingers dancing over scars.

"I don't know what I would have done if I lost you," Lucas whispered against Alex's lips. "When you said someone was attacking the house…I was terrified. I called everyone I could think of to get to you. I should have been there."

Alex kissed the rogue tears that rolled from Lucas's eyes. "It would have only given them more targets. They would have been hunting you as well. I was happy you weren't there."

He pressed another kiss to Lucas's lips, silencing whatever objections he may have had. He wasn't lying; he was happy Lucas wasn't home when he and Kyra was attacked. They would have been too distracting on protecting one another and Kyra, opening them up to their assailants. If one had been hurt or captured, the other would have tried to rescue them. It had happened before and had cost them dearly. Alex didn't want that anymore. He didn't want Lucas becoming vulnerable because of him. He didn't want someone weaponizing their relationship. That helplessness was a horrible feeling.

He rotated his hips as he raised them, lifting himself off Lucas's long length until only the head was still inside him, then slowly descended once more. Lucas made a little hiss and bucked upward to meet him halfway, not liking being teased. Alex repeated the action once more before picking up speed as those big hands grasped his hips once more. The creaking of the bed and slapping of flesh filled the room, mixed with soft grunts, cries, and the odd curse as Alex tightened his muscles and rode Lucas even harder. He pinched Lucas's nipples, wanting to bite and suckle them. It was something the other man got off on. The were pebble hard and a lovely shade of brown that was almost lost in his fading summer tan. He tweaked them instead, promising to pay them better attention next time. The whimper Lucas made at the simple connect, and his hips jerking, was all the invitation anyone would need; but they were in the wrong position for that, and Alex was not about to change where he was. Instead, he pinched and twisted them, taunting Lucas until it drove the man insane, and he bucked desperately up into Alex. It was almost enough made Alex roll over and let Lucas take control. Almost, but not enough. He stopped bouncing and pressed his entire weight into Lucas's groin, feeling every inch of the other man fill him. The impressive length seemed to push right into his stomach and should have created a bulge. It didn't, of course. Lucas was long and big, but not big enough to do that. Nonetheless, Alex's muscles clamped down on it, as if threatening to never let it go, that they would be trapped like this forever. A grin lifted his lips as he gazed down at Lucas's smiling face.

They were close. Alex could feel it. Lucas's length was virtually pulsing inside him, orgasm right on the edge. Alex placed his hand on either side of Lucas's head. They were sideways on the bed so he could grab the headboard for the next part, but it didn't matter. They were not going as hard and fast as he originally intended. Sometimes the slower pace was what they needed. He rotated his hips, loving the feel of Lucas's cock rubbing against his prostate. Not slamming into it or poking it, just rubbing, the friction delicious all on its own. Best of all, it drove Lucas crazy because he didn't have enough room to thrust upward. Alex rotated and rocked, keeping Lucas almost completely inside him, letting the friction build and build until neither one could handle it anymore, then began bouncing, going from slow and gentle to a fevered pitch that had both he and Lucas gasping for breath. One last roll of his hips was enough to have Lucas coming inside him with an anguished cry.

It wasn't quite enough for Alex. He gasped his aching length and pumped it in time with the movements of his hips, effectively thrusting into his hand while bouncing on Lucas's length. The familiar bubbling feeling in his stomach made it all the better and soon enough his seed was spilling over Lucas's stomach. A few more thrusts and they were both empty.

He flopped down on the bed next to Lucas, exhausted but feeling slightly better than he had in the last few days. Sex had a funny way of doing that for them both. Lucas wrapped an arm around him and pulled him closer until Alex curled against his side.

"Feeling any better?"

Alex's heart sank. For once, he wished Lucas had not said anything and simply enjoyed the afterglow of sex. Asking him how he felt made him think and his mind automatically went to the anger he felt at not being able to go to British Columbia to save Kyra and the betrayal he felt toward Lucas for siding with Caldwell and Michaels. Even so, Alex managed to keep his face a mask and his emotions hidden as he snuggled against Lucas.

"Yeah," he lied. His fingers carded through the dark curls of Lucas's chest hair. "Maybe you're right. We should start looking for a place to stay. It would have to be close to town for school. My students are probably already asking questions about what happened and why I'm not teaching today."

He had sent an email earlier in the day informing the principal he was taking a leave of absence. He didn't state for how long. It may only be a few days…it may be infinite this time. All he knew for certain was that he couldn't go back until he knew Kyra was safe.

Lucas rolled toward him and tucked Alex's head under his chin in the way he normally did when trying to protect Alex from the rest of the world. Normally, it made Alex feel safe. This time, it annoyed him.

"I'm sure we can find a flat somewhere," he mused. "Tomorrow, I'll get an insurance agent out here to see the damage and then we can decide what we're doing next. How about we take a nap and then find Elizabeth and James and go out for dinner? I'm getting tired of fast food and delivery."

"Sure," Alex agreed.

He rested his head on Lucas's shoulder and idly played with his chest hair as the other man nuzzled his head. They didn't bother scooting up the bed to sleep properly or get under the covers. Lucas could fall asleep almost anywhere, despite his sometimes-posh lifestyle. Military training and years of archeology had taught him that. It wasn't long before he rolled onto his back once more and soft snores began to fill the room. Alex lay next to him, wide awake, his emotions running rampant. After several long minutes, he got out of his bed and fished his new cell phone out of his jeans. It was a cheap one Elizabeth had gotten him from one of the local grocery stores, but it was better than nothing. He stared at the device for several moments before unlocking the home screen and pulling up James's contact information. He was thankful that he had been able to transfer most of the information from his old phone to it thanks to an app that backed up everything on his phone. He often used it so he could download information between it and his laptop or tablet. He never thought he would use it for another phone.

After one last glance toward Lucas to make sure he was sound asleep, he texted James.

Any luck?

Minutes ticked by before a reply came.

Maybe. Caldwell and Michaels are gone.

Alex nodded to himself. That was good. Without Interpol or the Armed Forces there, there would only be a few guards left, making it easier to move about without their every move being monitored. For all he knew, the room they were in could be wired and agents watching them. If so, he hoped they enjoyed the show.

Where's Elizabeth?

Back at the vineyard. She wants to help the police inventory everything.

That made sense. Aside from him, Lucas, and their employees, Elizabeth knew every inch of the vineyard. Having her there also meant she wasn't hovering over him and Lucas making sure they were alright. She was like a big sister to Alex, and sometimes, that could get annoying, not that he would ever tell her that. Their relationship was complicated at best.

I have a plan, but I need you and Lucas to meet me out back in ten minutes.

He glanced towards Lucas. No. Lucas was not joining him on whatever James had planned.

Ten minutes, he wrote back.

He placed the device on the dresser and began getting dressed once more. Ten minutes wasn't a lot of time. Once his boots were on, he went to the closet and fetched the small duffle bag Lucas had stashed there. Inside were the sex toys he had wanted to use on his husband but had forgotten about in his need. The black fur-lined cuffs sat on top of the rod case. They were meant to keep a person bound while not hurting them of from having the metal rub their wrists raw. Alex had worn them many times and in many positions. Now they would do the same for Lucas. He placed the keys on the table with a small handwritten note, then carefully connect the two pairs of cuffs together, attached one to the leg of the bed, the other to Lucas's right wrist which happened to be the closest to it. Had he been laying properly on the bed, Alex could have handcuffed both his wrists to the headboard, which would have been much better. Of course, had he done that, he may not be able to leave the room. There was nothing hotter than having Lucas tied down and virtually helpless, but that would have to wait for another day. After all, he just wanted to keep his lover safe…or delay him long enough so that he wouldn't get mixed up in Alex's quest to find and rescue Kyra. If Alex failed, at least he knew Lucas was safe. And so was Elizabeth.

Thankfully, Lucas didn't stir, the exhaustion of the last few days taking their toll on him. Alex took a moment to admire him. He really did love him. The very idea of leaving him behind hurt. It was a form of betrayal, but Lucas had also betrayed him in not fighting harder to allow him to return to British Columbia to find Kyra. He may have been trying to protect him, but Alex didn't need protection, Kyra did.

The hope for a clean get-away was dashed when the sound of a helicopter landing vibrated through the room. Alex looked toward the back door in surprise, having intended to go out through the hall. He wasn't sure if it was the same people who had attacked him and Kyra or if this was all part of James's plan. Either way, it awoke Lucas who tried to sit up only to discover one wrist cuffed to the bed.

"What in the world?" he mumbled, fighting back the sleep that still clogged his mind. "Alex?"

For a moment, Alex couldn't move, fear taking hold of him as his mind dove back into the attack. Panic filled him a moment later at the memory of Kyra being taken from him and disappearing into the night sky, carried away by a helicopter. He looked to Lucas, his frightened gaze meeting his husband's bewildered ones. Without explaining, he rushed past him and out the back door, slamming it behind him even as Lucas cried out his name.

It wasn't the same helicopter as had left the vineyard. That one had been black while this one was a bright orange and white, clearly an Emergency Medical Service vehicle. James was in the pilot seat and looked out the window at him before gesturing for him to get in. Alex hesitated only a moment before dashing around the vehicle and climbing in the passenger side. He grabbed the headset and put it on.

"Where's Lucas?" James asked as Alex buckled the harness.

"He's not coming," Alex answered. "Go."

James stared at him for a moment before nodding. He pulled back on the stick, lifting the helicopter back into the air. It turned, giving Alex a full view of the motel below. A very naked and angry Lucas could be seen running out of their room with one cuff still on his wrist. Alex stared down at him, guilt filling him. Lucas may be mad but he was safe and that was all that mattered to him.

"I have a plane waiting for us on the island," James reported.

"What about the police?" Alex asked. He tried to quiet his racing heart and guilt he felt. "Won't they be looking for the copter?"

James shook his head and gestured to the back of the vehicle. Alex looked back and was surprised to see an unconscious woman in an orange jumpsuit tied up on the floor.

"There's a missing camper near Providence Bay. That's where the plane is. So, I thought I'd get us a lift there," James explained. "When we get there, I'll hand this back to her and we'll take off. There

157

should be enough fuel to get us to BC. From there, we'll meet up with some of my colleagues and go rescue the kid."

Alex nodded.

"You sure leaving Lucas like that was a good idea?"

"No…it was probably one of my dumbest," Alex confessed. He took a deep breath. "But if Caldwell and Michaels are gone…then he won't be able to chase after us. He'll be safe."

Chapter Thirteen

The room was blindingly bright. The overhead lights were so bright that they hurt Kyra's eyes. The room she was in was small, with no discernable features but for the exception of a thin slat bed and small plastic covered mat. It was cold, far colder than the glass room, with no comforts. Not even a thin sheet to cover herself. She sat in the corner of the room, knees pulled to her chest and arms wrapped tightly around her, trying to stay warm. There were voices all around her. Not of her captors, but of something else…people trapped there, like her, but without physical form. They talked in unison, asking questions, demanding answers, claiming she was something she was not. Her hands covered her eyes, gripping her head with bruising force as she tried to shield herself from them. The only comfort she received was from Owen. His spirit wrapped around her, trying to shield her from the others, but he was only a spirit. He could not protect her from what the living humans that had taken her had planned. They were not like the others. These ones had cruel intentions and time was running out for her.

She tried again to reach out to Alex but she couldn't feel him. It was as if she kept coming up against a wall, perhaps even the walls of her cell. He was alive, she knew that much, and she prayed that he found her before her operation. She didn't know what these people were planning to do with her or what the operation was for, but she didn't want it. She didn't want any of this. She wanted to go home. She wanted Alex.

The fingers of his right hand drummed along the window sill as he and James drove the short distance from the landing strip to the cabin Interpol was using as their base point. They were approximately a forty-five-minute drive from the temple site, an area that was now a "no fly zone". They circled around it, having to detour almost an hour out of their way to reach their destination. Alex's heart pounded in his chest as time ticked by. It seemed to drag by and with every minute that past, his fear grew. He tried reaching out to Kyra, certain she was close, feeling a flicker of her in his subconscious, but unable to connect.

His right hand pulsed the closer they got to the temple site, a burning sensation with which he was very familiar. Turning it over, he studied the scarred flesh, the markings of the artifact he had used to open a portal years earlier. Still pristine, it was the perfect key to the alien vessels hidden with the temples. There was one here, he was almost certain of it. Was that why Kyra was taken here? Did her kidnappers expect her to open it for them? She was a hybrid but he wasn't sure if she could access the Vault. The ship was very particular. He curled his fingers into a fist, the strange burning sensation becoming too much. He hated the feeling. It raced up his arm and into his shoulder, like some sort of energy or electricity, the scent reaching his nose as if lightning was about to strike close by.

"Alex?" James asked, nervousness evident in his voice.

"Keep driving," he answered calmly. He had control of this. It hurt, but he could control it.

"If that keeps up you might kill the engine," the other man warned.

They were in a pick-up truck, the only vehicle available to them. It was handling the mountain drive just fine. There was no snow in British Columbia, but the further they went into the mountains, that soon changed, first with only a few centimetres of the white stuff, then several inches and icy roads. Given the location of the temple, there was bound to be much more.

"Just drive," he said.

He flexed his fingers, willing the strange energy away, and storing it for later. How he would use it was something he was still trying to figure out, but he knew it could be used as a weapon. It had stopped the Shadow-being, perhaps it could be used to stop the people who took Kyra. If not…he wasn't above killing them to get to her. A few years ago, such a thought would have frightened him. Now? He was just happy he wasn't thinking of feasting on their still beating hearts. The Celestial would have torn them apart. That bloodlust filled Alex now, minus the sexual nature that filled the creature.

There were a variety of vehicles outside the log cabin as they approached it, with a number of men and women patrolling outside, each one armed. Weapons were aimed at them as they pulled up.

"Be ready to break the line," Alex told James.

The goal was to go with the soldiers to the temple, not fight their way through. That didn't mean Alex wouldn't if he had to.

Two soldiers flanked their vehicle. One knocked on the driver side window, causing James to slide his window down.

"Doctor Jackson?" the man asked, startling both Alex and James.

"Yes?" Alex answered.

Unease filled him. He was about to tell James to reverse and get them out of there but a small group of soldiers now stood behind them as well as in front and to the sides. As much as he wanted to break the line and speed off to the temple site, he did not want to seriously injure or kill these people. Something prickled in the back of his mind and for one brief moment hope filled him. Had they found Kyra already? It didn't feel like her but was almost as powerful. Curiosity tugged at him.

"Please follow us. You too, sir." He nodded to James.

They exchanged looks. Alex sighed and nodded. James put the truck into park and they exited. The soldiers crowded around them and escorted them into the cabin, as if fearful they might try to make a break for the woods all around them. Their behaviour was odd but one thing was obvious, they were expecting them…Alex at least. How?

Unease turned to dread. Lucas. He must have called Caldwell and gave her a heads up that he was on his way and she would have contacted whoever was in charge of the team here. That meant he was going to be stuck here rather than helping rescue Kyra. That wasn't going to happen. He would fight them. He would lash out and do whatever was necessary to get to her.

The cabin was warm, the sweet scent of burning wood, and crackling fire greeting them as they walked inside. The cabin was large, housing well over a dozen soldiers, including, much to Alex's disappointment, Caldwell. Her blue gaze settled on Alex the moment he stepped past the entrance. It was cold and angry but nothing compared to the man standing next to her.

Alex's mouth fell open. It wasn't possible.

"Lucas…"

His husband's nostrils flared in obvious rage but he said nothing. His arms were folded across his broad chest, displaying the white and grey military fatigues he was wearing that matched those of the soldiers. Elizabeth stood on the opposite side of him, dressed the same, her long black hair pulled back in a thick bun. Her dark brown eyes held disappointment.

"Now that we're all here, let's finish prepping everyone," Caldwell announced.

Alex looked at her in surprise. He expected to be in cuffs and dragged off, not this. He looked questioningly to Lucas but his husband only frowned at him. He went to him, his stomach churning in a mix of guilt and fear.

"What are you doing here?" he all but demanded.

Lucas's face pinched, looking as if he was fighting the urge to yell at or even strike him. "We'll discuss it later," he managed to bite out.

Alex looked to Elizabeth. She shook her head, silently warning him not to push it, but that small movement made him feel even worse. He tried to listen to Caldwell as she and the generals laid out their plan to take the facility, but instead he kept looking at Lucas, wanting to take his hand. Now wasn't the time. He had betrayed Lucas and he was entitled to his anger, regardless how much it hurt.

"By the way," Elizabeth whispered, coming up next to Alex. "Military planes are much faster than whatever personal plane James brought you in."

He sighed. "I figured as much."

"You're fucking lucky I'm not drop kicking you right now. You better damn well have a good excuse, and not that you were doing this to protect us."

"I..."

She gave him a hard look.

"I couldn't lose him...or you. Not after Kyra and the winery. Not here."

She folded her arms over her chest. She was wearing a bulletproof vest like the rest of the soldiers. "So, to protect us."

"Elizabeth...I had to."

"No, you didn't. You choose to."

He sighed. "You wouldn't understand."

She pursed her lips and stared straight ahead at the generals. "The Celestial never left, did it? It's still in your head."

His mouth fell agape. "No. Look, we're not just dealing with a kidnapping and this temple...the Shadow is still out there and someone told these people where to find Kyra. If it's not Caldwell and her people then who and why?"

Her hands balled into fists. "Stop it," she sneered. "Whoever attacked probably knew about her and was already watching NORAD.

They would have attacked while they were moving her to Winnipeg if you hadn't taken her home. They changed plans at last minute and things got messy. You can't keep pointing fingers. We'll get her back and then you have to accept the fact that she has to go where she belongs. Wherever that is."

Their discussion had gathered the attention of the soldiers and even the generals were staring at them. The look on Lucas's face was clear. He wanted Alex to explain himself as well. Alex looked at each of them, but he had no answers just hunches. He looked to James but the Interpol agent shrugged, unable to help him. The plan had been to join the Armed Forces in saving Kyra. There was no plan after that. The fact was, Elizabeth was right. Whoever had attacked the vineyard would have gone after Kyra regardless where she had gone. He was making this personal when he shouldn't.

"Are we ready to go?" Caldwell asked, giving Alex a pointed look.

"As soon as they change," Elizabeth answered. She gestured to Alex and James. "Can't go into battle wearing red. You're walking targets. We need to be subtle."

There was a retort on the tip of his tongue but he bit it back. There was no time for arguing. He took the clothing he was offered and went to one of the back rooms to change. James did the same. The fatigues were lined with fleece on the inside, making them incredibly warm and able to withstand the cold. An armored vest went with it, as did sturdy, insulated boots. He had to loosen the laces on the right boot all the way in order to fit his prosthetic foot into it. The upper leather shaft of the boot went midway up his calf to protect from snow. It was a snug fit.

Alex sat on the edge of the bed once he was done and stared at the door, silently willing Lucas to come in so he could make amends. He should have known Lucas could get out of the cuffs quickly and find a way to get to him, even beat him to the site. After everything that happened with the Celestial, it was no wonder they thought he was still possessed. He thought he was protecting those he loved when all he was doing was endangering them more by making them chase after him. He was an idiot.

He waited only a few minutes longer before finally go back out to the others. Soldiers were already heading to the awaiting vehicles. Only Caldwell, Lucas, and Elizabeth were left waiting for him. James was already with the others.

"Doctor Jackson," Caldwell said as he returned to the main room.

Alex looked from Lucas to her but didn't say anything.

"Against my better judgement, I'm allowing you on this mission," she explained, even though that was obvious. "And not just because of you going out of your way to defy me, but because you're right. Kyra needs you. She has never responded to anyone the way she does with you."

"What does that mean for her after we rescue her?"

She glanced toward Lucas then back to him. "I'm not sure yet. Let's find her first then go from there. We're working in two teams. The lead team is going to take command of the complex while the second team goes in to search for Kyra."

"What about the remains of the temple and Vault?" Alex asked, not trusting her.

"If they still exist, destroy it. All of it," she answered without hesitation. "I don't want even a speck left of it."

He stared at her in disbelief, not seeing even a hint of a lie in her words or expression. She was serious. She had no interest in the temple or the Vault, only Kyra.

He nodded. "Good, because after I find Kyra, I'm leaving the place."

"Agreed." She glanced at Lucas. "That still alright with you?"

Lucas's expression didn't change. It was still a hard mask, his anger bottled up for the moment. He gave a curt nod. "I'll be going in with him. Elizabeth can hack their computers and guide us."

Elizabeth nodded but it was easy to see she wanted to do more. She was the best person for the job though and Alex knew the only reason Lucas would suggest her even entering the complex was because he trusted her to guide them better than anyone else. Elizabeth could hold her own in any fight, but if they wanted to find Kyra without a double cross, they needed someone who could watch everyone's move.

Caldwell agreed without any restrictions. Alex watched her as they headed toward the vehicles. Perhaps he had misjudged her.

Lucas climbed into the lead vehicle with her while Alex was escorted to another with Elizabeth. Without words, Lucas had pointed out he was not yet ready to discuss what had happened. Alex couldn't blame him. He only hoped they could still work together once they reached the lab. Regardless what he thought when he took off to recue Kyra with James, he needed Lucas and Elizabeth. They were all the family he had left.

"We'll find her," James assured, sitting next to the driver.

Elizabeth nodded. "Of course we will." Her gaze met Alex's. "Just stick close to James and Lucas when you go in…and don't remove your ear piece."

She handed him a small ear bud. "I'm taking control of the security room the moment I get inside." She pulled out a table and showed him the blueprints they managed to get of the compound of which they were heading.

"Where did you get that?" he asked in surprise.

She gave him side eye. "Seriously? After all these years you're still surprised when I get my hands on confidential information? Remember who was your dad's personal assistant. I didn't always get the information he wanted legally. These guys have computers on a network. I can hack it from the other side of the world. All I needed was to find their IP address."

She rotated her shoulders and sat back as Alex took the tablet.

"Everything is on a simple network. Whoever built the facility was in a rush. It's primarily prefabricated and looks as if it can be picked up and moved at any time. Their security is no better than a mall's. They rely primarily on mercenaries and cameras, of which they have an abundance."

"Okay, so how do we get past them?"

"Team one will create a distraction. We'll be going in behind them."

Alex stared at the tablet, using one finger to drag the image to try and get a better feel for the layout. He was hoping to spot Kyra's location but it was not marked. There were no prison cells, just endless labs. It wasn't a military facility but a research one. The question remained of who these people were and why they took Kyra. Whomever they were, they had had enough money to hire a small army to protect them and take Kyra. He was going to get her back, even if he had to fight his way through each one of them.

His hand was still pulsing, the energy building within it growing and waiting for release. It was getting stronger with every passing minute. More-so than every before. Something within him was changing but he no longer feared it. He embraced it because it might be the only thing that saved Kyra.

The caravan came to a stop just kilometers from what appeared to be a dirt road that Alex remembered was several kilometres from the facility. He had driven his father's research RV up it many years ago, leading a group of anthropology students up to where they would spend two months researching what they believed was an ancient Indigenous site. He felt Elizabeth's hand curl around his. Neither of them had been back since the attack that had wiped out everyone in their team. Elizabeth had been spared that horror when her and another research member had done a dump run to get rid of the camp's garbage as well as purchase supplies needed for the long drive across country back to Sudbury. Alex bore the scars of it. His heart pounded as he stared at the dirt road, the memory of their initial journey here playing over and over in his mind. He could hear his father's laughter as they led the caravan of trucks and campers up the dirt road, the excitement and hope they all felt at the possibility of making a ground-breaking discovery. Of nights around campfires, telling stories and joking around. Of a group of young adults with the whole world in front of them only to have it all taken away when they finally did make that discovery. Months of research not once interrupted, but shattered the moment they discovered the underground temple. Had they left when they were originally going to, every member of that team would be alive now, including Alex's father. Everything bad that had happened to Alex was because of that temple. It may sit in rubble now underneath the lab, but it would be dust by the time he was done. No one would find its remains. Never again.

They waited for the signal from Team One. That team was going through the woods, taking down any mercenaries they came across until it was safe enough for the second team to arrive. Team Two was able to hear the chatter from the other team as they moved toward the facility, avoiding, or taking out enemy cameras along the way. There were no loud bangs from gun shots only small pops as silencers were used to keep the noise level down. The last thing they needed was to alert more mercenaries or an outside audience from local residents and police. The Royal Canadian Mounted Police already knew what was going on and were keeping their distance but that didn't mean local police would do the same if enough people called-in concerned.

An explosion rocked the mountainside, startling Alex. His eyes widened as he stared off in the direction that it had come from. It echoed all around them, causing the ground to shake. Something in Alex broke, his mind delving back to years earlier when he and two others ran through those woods, trying to escape the terrorists only for one to be gunned down, another to die when they stepped on a landmine. Alex had nearly suffered the same fate when he had also stepped on a landmine. He remembered the searing heat, the shock of being thrown as bones shattered and his right foot was ripped from his body, the agony that filled him as he crashed through trees before landing in a broken heap on the cold unforgiving grown. It played over and over in his mind. His hands became cold and clammy, his breathing laboured.

He hadn't had a panic attack in years but he knew the symptoms. If he allowed it to take hold of him, he would be no good to anyone. He needed to calm down.

"Breathe," Elizabeth told him. She gently took his face in both her hands and made him look at her. "Breathe. You're here. You're safe. There's nothing in there but ghosts. Ghosts can't hurt you."

He stared at her for a long time before drawing in a shaking breath then another. She was wrong. There were more things than ghosts in the forest. Things that could kill them...would kill them. Ghosts were the least of their problems.

The vehicle they were in lurched forward, following the others onto the dirt road. Alex almost objected before remembering they needed to go up that road to get to the lab and find Kyra. His pulse was racing, fear making his blood run cold. Elizabeth made him look at her again.

"Just breathe, Alex. You've got this. It's not like it was when we were here last. The camp is gone. Everyone we knew...they're not here. Focus on the lab and Kyra, okay? We're here for her, remember?"

"Kyra..." he breathed, needing to say her name.

He calmed down. Kyra needed him. That's why they were there. He pushed back the memories, both good and bad, and focused on her. He made her name a mantra, reminding himself why he was there and to ignore all else.

They picked up speed as they travelled down the dirt road. For the first half of the drive there was forest all around them, as it had been when the anthropology team had arrived years earlier, but it wasn't long before they approached the clearing, a clearing that now had a tall fence erected right where the trees ended. The lead Hummer barrelled through the double gate, bringing it down. It swerved to the right, dragging it out of the way, the barbed wire tangling in the under-carriage. It didn't stop the vehicle. The Hummer corrected course and headed to the lab, the rest of the armoured vehicles following suit. Mercenaries rushed after them, firing weapons only to be taken down by Team One.

The vehicles headed directly to the front of the building. It was large, over two stories high, and spanned across over several hundred feet. There were no windows. It was like a huge metal box placed over the opening of the pit with the temple ruins far below.

"When I said rushed construction...I didn't mean this," Elizabeth said, looking out over the building. "What the hell is that?"

"It's the Vault..." Alex breathed.

"That can't be the Vault," she objected. She removed her seatbelt then grasped the back of the driver seat and scooted forward to get a better look as the neared to complex. "That's too big...isn't it?"

Alex shook his head. "No...that's the real thing. I don't know how they got it out but that's it."

It shouldn't have been a surprise though. The American Navy had managed to lift one from the depths of the ocean and move it all the way to Area 51 in Nevada. Lifting one out of an open pit with the temple already destroyed would be nothing by comparison. Creating a foundation to sit it on over the pit...that would have been more challenging. It looked so much larger outside the temple.

Now he knew why his hand had been pulsing so much. It wasn't just due to Kyra, as he had expected, it was the Vault. Whomever had dug it out had one of the many artifacts that served as a key. But did he? He was the key.

The moment their vehicle came to a stop, he climbed out and headed toward it, his focus on the slate grey structure. It was an alien vessel, the same as the ones so many other governments and organizations had been trying to get their hands on. Some had succeeded only to have it slip from their fingers as it was activated. Alex's senses reached out, that part of him that was still somehow connected to the Celestials that had created it. This one was damaged, unable to take flight or even open a portal. It was useless to anyone that didn't know how to bring it to life.

"Alex," Lucas called as he and the soldiers exited the other vehicles.

"Watch my back," he responded.

The ancient hieroglyphs seemed to light up as he neared. Elizabeth hurried to keep up with him, utterly confused as she stared at the blue prints on her tablet. It was obvious she had been given a fake. The Vault was shielded. There would be no way to get a copy of its layout, even if someone took the time to document it. It was all a lie.

Alex glanced toward Caldwell as she hurried to the entrance, weapon drawn and eyes on their surroundings. Her soldiers took point, guarding them from potential attack. The sound of gunfire could be heard all around them as the mercenaries fought back. There was no telling how many were inside the Vault waiting for them.

James stood next to Lucas, weapon in hand. He gave Alex a nod to show they were ready.

Alex looked to Lucas and Elizabeth, both also armed and ready. Squaring his shoulders, he placed his hand over the all too familiar engraving. At first look one might mistake it for an Aztec glyph. It was a lock with a specific key that could not be replicated. Most of the artifacts containing it were destroyed. Alex was the only known living key left, the previous dying before he was chosen by the Celestial. He placed his hand against it, lining the burned tissue of his hand against the lock until they connected. A wave of nausea filled him as energy raced up his arm, far more powerful than the pulsing and burning from before. It stole his breath. A moment later, the sensation was gone and the doors slid open.

"Let's go," Caldwell ordered.

Alex pulled his hand away and shook off the excess energy coursing through him. "Do you think you can hack an alien ship?" he asked Elizabeth as they hurried inside.

"If Humans are running this thing, then yeah, I can. Celestials...that may be more challenging," she answered. She held a handgun in a two-handed grip as they moved forward, ready to fight.

Alex's gaze swept over the bright hall. It was pristine white, but not like the other Vaults he had been in. They were darker, meant for the Shadow creatures to be able to roam and do their master's bidding. Whoever was controlling the Vault had retro-fitted it to meet their needs. That meant they would have a security room, or at the very least still have the command centre. Alex was pretty sure he knew where that was. So did Elizabeth and Lucas. He looked to Elizabeth who nodded in understanding, thinking along the same line as him.

"They would have tied into the main power source in the altar," she said. "I should be able to connect into their computers from there."

He nodded. "Lu..."

"Go with her," Caldwell told three of her people before Alex could finish telling Lucas to go with Elizabeth.

He opened his mouth to object but Elizabeth was already taking off in the direction of the control room with the three soldiers. He didn't like that. He didn't want her going alone as he still didn't fully trust Caldwell.

"So, which way do we go?" James asked, turning Alex's attention away from Caldwell.

Alex looked to Lucas but he had stepped back, letting Alex take the lead. Had this been a normal Vault, he would have known exactly where Kyra was being kept but the entire layout had been changed. He tried reaching out to her, to sense her mind. At first there was nothing, just his own racing heart and fear, then he felt her. It was like a sudden spark, a flicker of a flame in the darkness. She was on the move, being taken somewhere she didn't want to go. Fear wafted off her in waves.

He looked toward the right as they neared a juncture in the corridor.

"There," he said, pointing down it.

He took a step toward it but was stopped as armed men and women rushed toward them. Before he knew it, they were scrambling for cover as the mercenaries began firing at them. They obviously knew the Armed Forces were there for the girl. Lucas pulled Alex behind him as the soldiers took defensive position and returned fire. They needed to get down that corridor. It was the only way to Kyra. Lucas wouldn't let him move though, not while the entrance to the corridor was a firing range.

"How far down there is she?" Lucas asked, surprising Alex.

Alex shook his head as he tried to get a better feel for her. It was hard to keep the connection with the gunfire. She could hear it and was terrified. "Next level up and about fifty feet."

Lucas nodded. "Alright." He wet his lips and looked off in that direction. "I want you to get to the temple and make sure there's nothing left, then set up the bombs. Like you said...nothing left."

Hesitation filled Alex. "She won't come to you," he warned.

"She will," he promised. "Owen's protecting her, right?"

Alex's mouth fell open but he nodded. If Kyra can see Owen, then it only stood to reason that his spirit was somehow trying to protect her.

"Then we trust him to make sure she comes with me." He grasped the back of Alex's head and pulled him close until their forehead met. "Don't let ghosts distract you. Stay in constant contact. Plant the bombs and get out. We'll meet you outside."

Alex gave another nod. He wanted to kiss Lucas, it may be their last time, but he stopped himself from doing so. This wasn't their last moment together. They had been through much worse. They would make it though this just as they had everything else.

Lucas pulled back and stood next to Caldwell. "Make me an opening," he told her. "I'm going after Kyra. They rest of you protect Alex."

"You got it," she answered.

She waved to several of her soldiers. They moved in unison, coming out from their sheltered positions to face the mercenaries straight on. The move put them into a dangerous position, making it easy for the opposing force to take them down. One was shot almost immediately, but it also allowed them to have better aim. A spray of an automatic gun fire swept through the corridor injuring and killing enough of the opposition to create an opening for Lucas. The Archeologist took it and dashed down the corridor before the mercenaries could regroup. One of the soldiers tried to go with him but was gunned down as he broke the line. Soon, they were firing on Caldwell's people once more.

They were pinned down until the lights began flickering.

"I'm in," Elizabeth's voice came over the ear buds. "It's taking a little longer to hack into the system. Someone fused Celestial tech with ours."

"That's fine, just find the cameras and give Lucas directions to Kyra. He's enroute to her," Alex answered. He pressed a hand to his ear to hear her over the gunfire.

The lights went out for a moment before lighting up once more at half power, now on emergency power.

"Oops…sorry. Give me a minute. What language is this written in?"

Alex shook his head, grateful for the momentary darkness. "Russian?"

"No, this isn't anything from Earth."

He shrugged. His senses suddenly prickled, the strange burning in his right arm flaring in almost blinding pain as it had at the medical building in North Bay. The sulfuric smell returned with it. He looked around. The Shadows were taking on a life of their own. No wonder it had been so bright before. The Vault was the home of the Shadows. With the light dimmed, they were now free.

"About time," grumbled James.

Alex turned him as he stood, the Shadows leaping at his body. His normally dark blue eyes flickered to a sickly yellow.

Well, he now knew who their mole was.

Chapter Fourteen

Move!" Alex ordered Caldwell.

The Shadows swarmed the corridor toward the soldiers and mercenaries alike. He grabbed one of the flash grenades from a soldier, pulled the pin, and threw it at James. A resounding bang and flash of blinding light filled the corridor, chasing away the Shadows if only temporary. It didn't, however, chase away James. He stood defiantly in front of them and didn't even go down when one of the soldiers shot him.

"You're wasting your bullets," Alex snapped, calling for a cease fire. The mercenaries continued firing and the soldiers returned fire, either not seeing or caring what was going in the background. "The host body is already dead. Probably has been since the Shadow attacked us in North Bay."

It made sense now. When James covered for him as he rushed Kyra out of the medical facility at the airbase, the Shadow must have attacked him and possessed his body. Unlike Celestials, Shadows killed their hosts. James was dead, had been for days. The Shadow then connected with the rest of its kind, many of which must have possessed some of the mercenaries. That was how they found Kyra so quickly and why they attacked the vineyard. That was why they killed everyone but James. What didn't make sense was why they were working with humans. Why would bring Kyra here where the lights had been so bright that it chased the Shadows away? He was under the impression the Shadow had been trying to kill her. Were they working for humans? Had they sought out a new master after the Celestial abandoned them? Why were they hunting hybrids?

"Beth, I'm going to need you to fix the lights," he told Elizabeth as calmly as possible.

The flash grenades only lasted a short time and the last blast was already fading and the Shadows returning. They couldn't keep fighting on both fronts. They needed to set the bombs and get out of there. As much as he wanted to find out who was in charge and why they wanted Kyra, he knew how deadly the Shadows were. If they and the mercenaries didn't kill everyone, they would possess them, and that was a death sentence within itself, not nearly as quick as a bullet. It would be like having their soul torn to shreds. It only take a few moments but for the victim, it would be an eternity. James suffered greatly before his consciousness was snuffed out.

Elizabeth's voice crackled over the line. "We might have a problem with that. We've got Shadows coming out of the woodwork. It might be nice if you came down here with that hand-key of yours."

Alex grunted as another flash grenade went off, momentarily blinding him. Between the sound of gunfire and the grenades, his hearing aid was starting to get feedback. He had to remove it in order to hear Elizabeth over the earbud in his other ear. "We're pinned down. Forget it. Set up the bombs then get out of there."

"What about the girl?"

"Lucas has her. Get out of there."

At least he hoped Lucas had Kyra. Right now, he had to worry about how they were going to get past the mercenaries and Shadows. Worse, those possessed by the Shadows were impossible to kill, and it appear there were quite a few of them. Shadows could only withstand the light when inside a host. That meant light or no light, the soldiers were vastly out-gunned and out-maneuvered. Even if they could keep the mercenaries in one location – without the lights being at full power – the Shadows could corral them, block their exit, and take control of them. They were trapped, and the Shadow-James was now killing as many soldiers as the mercenaries were. In its host's body, the light no longer bothered it.

Lucas didn't hesitate to attack anyone who got in his way. His training with the British military took hold of him, but rather than gun down his opponents, that would have surely altered other mercenaries, he used his size and weight to take them down then slit their throats, not giving them a chance to call for help. It took him back to his youth, when he fought next to his brother on one of his first missions to Afghanistan, when they had to clear out a consulate that had been taken over by a terrorist group. Owen had been part of the special forces team and had convinced Lucas's commanding officer to let him join in. It was Owen's attempt to get him interested in serving in the army, something Lucas didn't care for. The training came in handy, though, as he fought took-down anyone who got in his way until he reached the second floor. From there it wasn't hard to find where Kyra was. The two guards at the door to a glassed-in lab was a dead-giveaway. Lucas didn't bother attacking them. He drew his gun and shot them both as he walked toward them, not giving them a chance to defend themselves. It shocked the scientists in the large room who looked out at him in shock. He aimed the gun at the window. It was probably bulletproof, but the threat was clear: unlock the door or risk him killing each of them once he got inside.

He glanced toward the child strapped to the gurney and the tools on the sterile metal table next to her. It didn't a genius to know what they were meant for. The small saw on the table was a craniotome meant for cutting into the skull. They were going to do something to her brain. He was pretty sure it wasn't brain surgery, despite Kyra being conscious. It looked as if they were about to do an autopsy. There were bone-cutters and a rib-spread meant to open her rib cage. They were going to harvest her brain and organs.

Horror filled him. Without waiting for one of the scientists to open the door, he shot the control panel and overrode the electrical system himself. The door slid to one side just as the power flickered off then back on dimmer than before. He heard Elizabeth apologize but put that to the back of his mind. As much as he wanted to be there for her and Alex, he was not about to let these people continue what they were about to do to this child. Under normal circumstances, he may have told these people to run, but disgust and rage filled him. He didn't bother asking questions, or try making sense of what they were doing. He shot each of them, all except one who backed himself against the far wall with wide, frightened eyes.

Lucas held the gun aimed at him as he used his free hand to undo the straps around Kyra's wrists. It was not an easy job with one hand. She watched him with wide eyes.

"What were you going to do with her?" he demanded as the child sat up.

"We were only told to harvest her," the man babbled.

"By whom?"

The man shook his head, clearly frightened.

Lucas shot the wall directly next to the man's head.

"I don't know! All I know is she can not reproduce and is no good to them. She's a living weapon but no good to them if she can not be bred. They wanted her brain and organs to study."

Lucas's nostrils flared. A Celestial would not want such things. They inhabited people and bred with humans; they did not perform science experiments on them. Whoever ordered this was human and had enough power to fund this entire operation.

"And you have no problem torturing a child to do that?" he asked as Kyra climbed off the gurney. She took his hand and pressed against his side, her small face against his arm. She was shaking, fear and relief evident.

The scientist whimpered. "I was only doing my job."

Lucas nodded. "Your job sucks."

He pulled the trigger, shooting the other man in the head. He didn't have time or the stomach to torture someone, and Kyra had already seen far too much for someone so young. The gun-shot had

179

made her jump and whimper in fear. Lucas turned her away from the bodies and made her face him.

"I take it you're Kyra," he said by way of greeting. She nodded. "Well, we haven't officially met. I'm…"

"Lucas," she answered with a sniffle. "I know."

He nodded. They had seen each other, even if for only a short time in North Bay, and Alex no doubt told her all about him.

"Alright, let's get out of here," he told her as he led her to the door.

"They're not going to let us go," she responded.

She pulled him to a stop with surprising strength as the guards he had shot got to their feet. They should have been dead. Lucas pushed her behind him as the first one entered the room. He glanced toward the scientists. They remained still as the dead…all but one that was now getting to her feet as well.

"What the fuck?" he cursed.

He backed away from them, keeping Kyra behind him. His eyes widened in horror as he watched their injuries stitched themselves back together, their wounds healing until it was impossible to tell that they had been shot at all. Their eyes bled to black, no longer human in appearance. He fired at them again only for the creatures to get up again and continue to advance upon them.

Kyra tugged at his hand. "They're Shadows," she told him. "This way!"

Confused, Lucas glanced down at her as she began tugging him toward a narrow sliding door at the back. She let go of his hand and quickly activated it. It opened to another hallway. Lucas kept shooting at the Shadows as he backed up through it. Then he took one of the normal grenades he was carrying, pulled the pin, and threw it in the room before the door shut. Then he used his last bullet to shoot the control panel. Only someone who knew how to rewire the panel would be able to open the door, but that would be unlikely as the grenade went off, destroying the lab and everything inside, including, hopefully, the Shadows possessing human bodies. It rocked the Vault, causing both Lucas and Kyra to stumble as they hurried down the corridor

He tapped his earbud, connecting him to the rest of the rescue team then reloaded the rifle. "Did anyone think it might be important to tell me the Shadows were possessing people?" he snapped, the comment directed at Alex.

"I thought you might have got the memo when I said the fucking things were possessing people," Alex shot back, sounding just as flustered. It would appear he was facing the same situation. "Do you have Kyra?"

Lucas fought back an annoyed growl. "Yes. She's fine. We're trying to find another way out. Our exit got blocked."

Alex cursed but agreed. "We need to destroy the Vault."

"Well, they're short one lab now. What's your plan?"

He stopped as they came to up to another corridor. Catching Kyra's arm, he pulled her behind him again then peeked around the corner. It was empty, their way clear. If there were any more of the possessed mercenaries, they were busy dealing with Alex and Elizabeth. He didn't like that. He had always made it his job to protect them, but both had proven they could handle themselves in a fight.

"Just find a way out. We'll meet you outside," Alex responded.

Lucas shook his head. "You know better than that. I'll find you."

Kyra pointed the way once more, leading him to the left, away from the front of the Vault.

"Are you sure?" he asked her. Instinct told him to go the other way.

"Owen says this way," Kyra retorted.

Lucas froze, his breath hitching at the sound of her saying his brother's name. He missed whatever Alex said next as he grabbed the child and made her stop. He knelt in front of her, getting to her height so that they had complete eye contact.

"What do you mean 'Owen says this way'?" he asked, his voice cracking ever so slightly.

Her eyes were wide as she stared at him, expecting to be in trouble. After a moment understanding filled her but rather than answer or pull away, she touched his cheek, her small fingers dancing over the scuff of his short beard. Electricity danced through her and into him but it wasn't painful, not like when he touched Alex as the same energy rode through him. This was gentle, almost welcoming. Currents ran through him, like the crashing of waves until it settled. He closed his eyes in an attempt to orient himself. He felt slightly dizzy and his sinuses felt as if he was underwater. Sounds were muffled. He could hear Alex in the background but not what he was saying.

When he opened his eyes once more, he was still in the corridor but he and Kyra were no longer alone. A tall muscular man stood behind Kyra, his large hand on her small shoulder. There were other people, dressed in attire from throughout the centuries, even tens of thousands of years in the past. They were the Guardians, the souls of those that had died guarding the temple and fighting against the Shadows to keep them from entering this realm. None of them mattered Lucas, only the one standing protectively behind Kyra.

"Owen..." Lucas breathed, too stunned to stand.

He blinked away sudden tears and wrapped a hand around Kyra's, afraid that if he lost physical contact with her that Owen may disappear. His knees shaking, he pulled himself back into a standing position and stood before the spirit of his brother.

"Is this real?" he asked, unsure if he was speaking to Kyra or Owen.

Kyra turned to stand next to him and look up at the large man. She didn't respond, allowing Owen to speak for himself.

182

"After everything you've seen, you still question the mystical?" Owen teased with a small grin.

Lucas shook his head, still refusing to believe what he was seeing. "You're dead. You died in Alex's arms."

Disappointment mired Owen's face. "Death is not the end, Lucas. You better than anyone should know that by now. Energy never dies, it merely transforms."

He gestured toward the Guardians, many of which looking familiar, anthropologists and researchers who had been killed at this very site, now serving to guard the temple. They had failed to keep the Shadows at bay.

As much as Lucas wanted to focus on Owen, the fact the Guardians had not been able to keep the Shadows contained brought about a new fear. "Is the portal open? How many Shadows escaped?"

"Thousands," said another being, one that looked remarkably like Alex. "They're searching for the hybrids and killing any that do not meet the Celestial's idea of perfection. The others are being bred with both Celestials and humans. They plan to finish what they began. Now they have humans working for them to help make a better, stronger hybrid."

That's why they were going to harvest Kyra's organs. She couldn't reproduce but they could experiment on her to see how to enhance the next generation. Horror and disgust filled him. They couldn't just destroy the Vault, they needed to shut down the portal before even more of the Shadows came through.

"I guess the family reunion's going to have to wait," he told Owen. He turned back to the other spirit. "Professor Jackson, can you take us to the command centre? I think Kyra can help us shut down the portal. I'll get Alex to meet us there."

Professor Jackson nodded as Lucas radioed the new plan to Alex. He didn't tell him about the spirits; he wasn't quite sure how he would explain what was going on just yet. It seemed too crazy to announce over an open line. He just hoped that there wasn't a timer set on the bombs that were already in place because he was certain this was going to be a long dash from where they were to the wherever command was.

"Hold on tight," he told Kyra as he picked her up.

Her arms wrapped around his neck. She weighed next to nothing, making it easy to run with her in his arms. Holding the rifle at the same time was not as easy, but he had a feeling he would not encounter another Shadow for quite some time. Not while they were surrounded by Guardians.

Chapter Fifteen

They were surrounded! Elizabeth threw everything she had at the Shadows as they crept through the vast room. They kept coming through the Void, but without Alex, she couldn't close it. All she could do was keep throwing flash grenades at them. She was running low on those and the number of soldiers by her side were steadily dwindling as they were picked off one by one. All that kept the creatures at bay were the floodlights over the altar to which she had managed to connect. They were part of a much larger network, but she couldn't hack into it while defending herself from the Shadow creatures. If she could, she'd get the overhead lights back on and flush the blasted things out of the Vault. As it stood, they would reach her long before that happened.

"Elizabeth!" Lucas yelled as he ran toward her.

"Shit!" she cursed, seeing the child in his arms.

The Shadows moved from her position and sped toward him only to come up against some sort of shield. They slammed into it before appearing to shatter, as if they were made of glass. It was a peculiar sight that startled Lucas as well. He stumbled for a moment then headed directly for her, the Shadows scattering in either direction.

"What the hell did you do?" she asked as he came to kneel next to her.

He set the child on the ground, panting heavily from the exertion of running such a long distance with someone in his arms. Kyra was incredibly light, but Lucas was still hauling almost a hundred pounds of equipment. It took a lot of strength and stamina to accomplish that.

"It's not me," he answered. His gaze moved to the child. "It's the Guardians. They can push the Shadows back and give you the time you need to get the lights back on, but it's not going to be enough to stop those inhabiting hosts. They're hard bastards to kill. We either need to use fire or shove them in the Void, but we need Alex to close it. Kyra can't do it. Oh…" He glanced down at the little girl. "Kyra, this is Elizabeth. She's a good friend of mine and Alex's."

The child nodded and held out a small hand to Elizabeth.

Surprised, especially given the situation, Elizabeth took her hand. "Hi, Kyra."

The girl gave a dazzling smile. "Hi!" she chirped. She glanced at Lucas. "Owen's right, she's pretty."

"What?" Elizabeth asked, gazing over the child's head to Lucas as well.

"It's a long story," he answered. "Let's just say she can see the Guardians and Owen…and Professor Jackson are part of part of them." He let his breath out slowly. "They're here."

"Oh…" was all she could say to that. She wasn't sure how to feel about that. Alex had talked about the Guardians many times but never came right out to say his father was one of them, or Owen. Her throat felt thick as she swallowed back the emotions that suddenly filled her. If Alex was correct, then everyone that had been part of their research team and killed were now Guardians, invisible to her, yet all around them.

She pushed those thoughts aside and turned back to Kyra. "Can you activate the altar?" she asked.

Kyra's head bobbed up and down. Her fingers danced over hieroglyphs much as Alex's would have had he been there. A clicking sound followed, then a thumping and whirling sound. For a moment, Elizabeth feared she may have activated the engines and was about to take them off planet. Instead, the bright LED lights powered up, becoming a steady hum as they reached full power. They were brighter than before. Elizabeth pulled her goggles over her eyes and looked at her tablet. She had full access to the entire facility once more. Everything but the Void. She tapped her fingers on the edge of the tablet. Perhaps if the Guardians could get the Shadows in the Void and then the soldiers threw the rest of their explosives, destroying it from the inside, it would keep them from coming back.

The Shadows fled from the light, retreating to the far edges where the light could fully penetrate. They snarled and hissed, lashing out at the light, desperately trying to reach out to anyone that may be foolish enough to get close to them. The light didn't affect those possessed by the creatures. They continued to fight and lash out, not falling under normal gun fire. They were steadily gaining ground and the soldiers were quickly running out of ammo. The only thing keeping them safe seemed to be an invisible shield of sorts. Perhaps it was the Guardians in some form or another. Whatever it was, the creatures couldn't get any more than a half dozen feet to them before being shoved back toward the Void.

Elizabeth kept Kyra between her and Lucas.

"Where's Alex?" she asked.

Lucas shook his head. "He's supposed to on his way here. James…"

She nodded. It was still hard to believe one of these things had managed to take control of James. He was a good guy. Had become a good friend. The idea he was dead and a Shadow was wearing his body like some human suit was mind boggling.

She shot at one of the hosts that got too close. The impact of the bullet sent the man staggering back a few feet. Then he righted himself, as if not injured in the least, and began to advance once more. Elizabeth fired again, but when she tried for a third time all she heard was a click. She was out of bullets.

"Anyone have another magazine?" she asked, looking around.

If anyone did, they were currently too busy to help her. She pressed her lips into a thin line. Why was this so hard? They had gone up against creatures like this before in Area 51 of all places, with half a bloody army under a Celestial's control and a general obsessed with gaining the alien's power. How were the Shadows harder to defeat?

While they others defended the altar, she swiped over the tablet, trying to access the cameras to see where Alex was, praying he was safe. If this was a regular computer or security system, she would have had complete control of it by now. This was alien. The fact that the people controlling the Vault had managed to adapt their systems to it was a mystery. Who were these people? How had they accomplished this? If they survived, she wanted to be there when they were interrogated. She had so many questions.

They had to survive first.

"Beth, get down!" Alex's voice echoed throughout the room.

She looked up instead, shocked by his sudden outburst, only to be blind-sided by a fist to the side of her head. It knocked her against the altar, her head bouncing against the stone with a sickening crack. Her vision blurred out, momentarily bleeding to white. Pain radiated from the right side of her head.

"Elizabeth!" Lucas cried.

She barely registered it over the sound of Kyra's scream as she was ripped away from them. Swallowing back the bile that bubbled up her throat, she forced herself to open her eyes. What in the world happened? It felt like someone had plowed right into her.

When her vision cleared, she was met with the worst possible sight, James…or what used to be James…had Kyra. One large hand was wrapped around her small throat and was backing slowly toward the Void. Alex and the remaining soldiers stood between them and Elizabeth while Lucas tended to her injury.

"Let her go," Caldwell said in a commanding voice, her weapon aimed at James's head.

The mercenaries possessed by Shadows circled James as his grip on Kyra tightened, making her gasp for breath. Elizabeth tried to keep focus but her head hurt and focusing became hard. She closed her eyes, consciousness slipping from her.

"Elizabeth!" Lucas yelled, catching her as slumped forward.

Alex looked toward them, fear filled him. He was torn between going to Elizabeth's side and fighting for Kyra. The child was whimpering in fear. His gaze met Lucas's. There was fear in his eyes but determination as well. He nodded toward Kyra, silently telling him not to worry about them but to focus on the child instead. Alex nodded and squared his shoulders, certain Elizabeth was safe with Lucas. He stepped toward the creature inhabiting James's body.

"Let her go," he said, repeating Caldwell's words. "You don't need to hurt her."

The creature's cold black eyes stared at him blankly. "She is a failed experiment. The humans damaged her. She is no good to the Celestials."

"Perhaps, but she's good to us," he insisted.

He raised his hands, showing he was unarmed. The gunfire had stopped the moment the Shadow grabbed Kyra. It couldn't absorb her life force while in a human body otherwise it would have killed her at the vineyard. It had had plenty of opportunities to kill her then. There was more to this than the fact she could no longer reproduce. It was keeping her alive for a reason. There was something within the Void waiting for her.

He stepped forward but stopped when the creature stepped back. "The Celestials don't want her but I do. She's a child, she needs a family. A father. Someone to protect her and love her."

"Her genetic makeup will be preserved to make another," it responded. It stepped closer to the Void, the other hosts following it.

Caldwell and the soldiers followed suit, weapons trained on them. They needed to get the Shadows in the Void, but they couldn't let them take Kyra. Alex made eye contact with Caldwell and shook his head, pleading for her to standdown. She opened her mouth to object, thought better of it, then held up a hand to signal her soldiers to stop. They would hold their place…for now.

Alex took a deep breath and turned his focus fully to James. "The Celestials are gone. Killing her only takes away one of their children. Her value does not lie in whether or not she can reproduce. Please…let her go. If any part of James still exists…let her go."

The burning sensation in his hand was almost unbearable. It wasn't painful though, just the thrumming of energy waiting for an outlet. He needed to connect with the altar to close the Void. He couldn't do that until all the Shadows were returned to it, and he wasn't going to let them take Kyra with them.

The Shadow James eyed him, its gaze on his hand and the way his fingers absently moved with the flow of energy. It seemed to make the creatures nervous. They shuffled back further. The Shadows without hosts surrendered to the Guardians, slinking into the Void with no more fight. That felt wrong. Why were they retreating? Alex could make out the humanoid forms of light moving around them, corralling the Shadows toward the Void. They could not do the same with the hosts.

"The Celestials will return," the Shadow James said in deep rolling purr.

It hefted Kyra off her feet, holding her only by her throat. She whimpered and kicked her small feet as her fingers grasped at his hand, clawing his wrists. Her face was turning blue from lack of oxygen. It looked as if the creature might snap her neck if anyone made another move toward them. The soldiers were on high alert. One gesture from Caldwell would have them opening fire. Alex wasn't sure what to do. If they made a move, she was dead…if they didn't, the same was likely to happen.

The choice was taken out of his hands when the Shadow creature suddenly turned on its heel and dashed across the short distance, diving head first into the Void with Kyra. The other Shadows followed suit.

"No!" Alex cried, echoed by Caldwell who reached out for Kyra.

He didn't think, he just reacted and dove into the Void after them. It was like hitting a wall of ice-cold water. He became weightless but it wasn't quite like floating in air, nor was it like swimming through water. The air felt thick, like inhaling smoke, heavy but not chokingly so. Swirls of purple and gray moved all around him. The Shadow beings disappeared, becoming one with the swirling clouds and disappearing to wherever they belonged. The ones in hosts had to discard their human forms to merge with the rest. That left Kyra floating amongst the clouds and smoke, the Shadows moving about her like whisps, snaking around her tiny form. Alex reached out toward her, moving swiftly in her direction until his hand wrapped around her wrist and pulled her to him. Her arms wrapped around his neck, clinging to him tightly.

"Alex, what are you doing?" Lucas's voice came over the earbud. "Please tell me you're alright."

It was surprisingly good reception. Alex couldn't help but laugh as he held Kyra close.

"I have her," he answered.

He had her but he had no clue how they were going to get out. Even as he watched, the Shadows were reforming and moving toward them. This was their realm. There was no fighting them here. If they tried to escape, the Shadows would follow them.

"Prep the bombs and throw them…all of them…into the Void," he instructed.

"Alex, no…" Lucas pleaded. "There has to be another way."

He closed his eyes and took a deep, calming breathe.

"Caldwell," he said, knowing she would listen. This was not only a matter of National Security but International. He pulled away from Kyra long enough to see her face. She understood what was at risk and gave a small nod in agreement. "Do it," he told the General.

Keeping one arm around Kyra, he removed the earbud. Lucas was yelling obscenities, pleading for Caldwell not to do this, for Alex to come up with a better plan or let them rescue him. None of that mattered to Alex. What mattered was keeping the Shadows from entering their world once more, from hunting and hurting other people, from paving the way for the Celestials' return. Destroying the Void would kill him and Kyra. It wasn't the outcome he wanted, but he didn't know how to escape without the Shadows following him. It wasn't his best plan, far from it, but he was content with it.

The cold increased, encasing his legs in ice as the Shadows wrapped themselves around him and Kyra. He held her a little tighter and raised his right hand toward them, praying whatever power that seemed to ride through him would work as it had in North Bay. He tried to summon it, the aim and fire, as if it was some sort of laser that he could channel. It didn't work as he wanted. No bright light shot from the palm of his hand. It did nothing until the Shadow tried to wrap around it. Then, just as before, the energy discharged, slamming into the Shadow with an explosion of blinding white light that completely shredded it and any others fool enough to latch onto them, while also propelling Alex and Kyra into the opposite direction. This time, rather than slamming into a wall, they tumbled together through the Void. It was impossible to tell if they were going deeper into it or toward the portal. There was no up nor down, only endless swirling smoke and fog, disorienting Alex more-so than he already was.

When Alex opened his eyes, explosives floated all around them. A mix of relief and sadness filled him. Caldwell had done as he asked. She would ensure the portal to the Void was closed forever from this Vault. For that, he was grateful.

Something warm and solid wrapped around him and Kyra from behind, shocking them both. Alex turned his head. His breathe shuddered as he met Lucas's concerned face. He shook his head, wanting to yell at him for being so foolish as to jump into the Void after them. Explosives were all around them. If they went off now, they would all die. The look Lucas gave him clearly said he didn't care and it took only a moment to understand why. A rope or harness of some sort was attached to him. The moment he grasped Alex, he tugged on it. Whoever held the other end began to pull them back toward the opening.

"Faster," Lucas called through the earbud.

The light from the energy blast was fading fast. The Shadows were reforming.

"Set the charges," Alex told him, hoping Lucas would relay his message to Caldwell.

Instead, Lucas shifted Alex into a one arm hold and pulled out a detonator. Caldwell had given him the detonator. Alex wanted to scream. Lucas wouldn't pull the trigger until the last possible second, which may be too late.

"Faster," Lucas repeated.

Alex glanced behind them. They were close to the opening, very close, but so were the Shadows. They were picking up speed, rushing toward them. There was no time for this. He held Kyra tightly in one arm and grasped the device, his hand wrapping around Lucas's. His gaze met that of his husband's. No words were exchanged. None were needed.

Together, they pressed the trigger, setting off the explosives.

They didn't go off all at once but in a sequence of bright explosions, each one more powerful than the last. Each explosion created a shockwave that propelled the three even faster toward the portal, while tearing apart the Shadows and the very fabric of the Void. They were thrown out of the portal and onto the hard, cold floor moments before another explosion tore apart its entrance, closing the portal for eternity.

Alex slumped against the floor, his head cushioned against Lucas's shoulder. He rolled over slightly so that Kyra was tucked protectively between them. Exhaustion filled him but he knew they couldn't stay there for long. The Shadows may be gone, most of them at least, but they still had to destroy the Vault.

He took a deep breath then looked at Kyra. He brushed her hair out of her face as she gazed up at him.

"Hey," he whispered, unsure what else to say. "You okay?"

She stared at him for a long moment before a sob tore past her lips. "Daddy!" she cried. She threw herself at him, her arms wrapping tightly around his neck.

Alex hugged her back, stunned by her words. He glanced at Lucas but the older man said nothing only pressed his lips to Alex's temple and hugged the both of them. Alex took a moment to relax, taking comfort in Lucas's strong arms and Kyra's slight weight. It felt right. Being called Daddy felt right. He gave Kyra a small squeeze then pushed himself off the ground and got shakily to his feet before offering Lucas a hand. His husband grasped it and got up as well. Lucas smiled at him and Kyra, squeezed his hand, then went to check on Kyra as the soldiers gathered their dead.

"How is she?" Alex asked. He shifted Kyra so that she was sitting on his hip, not yet ready to put her down.

Elizabeth was leaning against the altar, a hand pressed against the side of her head. "I'm fine. It's probably just a small concussion. Don't worry about it."

Of course, they were going to worry about it, but neither he nor Lucas argued with her. They still needed to get out of the Vault and there was no telling how mercenaries were left, or how many of them were possessed by Shadows. Alex looked around, willing the second sight he had gained after being marked by the artifact to overshadow his own vision. It had once nearly driven him mad. The ability to see spirits that no one else could was both a blessing and a curse. For a while it got to the point he could not tell the difference between the living and the dead, so he forced himself to say goodbye to the spirits, give up the gift, and focus on the living. It was not as easy as turning off a light switch. It meant retraining his brain to reject the spirit realm that overlapped their own, and to instead focus only the realm of the living. It was like building a wall between the two realms. Now, he let it down, if only for a few moments.

A small smile lit his face as the Light-Beings that roamed throughout the room took solid form. People of from cultures expanding ten thousand years into the past took shape, but none more important to Alex then the deceased members of his research team, his father amongst them. Emotions bubbled up in him at the sight of him but he held them in check and gave his father a small smile and nod, acknowledging that he could see him and he missed him. His father returned it in kind.

"Go," the professor whispered.

Alex nodded and looked to Kyra. "Ready to go?" he asked.

She glanced past him to the Guardians than nodded as well. "Yes."

Lucas placed a hand on the small of his back. "I think we all are. Caldwell, do we have enough charges left to blow this place?"

The General nodded. "We have enough to leave nothing but a crater in its wake."

"Good," Lucas answered. "Let's get the fuck out of here."

"Best thing I've heard all day," Alex responded.

He hesitated, debating between setting Kyra down on the floor or carrying her. Given how quickly the Shadow James had managed to grab her and hurt Elizabeth, he wasn't quite ready to allow such a thing to happen again.

"Hold tight," he told her. "No matter what happens, don't let go."

Her grip tightened.

It was eerily quiet as they moved through the Vault back toward the entrance. There was no resistance but the halls were not empty. Bodies littered the ground, mercenaries and lab technicians that had not been killed in the gunfight earlier. These bodies were drained, complete husks as if their very life force was taken from them. They lay in heaps, like discarded clothing.

"What happened to them?" Caldwell asked as they moved around the bodies, her rifle aimed at them.

"My guess? The Shadows discarded their hosts," Lucas answered. He had an arm around Elizabeth, helping her maneuver around the corpses. "It'll be easier for them to move without a corporeal form. They'll find new hosts."

Alex frowned as he looked at the bodies. A part of him wanted to ask Caldwell to have them gathered and removed from the Vault so that their families could give them a proper burial, but it would be foolish. For all they knew it could be a ploy by the Shadows. They would be better off cremating them with the alien ship. He was happy when soldiers stuck C4 to the walls along the way. It was going to be a controlled blast that would destroy the Vault and send it back into the pit and bring the mountain-side down on it. Thankfully, there was no one living in this area which meant minimal damage to those living in the region.

Once they were outside, everyone was loaded into vehicles and taken to a safe distance from the Vault as the demolition team took over. Soon there was an ear shattering explosion, the ground rocked violently. Alex watched from the Hummer he was in as the Vault buckled from the inside, collapsing inward before slipping into the pit below to fall hundred of feet onto the remains of the ancient temple below. A second explosion followed and the side of the mountain gave way. It flowed downward in a mix of rock and snow, tumbling into the now open pit, burying what was left of the temple and Vault. Thousands of tons filled the underground cavern until it was no longer seen and all that was left were huge pillows of dust and dirt.

"Is it gone?" Kyra asked from next to Alex, tucked between him and Elizabeth.

196

Lucas nodded from the front seat. "Yeah, it's gone."

"Finally," Elizabeth whispered, slumping back in her seat.

"How's your head?" Alex asked, twisting around to face her.

"I'll live."

"We need to get the medics to check you out," Caldwell said from the driver's seat.

Alex watched her as she radioed to the medical officers that were hanging back during the mission. Once they verified they were enroute, the General relaxed and leaned back in her seat.

"This wasn't supposed to happen," she said, her voice sounding strained and filled with exhaustion. She looked into the review mirror, her gaze settling on Kyra. "We should've have been in Winnipeg at the new facility by now. No one would have known about her."

Alex's hands balled into fists. She was still treating Kyra as a possession and not a person. He was about to comment but Caldwell continued speaking.

"It's probably a good thing though...not what happened. God, I never wanted anything like this to happen." She turned in her seat to face the girl and gave her a sad smile. "I'm glad you found each other."

Alex glanced to Lucas, utterly confused. This wasn't the same woman they encountered before and for one fearful moment Alex feared that Caldwell may have been possessed by a Shadow.

"I suppose it's time to let go," Caldwell continued. She drew a deep breath and sat back.

"It's alright," Lucas soothed. "She's safe. We're all safe now."

She nodded. "You two lost everything to save her. I may have a way to pay you back...if you'll allow me."

Alex exchanged a look with Lucas, unsure what think. He tilted his head, trying to get a feel for her, but it was impossible to tell if she was possessed or not. Once a Shadow took a host, the body became a shield for it. There was no telling it was there until it revealed itself.

Chapter Sixteen

T here it is," Lucas announced.

Alex leaned forward as the small bi-plane circled around the small lake. They were high in the mountains, far from any town or village. The closest one was a half hour by plane. There were no roads or other method of reaching the remote location, not even by boat. There were no other houses anywhere near the cabin below them. That was a little disconcerting. If there was an emergency, it would be hard for them to get immediate help. Given everything that had happened recently, he wasn't sure how to feel about that.

Kyra sat next to him, her pale blue eyes large as she peered out the front window. Elizabeth sat on her other side, just as transfixed. When Caldwell first suggested some place remote but under the protection of the Armed Forces, Alex had pictured an old military base that was no longer in use with multiple out-buildings, looking cold and desolate. This was something completely different. It looked like a Ranger station with an A-framed wooden cabin not far from up shore from the ice-and-snow-covered lake. There was smoke billowing out of the chimney, showing someone was already there. The only vehicles Alex could see were two snow mobiles parked in front of the cabin. That made him feel a little better. Snow mobiles and four wheelers weren't ideal for traveling into town for necessities, but it was doable. They had done that on a number of digs he had attended. Nonetheless, the cabin and location itself didn't look like any sort of military complex he had seen before. It didn't make sense for it not to have a road leading into it, or more structures.

"Don't judge a book by its cover," Caldwell answered Lucas. There was bemusement in her voice as she prepared to land. "This is an old site. A lot has changed since the 1920s."

"The cabin's that old?" Lucas asked, appalled. There was a glimmer of teasing in his voice. The cabin looked brand new.

Alex rolled his eyes. He could already see the list of objections forming in his lover's mind. Convincing him to move to the vineyard and their small home had taken a lot of convincing. If Lucas was in charge of deciding their next home, it would likely be a mid-modern flat in England or a new condo in a large city close to art and culture centres. A cabin completely isolated in the middle of the woods, in the Ishpatina Ridge. It was North of Sudbury and featured the highest mountain in Ontario. Quite a few small lakes dotted the landscape. The particular one wasn't very large but it was long and had plenty of room for a personal plane, or even a waterbomber, to land or gather water. The lake was frozen right now, but the plane landed with ease and coasted to a stop on the edge, not far from the cabin and next to a small dock.

Kyra quickly took off her seatbelt and reached for the door, excitement filling her face.

"Whoa…get your coat back on first," Alex reprimanded.

He undid his own belt and reached for the coats that they had stored behind their seat along with what few belongings he and Lucas had.

"Come on!" Kyra whined as he made her slip the coat on. "It's not that cold and the cabin is right there!"

"And it's winter and we're in the mountains," he retorted. "The wind hits harder here. The last thing any of us want is you getting sick."

"I'm half Celestial."

"And half human. Suck it up. You're wearing a coat, just like me, and Lucas, and…" He frowned as he watched Elizabeth exit the plane with only a sweater on. "Forget Elizabeth, she's built of Teflon. You're not."

Kyra's little face scrunched up in disapproval as he placed a toque on her head and had her stick her hands in her mitts. Alex imitated it, making her grin. It was easy to make her smile now that she no longer had to fear the Shadows…at least not for now. A part of him was still concerned about Caldwell and didn't quite trust her, but she had done nothing to harm any of them. It didn't necessarily mean she wasn't possessed by one of the creatures, but the likelihood was considerably less than it had been several days earlier.

Once he let Kyra go, the little girl ran after Elizabeth and took her hand. She looked at the woman as an aunt, happily chattering away about the first thing that came to her mind and asking endless questions about all the new things she encountered. Elizabeth took it with stride, seeming to enjoy Kyra's enthusiasm. Lucas came around and wrapped an arm around Alex's waist as he looked around. He didn't say anything and seemed more interested in taking everything in. Alex glanced around as well. They were in a valley area with mountains all around, but they were at a much higher elevation, not quite the highest point of the of Ishpatina Ridge but close. He could barely make out the old fire tower far in the distance. It wasn't manned but in the summer, hikers often travelled to the ridge. He wasn't sure how well anyone with binoculars would be able to spot the cabin. If anyone attempted the long hike up and down the long winding mountain sides to reach the cabin, it was sure to be treacherous.

"What are you thinking?" Lucas asked, following his gaze.

Alex hummed softly. "That if I make a Yeti friend up here I'm calling it George."

Lucas stared at him in confusion before shaking his head and laughing. "I'm going to guess that's a Looney Tunes reference."

Alex shrugged. "Kyra and I were watching it this morning."

"I ended up with two kids instead of one, didn't I?"

"Hey, you knew what you were getting into when you married me," Alex teased as they headed toward the cabin. "Now I have a better excuse to watch cartoons and eat Froot Loops."

"Ew…"

That made him laugh and lean into Lucas. They had a lot of things in common but they also had a few quirky differences. It made for an interesting relationship.

Alex's attention turned back to the cabin they when they heard Kyra's squeal of delight.

"Whoa…" he breathed.

The front of the cabin featured floor to ceiling windows that perfectly displayed a very modern interior that was fully lit. He paused before mounting the stairs and took in the surroundings. There was a huge solar panel system attached to towers that looked like they moved with the sun. More solar panels were connected to the house, going up the entire length. There didn't appear to be any lines leading to the small structure several dozen feet from the main group of solar panels. It was no doubt the battery house which transformed the sunlight absorbed from the solar panels into energy to power the cabin. The cabin was completely off grid.

His hunch was proven correct as they entered the building. It was much larger inside than it appeared from the outside. The main floor was completely open concept with a glassed-in fireplace in the living room that kept the building toasty-warm. Plush seating surrounded it and looked out over the mountainside and lake. It had a chalet-feel that Alex fell in love with. The eat-in kitchen was directly behind it and was a chef's dream. Large state-of-the art appliances with modern cabinetry and island gave plenty of preparation space. The island housed a large Farmhouse style apron sink with a flexible faucet and dishwasher next to it. Bar seats were tucked underneath. Kyra was already there, looking through the small gift baskets that had goodies inside. Elizabeth sat next to her, helping unwrap one of the baskets.

"This is almost like my flat back home," Lucas murmured as he looked around. "How many square feet?"

"Fifteen hundred," Caldwell answered. "There's two full baths and a powder room."

"Wait…three bathrooms in total? This doesn't look that big," Alex noted.

"The master bedroom is on the main floor over here," Caldwell answered.

She led them past the kitchen, pointing out the powder room and then past the curved staircase to a room just past it. It was larger than their previous master bedroom with huge windows letting in tons of natural light, a master bathroom to one side, and double closets. Patio doors led to a covered deck and what appeared to be a backyard oasis. It was hard to tell for certain under the snow, but there appeared to be a custom swimming pool, pergola, and patio, including a hot tub in front of a large retaining wall. This was definitely not something one would expect to see at what was allegedly a former base. Alex wasn't sure what to say but he could tell that Lucas was warming up to the idea of moving here.

"Wow," was all Alex could say.

This didn't feel real. It was more like going on vacation than looking at a potential new home. His shoulder tensed when he heard Kyra scream. His eyes widened and he rushed out of the room, thinking something was wrong. He took the stairs two at a time until he reached the second floor only to stumble upon Kyra in what he assumed to be her new room, gushing over the pile of new stuffed toys and princess bed in the center of the room.

"Why did you scream?" he asked only to be elbowed by Elizabeth. "What?"

"She just won the lottery," Elizabeth told him. She leaned against him. "Going from growing up in a sterile lab to being a princess? I'd be screaming, too. Look at that bed! It's huge and pink and looks as if it came out of a fairy tale. Lucas out-did himself."

"Lucas?" Alex breathed, momentarily confused.

A laugh escaped him a moment later. Caldwell may have chosen the location but Lucas had the chalet constructed. They had spent the last few weeks living in Elizabeth's small apartment while waiting for the insurance agency to approve their claim, something that could take months. During that time, they filed adoption papers for Kyra. Since she technically didn't exist, it proved surprisingly easy thanks to Caldwell. Everything was happening incredibly fast.

He took in the large bedroom, noting the closet and Jack-and-Jill bathroom that connected to a third room that was already set up as a guest room for Elizabeth. That room was just as elegant even if a little more sparsely decorated but there was no doubt who it was meant for. He left Kyra and Elizabeth upstairs and headed back downstairs. Lucas was waiting for him with the cat-that-got-the-cream little grin. Alex narrowed his eyes at him.

"You did this," he stated, not sure how he felt about Lucas doing something so big behind his back.

Lucas shrugged.

"How did they get the materials here? There's no roads and it's winter…the foundation."

"It's funny what money can buy you when you actually spend it," Lucas pointed out.

Alex opened his mouth than shut it. Despite having the vineyard and winery, they had been living a modest life compared to what Lucas was used to in England. Between what Lucas had banked away and whatever the insurance was giving them, they had more than enough to build the house of their dreams. Alex never imagined it would be here.

"How?"

Lucas looked thoughtful for a moment. "Remember how much I hate modular homes?"

"Yeah?"

"I found one I liked." He gestured at their surroundings. "A few calls and a long meeting with Caldwell...we had a team here setting down the foundation while she found a helicopter able to transport the modular and a construction team. The rest..." He shrugged, the smile still plastered on his face.

Alex stepped forward and placed a soft kiss on his lips. "I don't deserve you."

Lucas's hands grasped his hips. He pressed him against the wall and kissed his back. "You might be right."

If it wasn't for Caldwell, they probably would have began making out. Alex brushed a stray lock of hair from Lucas's eyes and gazed up at him, amazed as always that he had stayed with him after everything they had been through. He had even agreed to about Kyra, something that had taken Alex by surprise yet made him feel complete. They finally had a family of their own. And even though Alex had no siblings and rarely saw his mother, and Lucas's only brother, Owen, had died, his spirit watching over them, Kyra had people who loved her. Elizabeth doted on her and even Caldwell had warmed up to her, treating her as her own grandchild. After the events in British Columbia, she seemed much calmer, less on edge.

"One question," Alex asked. He placed a hand on Lucas's chest. "We're in the middle of nowhere. The only way in and out is by an all-terrain vehicle or plane and neither one of us have our pilot's license. How are we going to go shopping?"

Lucas hummed. "Well, if you check the closets, I had new clothing already delivered and the fridge, freezers, and pantry are fully stocked. We're good for two months, possibly three. Kyra can be home schooled, and you handed in your resignation already. So did I."

"Okay, but when we need stuff?"

"Caldwell has agreed to have a shipment delivered twice a month."

"So...we never leave?"

"No...I'm working on my pilot licence." Lucas grinned widely. "I was thinking you might want to get yours as well."

Alex gave him a slow blink in astonishment. "You hate personal planes. They scare the crap out of you!"

The older man shrugged. "It turns out that when I'm piloting...it doesn't scare me as much. I've already logged thirty hours."

"That's what you've been doing? I thought you were at the university."

"I officially resigned."

Alex shook his head. He wanted to object, ask how they would make a living, but he didn't. They both worked for Interpol as advisors regarding the Celestials. They were paid regardless if they had a mission or not. All their expenses were covered. Living off the grid made those expenses far less than they used to be. There were certain conveniences that he wanted to ask about such as internet and cell phone service but it would seem Caldwell had that all sorted out for them already as she led them back outside.

"See that tree," she asked. She pointed to a tall White Pine tree that towered over the others. "It's artificial. It's actually radio tower linked up to one of our satellites. The house is already linked to it." They walked through the snow toward it. "It was designed to help hikers call for help if they get lost. There are five more throughout the ridge. Search and Rescue can use them to triangulate their location to reach them faster. You'll have full Wi-Fi and cellphone service with encrypted passwords so that no one can track where you are unless you want them to."

"Well, that means we can still work from home but those online orders are out of the question now," Alex joked as they continued hiking the perimeter.

"I'm sure Elizabeth would be fine having items mailed to her and bring them up on her visits," Lucas answered. He took Alex's hand and gave it a squeeze.

"To be honest, I wish it was summer. There's something else I want to show you," Caldwell told them. She looked wistfully to the east then shock her head.

"You said there used to be a base here?" Alex asked, confused by the look on her face.

She nodded. "The base itself is gone but the security system is still fully operational." She turned and looked back toward the lake downhill. "This is a no-fly zone. For five kilometers all around, every plane or helicopter that comes here must radio in for clearance, including search and rescue. The Rangers can't give it. It comes from here or NORAD, or it used to. Now it comes from you."

"Us?"

"This is all yours. They can radio us but the final word comes from you. If anyone tries to land without permission, it triggers the security network and that plane is treated as a hostile."

Alex stopped walking and stared at her with wide eyes. "What happens?"

"It's brought down and troops are dispatched."

He looked to Lucas but his husband seemed perfectly fine with that, even when the ground seemed to open up and what appeared to be two defensive rocket launchers rose to the surface. They hummed loudly as they rotated, looking for a target, then returned to their previous position. A moment later they lowered back into the ground and the metal doors hiding them slid back into place, the snow now displayed.

"Are you kidding me?" Alex breathed in disbelief. "There's no way I'm going to live…"

"It's for Kyra's safety," Lucas said quickly, stopping him from panicking. "Look, the Shadows are still out there. We may not be able to stop them in their natural form but these will help deter them in their hosts. Someone was working with them. We would be fools to think they won't try coming after her…and you…again."

"So, you had cannons installed?"

"They came with the property."

Alex shook his head. "We're not staying here. This is a potential death trap...and not just for some group of possible terrorists. No...I'm taking Kyra and we're going back to the city."

"Wait!" Caldwell called as Alex turned to head back to the cabin to gather Kyra and Elizabeth.

He turned back to face her, daring her to give him a good reason to stay. He watched her, seeing more emotion appear on her face then he had since they met.

"The cannons are meant to protect something else, not just Kyra," she explained.

"That type of armory wasn't available in the 1920s," he pointed out. "You don't see them in the middle of a forest let alone in the mountains. What are they? Heat seeking? Do you know how dangerous they are? And you expect me to raise a child here?"

She closed her eyes and took a deep breathe before retaining her composure. "They were installed in the mid-seventies just before the base was officially closed with only a small group staying behind."

"Why?"

She fell silent for a moment. "I think it's better if I show you rather than tell you. We'll need the snow machines. It's a fair distance from here."

Alex gave Lucas a dark look but his husband seemed just as surprised. He knew about the defences but not this. It brought a bad taste to Alex's mouth. Nonetheless, he followed Caldwell, his curiosity getting the best of him. They took the snow machines and followed Caldwell deeper into the forests, further up into the mountain ridge to an area so dense with woods that the path became narrow. It soon became apparent that few, if anyone, travelled this path. It wasn't well cared for and if not for Caldwell leading the way, one could get lost very quickly. There were absolutely no markers to let anyone know they were going in the right direction.

After nearly twenty minutes, they came to a what appeared to be an old mine shaft. Alex's stomach immediately knocked as Caldwell began pulling aside carefully placed logs and brush that hid the opening. A part of him wanted to run, instinctively knowing what was hidden in the mine. Another part made him plant his feet firmly where he was. It was quickly apparent that it was not a usual abandoned mine, as Caldwell began going through a whole security procedure that seemed a little over the top. After a few minutes, she pushed open a heavy iron door similar to the one that led to the underground NORAD bunker.

Alex shared a look with Lucas who seemed just as surprised. They followed her into the mine for nearly a hundred feet until the reached a lift. The familiar itch came to Alex's hand as they descended into the mine. They shouldn't be here. They should leave. Yet he couldn't. His body seemed to move all on its own, as if he was drawn to whatever Caldwell was leading them to. He grasped the rails of the lift, his knuckles turning white with the force he held it. He knew what it was before they even entered the vast underground cavern.

"You've got to be kidding me," he breathed as it came into sight.

It was a temple, fully intact, as if built recently, the white marble and limestone glistening in the dim light of overhead lights that someone had installed overhead. Alex's heart beat wildly as he stared at it. He felt transported back to the first time he saw the one in British Columbia, the same awe and astonishment that something so large could be built in the mountains and them moved underground when human rebelled against the Celestials.

"You're one of them," he said, not bothering to look at Caldwell.

Silence met him as they continued to descend into the underground chamber. This one was slightly different from the others he had seen. There were other structures around the temple, like a small village despite no one being there. A flowing river cut a path through the rocks, bring fresh spring water from the nearby lakes. The crystals embedded in the rocky terrain reflected the artificial lights installed into the ceiling, giving the chamber an almost ethereal look.

"Yes," Caldwell answered.

"You're a Shadow?" Lucas said, fear in his voice as he grasped Alex's arm, ready to defend him.

Alex gave a hollow laugh. "Worse, she's a Celestial."

The lift jerked to a stop as they reached the cavern floor but none of them got out. He turned toward her and leaned against the rail. He kept one hand around Lucas's wrist. There was no point trying to fight a Celestial. Even if they tried to kill her, the alien within would only heal the damage. Alex knew that from first hand experience. It was better to keep their calm.

"Why did you bring us here?" Lucas demanded, clearly angry to have been played. "Why help me set up the property if you're planning to kill us?"

That surprised Caldwell. "I'm not going to kill you...either of you," she responded, clearly bothered by the indication. She removed her toque and ran a hand through her short salt and pepper hair. "That's not why I brought you here."

"Then why?" Alex countered. "And how is this temple still intact? I thought all the Celestials left. The Vaults destroyed the remaining temples as they left the planet."

Caldwell shook her head. "Not all the Celestials have left." She leaned against the other side of the lift and stared wistfully at the temple. "There's a fraction of us that fought against the ruling class. We didn't want to rule. We wanted to live in peace, become "one" with you, but we had to take a corporeal form to do that. We didn't want to create a new species of humans, we simply wanted to be one of you. To be free." She drew in a deep breath. "The ruling class objected to this. Humans were just another race to experiment on.

Their bodies nothing but hosts to help spread our genetic make up and create a superior race."

"That's why you had Kyra's reproductive organs removed," Lucas breathed.

"Yes. I killed her mother and the other hosts. I stopped them from creating more hybrids. I should have killed Kyra as well, but I couldn't bring myself to do it."

"So, you tried to raise her as your own," Alex finished. "You weren't planning to take her to Winnipeg. You were going to bring her here."

"She's a living weapon. They all are. Doctor Jackson...Alex...you're right. The Celestials will be back. The human race isn't ready to defend against them. They're not strong enough, not against ethereal beings that can possess them. I took this host while she was in her youth, lived amongst your people and tried to prepare them, but you're not ready. The hybrids are the only beings strong enough to defeat them. The Celestials cannot possess them. They are the Celestials' greatest weapons and biggest weakness. If we can find them, train them, we can stop the Celestials from conquering this world." Her gaze shifted from Alex to Lucas then back. "I wanted to bring Kyra here, away from the labs so that she could be trained to fight them. Just as I hope to do with every hybrid once they're located."

Alex looked back over the tiny village of buildings around the temple. There were dozens of them with room for more. "If they can keep the Celestials from possessing them, why not let them breed with humans and strengthen the race? Don't you breed? Isn't that the whole point behind taking a host?"

"No. Humans are already bouncing through evolution at an incredibly dangerous rate from mating with hybrids. If it continues, they will destroy this planet more thoroughly than any Celestial invasion. It needs to stop. Mankind needs to take a step back. I'm not going to add to their troubles. Believe it or not, I love this planet and its people. I want to save it but I can't do it alone."

"What do you want from us?"

She pushed away from the rail and stood next to him. "You know more about Celestials than any other human. You've been a host and survived. I'm offering you a chance to help me prepare the next generation to stop them. To fight back. While you're at it, you can explore this temple, and its Vault, to your heart's content. Learn everything about it. All I'm asking in return is for you to protect it, and Kyra. When she's ready, she'll be trained to defend this planet while I search for more like her."

Alex nodded in agreement. He could live with that. "Was your host a soldier before or after you possessed her?"

"After. NORAD seemed like the best way to keep track of airwaves in case the Celestials awoke. Most of us were in hibernation within the Void for a very long time until the temples began being rediscovered. This is mine. It was discovered by miners in 1890. I've kept it secret until now."

It was a lot to take in. Alex didn't trust Celestials. He didn't trust Caldwell, but the itch in his right now wasn't as powerful as it had been when dealing with the Shadows. It was a dull ache, not demanding attention or pulsing with energy. It was like his body was telling him he had nothing to fear.

"What about the Shadows?" he asked, concerned because they had not recognized nor bowed down to Caldwell when they attacked, as if she held no authority over them.

"They will be dealt with."

Alex nodded to himself as he took it all it. "Remote location, massive security, hidden underground temple, and a new adopted daughter…" He turned to Lucas who also seemed deep in thought as he looked out over the temple. "What do you think?"

Lucas shook his head. "I'm still trying to wrap my head around the fact she's a Celestial." He sighed and looked at Caldwell. "If we agree to this, its on our terms. We raise Kyra. We decide on her training. You don't just show up and declare what we do. We make all the decisions. If we choose to leave, Kyra comes with us and you never make contact with us again."

The Celestial's mouth fell open, as if she was about to object. Then she sighed and nodded. "Agreed. You are her legal parents now. All I ask is you allow other hybrids access to the temple when the time comes. The Void is inaccessible from this temple. The Vault inoperable. There is no fear of the Shadows or other Celestials coming through. In fact, I believe we may have destroyed the Void, or at least made it a less desirable access point."

That was good. It gave Alex a little peace of mind. "So, in essence, you're asking us to be living Guardians of this temple."

"In essence."

"What about the Guardians that already protect this temple?" Lucas inquired.

"They're here," Caldwell assured. "They're all here. Including your brother."

A smile pulled at Alex's lips. He could feel them. If he allowed himself to slip into his second sight, he knew he would see them. Not just the Guardians here or Owen, but he was almost certain his father and the members of his old research team were here as well. They had followed them there. His gaze fixing on Owen as the spirit moved toward them with the same protective nature that made Alex fall in love with him and Lucas so many years ago. His eyes closed for a moment as Owen reached out to him, his large ghostly fingers, brushing through his hair and along the right side of his head to curve around his ruined ear. His fingers felt warm and almost solid, as if he was still alive and with them in life. It made him feel safe despite their location.

"We'll do it," he said firmly.

"What?" Lucas asked in surprise, no longer able to see his brother. He would need Kyra to grant him that temporary gift in order to do so again.

Alex turned away from Owen to face Lucas directly, wanting to tell him about Owen but choosing not to. "Lucas, you just spent a ton of money building us a new home in one of the most remote parts of Northern Ontario without sticking us so far North that we couldn't rebuild the vineyard. Here…it'll be tricky but we can do it." He stroked Lucas's cheek. "And as much as I hate to admit it, Caldwell's right. We need living Guardians to protect the temple. The ghosts…they've tried. They can fight the Shadows and even the Celestials to a point, but they can't fight humans. We can't let another terrorist group take control of a Vault. And for the first time, we can actually investigate the temple and Vault without fear of being attacked. Kyra can grow up knowing her history and be prepared for whatever lies in the future."

Lucas leaned his cheek against Alex's hand. "Are you certain this is what you want?"

"Yes," he answered. He had never been more certain in his life. Everything he had lost was now here. His father, his team, Owen…they were all here.

This was where they were meant to be. Everything that had happened over the years had been leading them to this moment. Why else would all the Guardians converge here? For once he didn't feel threatened or anxious. He felt at ease, like he belonged. He wasn't even angry that Caldwell had kept them in the dark about what she truly was. If anything, he felt foolish for not seeing past her disguise. He hadn't felt the Celestial within her, had tried to force the memory of his own possession out of his mind. Unlike when he was possessed, Caldwell and the Celestial seemed to be one. It took time to form that bond.

"So, we're staying?" Lucas asked for confirmation.

Alex glanced down at his hand, feeling the faint trails of energy that flowed through it and connected him to the temples and Vaults hidden within. "Yeah," he answered. "We're staying."

It was an odd arrangement and living so far from town took some getting used to. Lucas stayed true to his word and got his pilot's licence. Eventually so did Alex and Elizabeth. Caldwell made sure they had the best trainers and provided them with two bi-planes, one that stayed at the cabin, the other outside Elizabeth's new house along Lake Ramsey in Sudbury, making it easy for them to get back and forth on short notice. Kyra received the best education possible. Being home schooled by an anthropologist and archeologist meant she got the best of both worlds. When Elizabeth visited, Kyra learned the ins-and-outs of technology, staying up to date on programming to hacking and everything in between. Alex thrived being a father. Both he and Lucas doted on Kyra but he was the one who went out of his way to learn how to style her hair and play with her while Lucas taught her culture and how to dance, often letting her stand on his feet while he did the dance steps. Eventually a new vineyard was created, along with a new, much smaller winery. Tending to it became one of Kyra's passions. It wasn't easy given the terrain but it was doable. Teaching Kyra about the Celestials wasn't easy, if anything, that proved to be the hardest part. Making sure she knew who and what they were without sounding prejudiced was a trial in and of itself, but Alex made sure she knew first hand about her heritage. Many of her archeology and anthropology lessons were conducted underground, inside and around the temple itself.

Caldwell kept to her word. No one else knew of the temple's existence, believing as they had that they were all destroyed and the Celestials gone. As the years passed, the Celestials became nothing more than a memory to the rest of the world, an urban legend like the Roswell UFO and Loch Ness Monster. People forgot, as they tend to do, but Alex and Lucas didn't. They waited for the day Caldwell would show up at their door with one simple sentence.

"It's time…"

About the Author

Canadian born and raised, M.J. writes primarily urban fantasy, erotic paranormal thrillers, young adult fiction, branching out into short screenplays as well as children's fiction. She enjoys mentoring young authors in the craft of story telling and writing.

To become an ARC reader and join our newsletter for chances to win swag and/or gift cards visit:

www.mjspickett.ca

www.ingramcontent.com/pod-product-compliance
Lightning Source LLC
Chambersburg PA
CBHW031958240626
47153CB00003B/1019